We'll Never Be S
In A Synchron

By

Mick Whitehead

Copyright © 2024 Mick Whitehead

ISBN: 978-1-917425-74-2

All rights reserved, including the right to reproduce this book, or portions thereof in any form. No part of this text may be reproduced, transmitted, downloaded, decompiled, reverse engineered, or stored, in any form or introduced into any information storage and retrieval system, in any form or by any means, whether electronic or mechanical without the express written permission of the author.

This book is a work of fiction. Names, characters, places, organisations and incidents are either products of the author's imagination or used fictitiously. Any resemblance to actual events, places, organisations or persons alive or dead is entirely coincidental.

For Sue, Craig, Harley, River and Maya
and all my family

Very special thank you to my editor
Paul 'Haddock' Osman

This book is a further Mark Byrne Adventure

Also by the same author in order of publication

We'll Never Be Sixteen Again
We'll Never Be Sixteen Again - Part Deux
We'll Never Be Sixteen Again - At Sea
We'll Never Be Sixteen Again - In The Caribbean

All the above fiction novels are available to buy Online
In Ebook or Paperback Formats.
And from major high street bookstores.

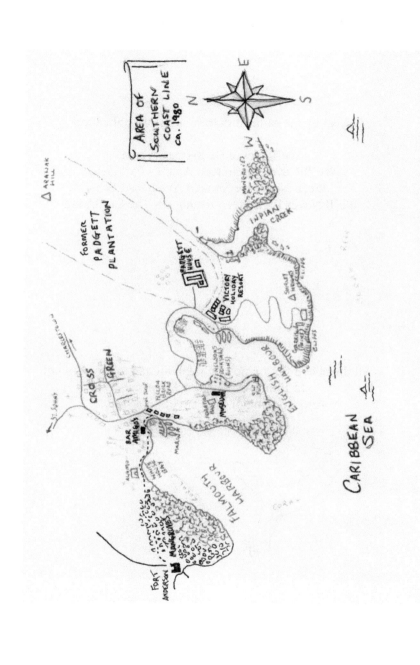

'Synchronicity is an ever present reality for those who have eyes to see.'

C.G. Jung

Chapter One
A World Away

This was just another of those distant African countries, whose land, population and resources, like many others on this incredible continent, had been robbed and exploited for more than three hundred and fifty years. Signed between the banks of two great ocean going rivers, sealed by a sixteenth century handshake and delivered by the unequivocal law of a loaded cannon.

These vast, sprawling, fertile plains and gentle sloping hills were once mineral rich, unpolluted and free. Not that anyone who lived here now could remember those times. In more recent decades they'd been shoved harder against a wall when the great empires of the world started to crumble and fracture spawning their looming shadows of revolution. For the oppressed majority, united in their fight for independence (the so called "little people"), the hour was long overdue.

A littering of shallow graves had flowed unstaunched for a full fifteen years and yet this bitter conflict hadn't rated very highly in the western newsrooms, except on the odd occasion when the rebels had managed to interrupt the flow of oil for a week or two. Day by day, these struggles seemed endless. Then suddenly, during the severe drought of 1976, the Colonials hurriedly departed and against all odds and against the might of a selfish capitalist regime, the war for the independence of Ambundu came to an end.

The memory of those short-lived, jubilant days that followed faded, even before the nation had had time to bandage its wounds. For, an even deadlier and more bloody conflict exploded from the severed scraps of power and what little else remained intact: half a dozen oil wells and a bankrupt economy.

Many of the more remote villages and farmsteads, those that contained some of the poorest rural tribesmen and women who had yet to enjoy their song of victory and freedom, were not even aware that they were about to be engulfed by the murderous implosion of a civil war.

At the centre of a small, cultivated field on the great rolling African plateau, the close-knit community of Mittende had existed for a thousand years. That was until the morning it was obliterated by the soldiers, a rag-tag mob armed with grenades and Kalashnikovs.

There would be many such atrocities. Unrecorded and unknown, they were erased from the map forever, for the sole reason that they were caught in a 'no man's land' between the two warring factions: the Popular movement and the Nationalist movement, the left and the right. They were neither right nor righteous. In the escalating violence and destruction, neither of these two remorseless groups could declare any form of innocence.

Iko Kaloode was just thirteen years old when he lost his parents and all seven of his younger siblings. Had it not been for the fact he'd been rushed from his ancestral home in Mittende, a few days before, to have his appendix removed at the military hospital on the outskirts of Lusalgo City, he would, by now, have become just one more worthless, wind-blown, pile of ash, trampled into the dusty earth.

When, after a week, no one came to collect him, the doctors knew Iko's only place of refuge would be found in the neighbouring orphanage for misplaced children.

'Orphanage' was unquestionably far too grand a label to pin to the canvas collection of makeshift shelters where Iko was sent, to recover from his physical and emotional scars. Luckily he wasn't alone, but it would've helped his cause had there not been quite so many unfortunates in the exact same plight as him-self.

There were approximately fifty children, of all ages from six to fifteen. They were seldom supervised and were unschooled, left to their own devices, with only a meagre handful of bread and fruit, handed out at irregular intervals to keep their hunger at bay. Iko soon learnt he had to be resourceful if he was to survive. This meant taking risks and plucking up the courage to enter the military barracks at the opposite end of the encampment. Not all the soldiers billeted there welcomed his intrusions. Iko quickly recognised which ones to avoid and which would reward him for performing menial tasks such as: washing dirty uniforms, or scraping the bloody mud from their boots.

This brigade of international 'advisors', on whom Iko depended, was fighting alongside the Populist soldiers of the now dominant ruling party. He had made up his mind, despite the fact most of them spoke a different language, that, these smartly dressed, well-armed foreigners were at least on his side. These were Allied forces, at war with the guerrillas that had slaughtered his entire family and friends and every single one of the other one hundred inhabitants of Mittende.

In the weeks that followed, Iko's existence was no picnic in the park. From sunrise until sunset there was little hope that things would ever improve. Fear and starvation dogged each day. But the most unbearable sufferance by far was when the soldiers returned from battle with their captives. The smaller children cried throughout the night whenever the tortured screams of prisoners rang out across the encampment. They burned away the memory of youthful innocence. The violence was deeply shocking and inescapable. In the end the brain taught the body how not to shake, how to shut it-self off, how to be punch drunk and numbed until the eyes and ears could even ignore the sudden, shuddering, crack, crack, crack of dawn executions.

After a year in the camp, Iko had learnt to speak their lingo and understand the ins and outs of barrack room banter. He was fascinated by their equipment, the uniforms and armour, which constantly littered the floors of their quarters. In particular, Iko was spellbound by the strange, white machine, in the corner of the room, which kept everything that was stored inside cool and sweet. It was the first time Iko had ever seen a refrigerator.

Of all the billeted soldiers he fetched and carried for, he had one benefactor whom he greatly admired – Captain Juan Miguel Martinez. And like all the other foreign soldiers at the encampment, 'El Capitano Miguel' and his company had been flown in urgently, just over a year ago, from Cuba.

Along with a handful of the senior orphans, Iko had become entrusted to clean the soldiers' weapons. Captain Miguel had taught him how to strip the rifle down to its component parts, how to lubricate the firing mechanism and rod through the barrel and occasionally he was even allowed to fire the Russian made AK47, at a target fixed to the perimeter fence. With the rifle pulled tightly against his shoulder, for the first time in his life Iko felt truly empowered.

He also particularly enjoyed accompanying the uniformed men on their short tours and sorties, although he struggled at first to carry the heavy weapons over long distances. But, the excitement of being away from the hovel he called home and being in amongst the action overrode all his fatigue. During these skirmishes he faced many brushes with death: dodging the bullets or, as befell the less fortunate ones, stepping on a landmine.

As much as Iko admired the El Capitano, Miguel was equally impressed with Iko's fearlessness in the face of danger. He was a fast learner, followed every command unflinchingly and was by his side at the critical moments, with a fully loaded magazine of bullets. It wasn't long before Iko was allowed to keep a weapon of his own, which he'd rescued from a fallen comrade. Carrying a weapon also meant he was invited to bed down at their barracks. He'd won their respect with his thirst for killing, driven by the urge to avenge the loss of those he had known and loved as a child.

When a group of captured guerrillas admitted, under interrogation, to having been responsible for the massacre at Mittende, Iko personally executed each one of them.

Captain Miguel was anxious and concerned that Iko should not turn into a bloodthirsty savage. He began to teach Iko about his beliefs and philosophy and the reasons for fighting in faraway lands. He no longer saw Iko as a lost African child, but as a human being on an equal footing and from this point forward he wanted to share as much of his own wisdom as he could.

When the Commander in Chief, Fidel Castro paid a morale-boosting visit to the ruling party in Lusalgo City, Iko was part of the armed escort and as a consequence heard all of his public speeches. Iko was particularly impressed with a phrase that Castro repeated many times about his desire for the rights of the poor to have free access to health and education and to share in the support for Internationalism among like minded countries who were under siege from Imperialists who, in turn, sought to overturn these 'monstrous' social reforms. Iko routinely experienced, at first hand, what Castro had remonstrated against in the language of freedom, as the civil war dragged on and on. Each day, more and more, the opposing forces of the Nationalist party kept on coming, reinforced by invading troops from South Africa and Zaire: mercenaries armed with American tanks, guns and artillery.

When the time came for Captain Miguel to return to Cuba at the end of his two-year stint in Africa, he brought Iko along with him, determined that he should be given further opportunities to improve himself and serve the Communist cause. Miguel knew that more than anyone he'd fought along side, this gifted young man had earned the right to an alternative life, something other than the short one he was destined to lead in war torn Ambundu.

Iko was kitted out with a pair of green, army fatigues together with a pair of calf length black combat boots. He was encouraged to stand on a table in the centre of the barrack room to the applause and cheers of the company. For the first time since Captain Miguel had mentioned taking Iko with him to Cuba, it began to feel like it was actually going to happen.

"Pack your belongings, Iko. You've a plane to catch tomorrow."

When the Soviet built Ilyusin Il-62 took off from Lusalgo City airport it was full to capacity, with two hundred soldiers on board. With the military code suspended, the atmosphere in the long narrow cabin was buzzing with song and laughter. It was also dizzy with smoke too as most of the men were puffing away on their fat Cuban cigars. Even the two military flight attendants had one gripped between their teeth as they handed out drinks. It wouldn't have been beyond the realms of fantasy to find a 'poule roti', slowly turning on a spit in one of the tail end toilets.

After eight, airborne hours the aircraft landed at a military base in Portugal to refuel. The men were encouraged to take a stretch outside, but the temperature out on the concrete apron was like stepping into an open oven. Most only lingered to take an uninterested glimpse at their surroundings before climbing back up the steps to the air-conditioned comfort of their seats.

As exciting as it was for Iko to be in the air again, he found the prospect of another nine-hour flight from Portugal to Havana to be a weary experience. On top of this was the fact he hadn't slept at all the previous night and as the bravado amongst the men subsided, Iko was just one of the many who slept for the whole remainder of the flight.

The reception, which awaited their aircraft at Jose Marti International airport, came as a complete surprise. A marching band struck up the introductory notes of La Bayamesa as a grey bearded General greeted the disembarking soldiers with handshakes and salutes. Even the city press photographers had been invited to record the action. The Cuban army was never one to shy away from self-promotion, especially in the limelight of victory.

Iko was confused at first when Captain Miguel suggested they shoulder their kit and find a bar to take lunch. Iko had left Lusalgo City just after breakfast and had flown the equivalent of a long day and yet it was still only lunchtime.

"I'll explain later," replied a cheery Miguel. "Come on, let's grab a cab."

Iko had his head stuck out of the window the whole time on their short ride into the heart of Havana. The city smelt very different to what he'd known back at the encampment. It was alive and fresh, exotic and sultry, a paradise like he could never have imagined and music appeared to ooze freely out of every building. People owned the streets and cars hogged the highways. The architecture looked very palatial and yet most of the buildings were occupied by ordinary people wearing their work clothes. They were either in constant motion, or parked in bars and cafés. Children played in the streets as housewives hung out their washing high above them. The men all smoked and the young girls giggled as they glided by.

"Well, Iko," Miguel said at last, "What do you think of my city?"

"There's so much happening at once," smiled Iko. "Is every city in Cuba like this? I love it."

"Wait until you see the Hotel Riviera and the playa," grinned Miguel.

****

Straying only a few hours away in time, but at least one hundred and eighty degrees along the political dial, one would find a land of immeasurable opportunities, the United States of America.

If there was one thing the American political parties knew how to do in overdrive, it was the razzmatazz surrounding the build up to a presidential election. It was already starting to dominate the news: every evening, on every TV channel in every State and it was still only the second of February and still practically ten months to election day.

Not even the dull, foggy skies across California could dampen the expectation that 1980 would be ringing in the changes of power with a stiff-arm charge to the right.

The present incumbent dithering behind the desk in the oval office had shown far too much weakness when it came to the U.S's foreign policy. It was no secret that; the Ayatollah of Iran was still laughing at the West, Brezhnev was gathering up new territory in the Middle East, Castro ruled unopposed in Cuba and also knocking at the back door, civil war raged, unabated, across the hills and jungles of Central America, and all, despite, the immense CIA funding that had been squandered there by a succession of puppet, militia styled rulers.

Times were a-changing. Three and a half thousand miles north-west and a world away from say the quiet marina in Cross Green for example, a key political meeting had been urgently ordered. The Campaign 'O-line' was calling a 'time out' on Democracy in the name of restorative justice.
Even before the fanfares and flag waving, parades and rallies were being written into busy schedules, there was always a flip side to every, orchestrated decision. And for the vast majority of people who would be later asked to cast their vote, well, they had to believe they were doing so on the evidence which they'd seen and heard discussed and debated in public.
But the 'politically motivated' flip side operated to a very different set of rules. One could say, there weren't any rules at all. This particular urgent meeting was definitely not a huddle of old timers discussing last night's game.
Within the bland walls of an insubstantial commercial building, on State Street in downtown Santa Barbara, California, a group of strategically selected strangers were about to assemble for the first time. In the guarded, square shaped room with no windows, there would be very few distractions and the two heavies outside the solid wooden door would ensure there'd be no interruptions either. The room was bug free and nothing was about to be recorded. The unimaginative interior and polished linoleum floor were clinically clean and as the occupants took up their seats they could be forgiven for thinking it was some kind of a surgical theatre. But a theatre by another name would describe this meeting of minds, perfectly.

On two sides of the sturdy oak table sat six men, each of them an expert in their own particular field of operations. At the head of the table was John Arfield. He was by far the most senior person present, in age and in rank. He had retired from 'intelligence' work ten years ago, but still kept himself keenly up to date with the latest coming and goings, thanks to his old boy network. It was an arrangement that worked both ways. 'You scratch our backs, John, and we'll scratch yours'.

Arfield had risen to prominence as a field agent for the CIA during the successful US backed coup d'état to overthrow President Veraz, in San Albarra in 1952. He had been part of the team responsible for training the rebel forces who had attacked and ousted the democratically elected government. It'd been his job to impart methods of psychological warfare and assassination techniques. He was a willing volunteer and even contributed to compiling the first assassination manuals. It didn't matter to him for example that he'd no evidence to confirm Señor Veraz who had only been in office eighteen months was indeed a communist. In John's words, 'he was the nearest thing they had to one, and he'd do just fine, until a real one came along.'

Once the meeting door behind him had been firmly closed from the outside and his audience had settled into their high back chairs and had helped themselves to cold drinking water, Arfield rose to his feet and walked behind the seated men, placing an identical, closed red folder on the table for each of them to read at the appointed time. The folders were ambiguously marked 'Foreign News'. It was obvious by the blank faces on everyone around the table that they had absolutely no idea why they'd been summoned here.

"What's this all about John?" The only person present to have met Arfield recently was Allan Klein, the assistant presidential campaign director. His curiosity was getting the better of him. He knew he had to speak before he began his uncomfortable shuffling and scratching his imaginary nervous itch. Although Klein didn't know the man at the head of the table personally, he respected his authority. He had observed him recently in the Party candidate's company on several occasions, albeit from a short distance away though alas, too far to eavesdrop on their intimate conversations. For now, Klein could only assume that Arfield had most likely promised the largest contribution to the campaign fund. Clearly, he had a large stake in the candidate's future.

"Before we get into that Allan, let me introduce you all to one another. Immediately next to me is Allan Klein, assistant director at campaign headquarters. We've met on only a handful of occasions so far, but we're both committed to the long haul. That's right, isn't it Allan." Arfield allowed himself a wry smile. "Next to Allan is Julian Glendenning from PR Incorporated and further on my right is Jim McGarry, head of campaign security. Thanks for sparing the time today Jim, I know you've your hands full at the minute." There followed a brief appreciative nod between the two heavyweights.

"On my left," continued Arfield, "Robert Stockley, our press officer. Next to Robert is Felix Schwarzkopf, operations executive, and finally furthest on my left is Ben Hansen, formerly with the Drug Enforcement Administration and now a freelance detective."

In the brief pause that followed Arfield's matter of fact introductions, there resulted a few quizzical glances from the other party supporters with regards to the presence of Hansen.

Arfield was still standing. He lent forward with his arms stretched out and gripped the edges of the table with his taut hands. His mood took on a more serious tone.

"Welcome everyone. As you're all aware this year's presidential campaign is ours for the taking. It's in all our interests to get our man across the line first. And one of the biggest draws in our favour will be taking a strong line of attack at our recent disastrous foreign policy. It's not necessarily a bad thing that our candidate has already been labelled a dangerous right wing extremist." Arfield paused to allow a few chuckles to subside. "We can put a positive spin on any label the media sling at us. But we have to keep a tight lid on any skeletons that might pop out of the cupboard and bite us in the ass."

This sounded like political rhetoric to the senior heads at the table. Arfield noticed a few nonchalant looks on the faces of the men beside him. But, he was a 'Commie-Bashing' bully who had ways of bringing the unenlightened and the most sceptical opponents around to his way of thinking.

"Gentlemen, please open the folder in front of you."

Each of the red folders contained a selection of intelligence photographs and on the reverse of each one was a brief description as to regarding what they were looking at. Most of the scenes showed a solitary building on fire surrounded by a miss-matched bunch of foreign troops. Black smoke could be seen pouring skyward from several windows. The soldiers on the ground looked on with what appeared to be a casual indifference. Some even stared directly into the camera, smiling.

Arfield allowed the men at the table to absorb a few details before he commenced to fatten out the facts. "What you're looking at occurred three days ago in San Albarra city. The burning building belongs to the Spanish Embassy. There were around forty people trapped inside. They all perished."

"This is the same San Albarra that we crushed in '52, I presume?" commented Felix Schwarzkopf.

"That's right Felix. The man we installed as president after we persuaded Veraz to move over is still in command down there. The official line from the Presidential palace in San Albarra is that the fire was started by a group of peasants from the Peoples Collective. Allegedly they'd gone there to inform the Spanish ambassador's office about some massacre in one or other of the hillside villages. The Presidential Office got wind of this little gathering and sent in three hundred assault troops to deal with the matter quickly. The peasants were ordered to leave, but instead they barricaded themselves inside and became martyrs to their cause, eliminating the embassy staff too for good measure."

"Goddamit, what has that to do with our campaign? We can't be held responsible for every damn tragedy that occurs in

Latin America," bemoaned the blustering voice of Jim McGarry. "Hell, they probably deserved to die, anyhow."

"I'm not sure the Spanish Government will share your appraisal, but I take your point Jim," replied Arfield. "We still have some reliable people down there and the real news, gentlemen is that the assault troops barricaded the embassy from the outside and set the building alight before any of the local TV crews arrived. Our agent has since discovered the peasants took their own Journo with them who managed to escape the burning building with a handful of film rolls." Arfield paused to see the reaction on the faces of the men around the table. It was Felix Schwarzkopf who reached the conclusion first, that this could damage their candidate's foreign policy if it became known we were responsible for putting murderous gangsters in charge of our neighbouring countries. "Do we know who this journalist is?" he enquired.

Arfield smiled; he already had the answer. "If you turn to the next photograph, gentlemen."

The black and white photograph showed the portrait of a young, good-looking women, crouching forward and holding a camera up to her chest.

"She's just a gal," scoffed Jim McGarry.

"Don't be fooled by her looks," replied Arfield quickly. "That bitch could scupper our whole campaign. Her name is Ilena Romero. She's of Spanish decent, but holds a French passport. She's a freelance who specialises in war zones. Her dossier is quite impressive. Off the top of my head..." Arfield recalled a few of her major assignments. "Soweto in '76, Santiago in '77, San Carlos de Bariloche in '78."

"And now San Albarra, so she specialises in cities beginning with S." interrupted Jim, again, "Big deal."

There were one or two laughs before Arfield continued.

"Well we know her form, Jim. She likes nothing better than to find a scoop and get her pictures in the nationals. She has a contact with the Chronicle and Herald over in Washington and we all know where that can lead."

Felix was the first to close his folder and he tapped the red cover as he spoke. "So how do we silence Miss Romero? Do we know where she is now?"

There was some uncomfortable shuffling around the table, mainly from Allen Klein who'd begun to scratch the back of his neck. Surely they weren't all here to discuss how to bump off a foreign journalist.

"According to my CIA contact, she's managed to evade our agent in San Albarra. She gave him the slip at the airport down there, by changing flights at the last minute. What we know is she's heading for Antigua, before possibly obtaining a passage to Florida."

Most of the players around the table were still absorbing Miss Romero's bio. Up until this point, Ben Hansen had not uttered one sound. He had wondered why he'd been invited to this particular meeting, but hearing the Chairman mention Antigua it was becoming clear to him, having spent the last two years of his service in the DEA, in and around the Caribbean. He'd nothing else in common with any of the other men around the table apart from the fact he had voted for the Party at the last election. He was a former law enforcer and was only here because there was a big payday promised, although he wasn't about to get involved with anything underhand. His first impressions of John Arfield was that he appeared to be a person who operated on several different levels. Ben noticed Arfield also had a slight flow to his Texan accent whenever he sensed any kind of threat. Particularly, the way Arfield's voice had the habit of crunching down on the first syllable of a word of command. Without doubt, his natural air of authority was the sort that most fighting men would follow.

Arfield's next statement was directed solely Ben's way. He'd anticipated it coming.

"Ben, you've valuable experience in that part of the world. How do you feel about taking a trip down there and locating Miss Romero for us? We don't have much time. Are you able to do that?"

"Am I working alone on this, or are you providing a couple of extra pair of hands?"

"Sorry Ben, it's down to you and you alone. Unless you have some reliable people you can use in Antigua. What sort of a time scale do you anticipate reaching a conclusion on this one?"

"If I fly down there today, Antigua's only a small island, maybe two more days at the outside to find her. And then what?"

"Just keep an eye on her for us until we send a negotiator to meet with her." Arfield looked into Hansen's eyes for a reaction, but there was no sign of emotion. "That's all for today gentlemen. Please leave your folders on the table. It goes without saying that anything we've discussed here this morning remains solely inside this room. The nodding heads was a sign for Arfield to press the buzzer beneath the lip of the table and within two seconds the exit door was opened, by one of the two heavies who'd been guarding the room.

"Oh, Ben, can you spare me a minute whilst I give you my contact details." Arfield waited until the last man had left the room before handing Hansen his business card. "This is my personal phone number. You can ring me anytime, day or night, as soon as you locate her. The faster you can do that, the bigger the cheque you'll receive from us. I hope I've emphasised how important this is to our candidate."

It was Ben's turn to stare into Arfield's eyes for a reaction. The deeper he looked the less he liked what he saw. He wouldn't trust Arfield, no matter how much he was paid.

But he'd made up his mind to take his money all the same. If there was one thing that drove him on in life it was his sense of duty. He recognised the American way of life was under threat from outsiders. Not that he agreed with any of the misdemeanours that politicians these days got away with in office. But if there were any changes to be made he would rather they came from an American citizen like himself.

****

When Captain Miguel's 'R and R' came to an end, after six weeks of games, girls and grandiose living, it was time for him to report back to duty. Before doing so, he had a firm plan up his sleeve for Iko. During their break from the struggles in the world, he'd taught Iko how to get by in Havana, as well as how to navigate at sea and crew his boat, how to read the tides and the waves and where to find the biggest fish. Iko had managed to conquer his fear of the water, but was unable to stay afloat without a life jacket. No matter how he tried, he just couldn't swim. In the final days, Miguel had called in a favour from an old sweat at the Special Operations office, who had agreed to enrol Iko, once Miguel had returned to his company at the military base in Santiago.

The old sweat was one Alfonso Chiquata. He was a veteran from '53, one of the originals of the 26th of July Movement. He'd semi-retired a decade ago, but was unable to completely back away from running a sort of school for spies. Once every couple of years a candidate would successfully pass through his classes and join one of the illustrious, worldwide undercover networks. But the quality of recruits in recent times had greatly disappointed Alfonso. 'I don't understand the kids these days. Most are only interested in being in a band and smoking weed.'

Iko was paid a small wage to attend Alfonso's classes, which enabled him to pay for a room in a shared house in the old quarter of Havana. When not attending classes, Iko kept himself to himself, but he shared the same easy way in which people just got on with life, despite the hardships imposed on them by the international trade sanctions. Everyone accepted the frequent power cuts and even when their taps temporarily ran dry, they were content to live as they did, because they had their freedom and in all honesty the nation's standard of living had improved significantly since the revolution, despite the fact they were largely cut off from the rest of the world. And yet still encompassed by all these disadvantages and inconveniences, Cuba could produce fine artists and musicians and sporting heroes that won gold medals at the Olympic games.

Iko continued to impress his military coaches at the school of spies. His physical strength was exemplary. He'd shown he could adapt to all their initiative tests with a killer instinct to the like they had never seen before. Iko persevered with most difficult challenges and in doing so he also managed to swim a short distance at sea. Even Alfonso began to take notice. Maybe he had a champion on his hands once again. In just twelve months Iko had also learnt to speak English, or at least an Americanized version of it. What his instructors hadn't noticed in class was his inability to socialise outside the office. He had no real friends at his digs and for a girlfriend, he relied on the local brothel for his comforts. It was the policy of the school that any successful candidate would be placed in an environment where they could circulate unnoticed. Iko's prospects were limited, but not impossible to overcome.

When the Cuban forces were sent to shore up their beleaguered comrades in Latin America, they faced many logistical problems. They had to probe new ways and routes for supplying their military aid to their friends into countries like San Albarra. They quickly realised they must secure a beachhead, closer to the South American coast line, especially since their favoured shipping routes to Mexico where under constant surveillance by their arch enemy, the U.S Navy and Air Force.

So, Alfonso and his colleagues came up with the scheme of sending Iko to the Caribbean to find a suitable location. His brief was to locate a deep-water harbour in a remote area. At first, Iko thought it was just another field exercise or an extravagant initiative test. However, when he was given a new identity and informed he must leave his digs immediately, he knew this must be the real thing. Just before he left Havana, aboard a smelly old fishing trawler, he was handed a bag containing more bank notes than he'd ever seen in his life. He was given the name and place of his contact at Station Z in St. Georges, on the Caribbean island of Grenada. This trust worthy communist would pass on further instructions to him.

On the day of departure, Alfonso called Iko into his office for a few final words of advice. He spoke to him in English.
"How do you feel about what we are asking you to do?"

Iko answered without the slightest hesitation. "You can rely on me, comrade Alfonso."

Alfonso beckoned Iko to relax a minute and be seated. "Listen, don't worry if it takes you a while to locate what we have asked you to find. You might not even find anything suitable at all. The important thing to remember is to establish yourself in the local community. Put down a few roots, stay out of trouble and don't forget to maintain a regular correspondence through your controller. I know you're going make a success of this." Alphonso smiled and for a moment, he was held by a drifting memory from his own younger days. " I wish I was coming with you too," he said wistfully, "And have my time all over again and if I could, I would do everything exactly the same." Alfonso lifted himself to his feet and respectfully saluted his protégé.

Iko sprang to his feet and raised his right arm sharply in reply. "Thank you, for the things you have taught me. I won't let you down."

Chapter Two

Bar Amigo's

I was lying on my side in bed, watching Fionn as she rolled over to face me. She opened her blurred eyes for a brief moment and without speaking closed them again. Our little rest room above the bar was bathed in the full light of the morning sun and by the east facing, half open window the muslin drapes performed a lazy dance. Knowing it was my morning to get up early and set up the tables for our guests, I thought I'd try my old routine of kidding Fionn into doing it for me.

"Hey, wake up Sleepy. It's your turn to do the breakfasts."

Fionn's eyes opened in an instant at my absurd suggestion. "Ha, ha, same old jokes," she moaned, "Just get on with it Byrney."

I kissed her on the top of her head and gently rolled out of bed. Fionn's little travel clock was pointing to six a.m. - time for me to move. Despite a soft sea breeze and an additional overhead fan stirring the morning air, the temperature inside our room felt to be at least eighty degrees. Still, the electric fan's hypnotic movement did it's best to convince us that without it our room would feel much warmer, perhaps even eighty-two.

My first task was to ride up to the bakery in Charlestown, to pick up our daily order. Somehow during the last twenty months of our occupation of Bar Amigo's, we'd acquired most of what we'd lacked through hand-me-downs and second hand purchases which, thanks mainly to our friends and neighbours, had fallen into our laps with very little exhaustive searching on our part.

The little Honda step through motorbike was one such splendid example that had been loaned to us for free, from Sly at the Barracuda Dive Shop. Okay, so it didn't do much for my street cred, but this was Antigua, not West Lancashire and besides, look at how I was dressed: an open face helmet and sandals? Well, I guess that would've meant me riding past pavements full of derisive laughter, back home in England. As for looking the part right here and now, it didn't seem to matter since I'd found a satisfying inner contentment; I'd got the perfect partner and lover in Fionn and a fantastic little business of our own, in the kind of laid back lifestyle that most people would give up their right nadger for, as my old mate Lewis would say. And besides: this old step through fired into life with the first kick and even though I'd never tinkered with her much, she never let me down. (I smiled and had to remind myself I was referring to the motorbike, in case anyone passing could read my thoughts.)

The only other essential item a motorcyclist needed when riding anywhere around the island was a pair of goggles. The larger vehicles kicked up clouds of dust, which inevitably hung around in the roadside vegetation and swirled about in the breeze, even when you had the highway to yourself. And one had to remember to keep ones mouth closed too, at all times, as the many winged insects took great delight in zooming to the back of your throat, whenever you least expected it.

A quarter of an hour inland from the marina at Cross Green, I popped the little Honda onto her centre stand and unfastened the bungee cord which secured my plastic shopping basket to the back of the seat. After parting with twenty dollars for our order, I'd almost managed to get away from the counter when in walked police sergeant Fred 'Hawkeye' Hawkins, from Charlestown police station. 'Typical', I thought. No matter how I tried to vary my time of arrival and departure from Lukemans's Bakery I always ended up bumping into him; not that he was an aggressive or unfriendly sort. In fact, something more like the opposite was true, in my limited experience of dealings with him. Like the rest of the customers, he'd obviously been lured here by the same irresistible scent that filled the streets either side of the hot ovens. The thing I'd prefer not to come face to face with was the sight of his uniform and the way he slapped his holstered truncheon with the palm of his hand - always put me right on edge. Why did policemen always make me feel guilty whenever I looked at them? Must have been my guilty conscience. But, here in Antigua I had a clean slate and there was nothing for me to feel guilty about; more than that, not only had I turned my life around in the last four years, I'd become a minor celebrity. If only I'd been allowed to shout about it. Only Fionn, Leyda, Raoul, Pug and the chairman of Manners Bank in St. Johns were aware that I ought to have been treated as a conquering hero, a fully paid up member of the three adventurous cave diggers who'd discovered the long lost Potosi Cross. For the time being, it was still lying, locked inside a bank vault, away from the clutches of British red tape, until the day of Antiguan Independence had been granted.

"Are you stealing my croissants, Byrney?" declared the 'Tannoy' like voice, almost imitating a railway station announcement.

I looked up at the sparkling looking, uniformed policeman. His broad grin put me at ease a little and gave me time to put a variation on my standard reply. "These are all yesterday's batch, Hawkeye. I saved the fresh ones for you," I replied, pointing at my stuffed basket. There were only two, lonely, crescent shaped, croissants left on the counter. I didn't have the heart to take them all, unlike Fionn who always fulfilled our order completely.

I began backing away to make my escape.

"Bye Byrney. Stay outta trouble," he bawled as he followed me all the way to the door, with his halogen eyes.

As I returned my motorbike to the back of Amigo's I noticed the early risers amongst our guests were already seated: under the cover of our palm leafed veranda, tumbler glasses in hand and sipping their freshly squeezed juices, half a dozen, yawning, sun tanned faces. The young ones were half dressed in sandy shorts, whilst the older clients wore expensive looking baggy clothes. They each conducted their private conversations through whispers and giggles. I was pleased they all at least appeared content, all except our regular, morning visitor, whose sweat still leaked over his prominent brow and down his large, dark brown face. He gave me a silent nod. Pug Walker was a man of few words, which made it all the more important to listen when he did speak. The only exception was when he nervously rubbed his worry beads in his spade like hands. On these numerous occasions, he was liable to rattle off any number of incoherent words of mumbo-jumbo. But, for now, he just bowed his head at me and continued to stare down into his coffee cup.

"At last," announced an exasperated Fionn. "What kept you?"

It was her customary, rhetorical greeting which as usual I chose to ignore. The way we'd started bumbling along together recently, like an old worn pair of gloves, reminded me of Madge and Edward at the Friary in Crowston: always behaving slightly at odds in everyone else's eyes, but nevertheless deeply in love with each other when they were alone. We must be getting older too I thought.

"I see Pug's arrived already. Didn't take him long to tidy up Leyda's paths today," I commented as I handed Fionn the basket of loaves, which she immediately began dispensing into the worn rattan bowls, ready for our diners."

Fionn began to recount a tale as she distributed the croissants. She was good at that sort of thing, doing several tasks at once. "Well, you know Pug. He probably set out four or five hours ago and whilst you've been swanning around the island you've missed all the excitement," she smiled teasingly.

I broke the end of one of the crusty loaves and gathered up a large flake of the white fluffy dough and stuffed it into my mouth. "Oh yer, what was that: three pelicans doing a sand dance like Wilson, Kepple and Betty?" I did a quick demo by shuffling my feet. There was always plenty of loose sand lingering around our floor.

"Byrney, be serious for a minute. It actually gave me quite a fright to begin with."

I placed the loaf down on the chopping board and gave her my full attention. "Go on."

"When I first came out onto the veranda this morning there was this ugly, giant iguana. It must have wandered over from the mangroves. It was just standing there, perfectly still, like a frozen statue. The only thing that moved was his long, wiry, black tongue, which kept flipping in and out. It almost freaked me out. You must have seen it when you left earlier?"

"No, I didn't notice anything."

Fionn raised her eyebrows with disbelief. "Well it was just as Pug arrived too. The moment he saw it, he began rolling his eyes. You know what he's like. He kept saying it was an ill omen and that by the end of the day something dreadful would happen."

I began to laugh. "Argh, Pug's always like that, full of dread and superstition. Take no notice. If anything dreadful happens, I'll protect you."

"Oh, is that right?" scoffed Fionn, "You mean the same kind of protection whenever there's a bump in the night and you make me get out of bed to check. Here, take these out to our diners before they wander off too, in search of somewhere else to eat."

"Thanks, Madge," I replied trying to hide my blushes. It's not my fault I'm a heavy sleeper, I thought.

The travel agents: on Main Street, in St. Georges, was named Queen Conch Travel, but in Havana circles and to a select few it was referred to as Station Z. The window front was emblazoned with posters and photos and boasted the names of exotic locations, throughout the Americas. It looked very much like a well-travelled leather suitcase that might have been found languishing on the shelf of a lost property office. The offers on display here, to a would be tourist, looked very tempting, even for someone as young and inexperienced in these matters as Iko. He'd returned to where he'd begun, having come full circle around the coastline of Grenada. His search for a suitable beachhead location had been unproductive, but not a complete waste of time. He'd enjoyed every minute of it and it had further inspired him to do better at the next location - Station Y.

He was about to discover where exactly that was from the comrade behind the desk, but he'd have to wait for the moment when Desmond Riley finished his call. It sounded like he was in the middle of taking a client's reservation for the coming weekend's cruise to one of the many cayes in the area. Iko had already seen the hand drawn poster in the shop window. This week's charter was bound for Spanish Caye - a tiny island with no domestic or commercial buildings: just a watchtower and a few coconut palms and no doubt, stored away somewhere, there must have been a home made grill for roasting burgers. Twenty dollars guaranteed you a seat on the boat and a day of unspoilt bathing with food and drinks thrown in for free. Desmond had got his sales pitch down to a fine art.

He put down his phone and smiled at the Havana agent entering his shop. "Doctor Livingstone I presume?" Des was fond of jokes, even bad ones. He'd picked up a Yorkshire accent too, during a three year stint of driving the buses for the Bradford and Bingley Bus Corporation. At that stage in his career, if you could call it that, he'd not yet discovered communism as a way of settling a few scores in life. No, he'd been encouraged to emigrate to England, by his uncle Malcom, who'd found Des a job in advance. It was all the rage back in the sixties. According to Malcom, you could walk into a job any morning of the week and if you didn't like it, there was another one waiting for you at the labour exchange the same afternoon. But Des didn't need to change. He loved driving the buses. He got to meet lots of characters, real people - 'Salts' he called them. Lots of old dears moaning about the weather and the young as they struggled with their shopping bags and tartan trollies, always harping on about the old days, when they had ration cards and Hitler.

These happy times for Desmond and Malcom, in West Yorkshire, turned sour when racism became more widespread. He didn't mind being called Chalky by his mates at work. He knew that, for them, it was only used as a term of endearment. Then, one night after a late shift, he was badly beaten by a gang of Nationalist Skin-Heads. Des simply couldn't understand their hatred towards him. No one should have their head stamped on, just because of the colour of their skin. Des couldn't get away fast enough. As soon as he was well enough to travel, he sailed back to the Caribbean. But, when Des arrived home again to Grenada, everything had changed. There was a new political movement in charge of government. Lots of new schools and hospitals were being built, supported by training programs for teachers and doctors, all aided by foreign investment from Cuba. Armed with his experiences, Des was handed the opportunity, quite by chance, to pursue his dream of being a stand up comedian in one of the many night clubs that had begun to spring up in town, with the onset of the blossoming tourist industry.

Then, one night, he was approached by an interesting character, who happened to be sitting in the audience. Des's act included a lot of anti-imperialist type stuff: jokes about capitalism and how the wealthiest people tended to do the most stupidest things. His admirer turned out to be a high ranking official from Cuba and what he had to say really resonated with him, in relation to his past experiences.

After a couple more meetings between the knowledgeable older man and the comedian, they struck a deal. He agreed to set Des up in the travel business. All Des had to do, in return, was look after certain tourists, which were sent to him from Cuba, and maintain a line of communication with the Special Operations Office in Havana. It seemed almost too good to be true. The only down side to becoming a casual member of the communist party was that once he'd been recruited and put in place, he'd have to give up his act. However Des continued to be funny. The most frequent instruction he'd been given was that he should try to blend into his surroundings. And so he figured that no one would suspect a clown of passing information to a foreign power. In reality Des was never in any danger, it wasn't as if he would ever be asked to kidnap or kill anyone.

He smiled at Iko as he opened his top drawer and handed over a large brown envelope. "This came for you yesterday Mr. Delgado. Looks like you've won first prize in this week's lucky draw. Could be a twenty four hour pass at Lily's," he joked, winking at Iko. "Second prize is a forty eight hour pass at Lily's, so don't come running to me if it hurts when you take a pee."

Iko ignored his remarks as he ripped open the top of the envelope. It contained a book of travellers' cheques, a Grenadian drivers licence and a passport in the name of Eldridge Delgado. There was also a hand written sheet of directions of where to meet his next contact. Iko pulled out the book of travellers' cheques, which had been made out to his new identity. Each one was printed to the value of one hundred dollars. He quickly flipped each of the thirty leaves to see if they were all the same. As Des watched he began to whistle in appreciation. "Where are they sending you to next, Iko?"

Iko picked up the sheet of handwritten instructions and details regarding his assignment at Station Y. Iko knew it was okay to tell Des where he was heading. He probably already knew. "Antigua, I'm to find a man called Orr at the Dockyard museum," he replied.

Des couldn't help chuckling to himself. "Oh, you're in for a jolly jape with old Norman. Watch out, he has some very interesting torture techniques, like boring the pants of his victims. Half an hour in his company and you'll be begging for mercy."

Iko smiled as he turned to leave. "Adios Des. Be careful you don't injure yourself with a splinter from your chair."

"Hey that's not bad for one of yours. Would you like me to let the girls at Lily's know you're leaving?"

As Iko closed the door behind him, Des watched him walk away before picking up his other phone, the red one marked top secret, in hand written felt tip pen. He dialled long distance and when his call was connected he spoke in Spanish, commencing with a series of coded numbers. After a few seconds the operator transferred his call, to Alphonso Chinquata.

It was very early morning when Iko received a knock on his cabin door; he wasn't sleeping, having already been alerted by the footsteps moving towards him along the corridor. The crew of the 'El Alca' were signalling that he'd shortly reach his destination at the head of Falmouth Harbour. They were happy to have the temporary distraction of a paying guest on board for their outward journey. Their normal vocation however was 'trolling' for Yellow Fin. They had a four rod spread, all rigged up and ready to go and as soon as they'd dropped off their man below deck they would head out to the seasonal fishing grounds once again. Only last week they'd landed a four hundred pound tuna and at five dollars a pound they were hoping for an even bigger fish this time, maybe one of the 'Granders' if they were lucky. They intended to start hunting as soon as they were free.

The sleepy marina at Cross Green was in permanent holiday mode, as usual. When the bow of the El Alca kissed the point of the wooden jetty and dropped the gearbox into reverse, the narrow gap between the hull and the pier remained just close enough for Iko to leap ashore, with his kitbag slung over his shoulder, before the fishing boat hastily accelerated away towards the open sea.

Iko headed down the jetty towards the deserted quayside bouncing over the loose planks. At the end of the quayside he paused to get his bearings. He had studied the map of the southeast coastline the previous night, so that he wouldn't have need of it once he'd arrived. There was nothing more alien than walking around clutching a map, if you wanted to pass for one of the locals. As he turned right into the yellow, dusty road he had to leap out of the way of a red motorcycle, which hurtled past him, with an empty basket tied to the seat.

From the marina at Cross Green, Iko had calculated it would be a brisk twenty-minute walk down to the old dockyard. He studied all the historic buildings along the way, some of which were in a ruinous state of repair, like the two rows of giant rounded obelisks leading down to the seafront. He had no idea as to what purpose they served. The morning breeze lifted the union flag that laid claim to the crescent shaped bay, a typically tropical, sandy scrubland.

Behind the solid garden wall to his right, stood a two story white building. Its large, symmetrical windows were gaping half open, lazily breathing in a taste of the sea. Iko walked through the open, iron gate, which was hung from hinges seized by a coating of weather worn rust. 'All this grandeur', he thought, 'redundant and left to rot'. His first glimpses of the residue of British imperialism made quite an impression on him. Even the hanging Museum sign creaked on its chains.

He followed the path up to the main entrance and eyed a comfortable place to sit whilst someone came to open up. To his surprise, the door began to slowly open before he'd reached the first step. The figure of a grey-haired man, half hidden by the oak door waved him forward to enter. Then, immediately after Iko stepped inside, he noticed the museum keeper's head peering back down the path and glancing hastily from side to side, as if he was checking they weren't being secretly observed, before locking the door behind him.

"Step this way, Señor Delgado." The middle-aged man said nervously, having been set on his back foot by Iko's strong, physical appearance. He'd had precious little time to prepare for Señor Delgado's arrival since his weekly call to Havana, but had he been given more time it would still not have lessened the shock of coming face to face with a real live spy at his own front door.

He'd made the same routine call for the last five years and yesterday had been the first time he'd been asked to set out the ground for a fellow agent. For as long as he could remember he thought Station Y should have really been named Station 'y bother'. He had been forced to act quickly during the last twenty-four hours and it was a testament to his own network of contacts that he'd managed to organise a role for his guest and a place from which he could carry out his mission. But, as Orr's nerves were now starting to get the better of him, most of all he was just hoping there'd be no funny stuff. 'Be courteous and polite and hopefully, he'll soon be on his way'.

The muscular, dark stranger nodded at his host and spoke softly, "Please call me Ellie," replied Iko, referring to his new identity. Iko noticed the name tag pinned to the old man's shirt - Norman Orr, Dockyard Museum Guide.

As Orr led the way through to the large gallery showroom, Iko began to absorb his surroundings: the framed photographs on all the walls and the table top cabinets, filled with Naval memorabilia; ancient weapons and uniforms and more mundane items like pewter mugs and plates.

"Quite an impressive collection, don't you think?" regaled Norman. "Most of the exhibits here are over two hundred years old, from Admiral Nelson's era." Norman was determined to try and engage Ellie in conversation, "You'll have heard of him, no doubt?"

Iko peered into one of the glass cases to get a closer look at one of the rusty canon balls as the jittery repartee continued unabated.

"And there are more salvaged items stored here, which haven't seen the light of day yet. We're having the upper floor renovated, you know." He was about to explain further, but his mouth was running dry, so he just pointed up at the ceiling as his voice faded away. "Should be ready, any, day, now."

Iko couldn't stop himself from yawning. He'd already switched himself off from Orr's commentary and found himself thinking about his own, shorter history. Seeing all the items of militaria reminded him of the barracks at the encampment in Lusalgo. It had been a bitter sweet decision to leave his ancestral country of birth. He'd not thought about the orphanage and especially the other children since he'd left them all behind.

Norman had regained his composure and commenced rattling away again to himself. At the same time, Iko began to wonder where his new quarters were to be found and how quickly he could reach them, hopefully not with this boring *pendejo*. To Iko's thinking, Orr just didn't seem the type of person to be a sleeper agent. Maybe someone else was using Orr's name badge. He thought about probing him with questions of his own, to confirm he was actually who he was supposed to be, but at this precise moment he'd more pressing issues to resolve.

Orr noticed Delgado becoming restless and by the steely look in his eyes, Orr realised he'd better get on with the business in hand. He turned away from his desk, opened the curtains behind him and removed three large boxes, to reveal an old iron safe in the corner of the storage room. Then, he removed a ring of keys that were chained to his trousers, selected the longest one and slid it into the lock. Iko looked on with interest. When the safe door opened Iko noticed a small pile of documents and below, on a shelf of it's own was a leather bound book whose page ends were rather worn and bulky. Whatever secrets it held Iko thought they must be of special interest to his host to warrant such secure precautions. He made a mental note of it's location for future reference.

Orr removed the top document and smiled at Delgado. "All your instructions are in here. You'll be working for the local government Marine Observation Team. They have officers posted at various points around the island based in some of the old Naval forts. But don't worry about learning as you go. It's a newly created agency, so you'll all be in the same boat, so to speak. You've been allocated to Fort Anderson. It's about five miles up the coast from here. There's a path from Cross Green leading through White House Bay. Fort Anderson is at the headland on the other side of the mangroves." Orr paused to check that Delgado was still keeping up to speed. He needn't have bothered. "As you've got all your kit with you, I can lend you our Land Rover. Take the coast road to St. Johns. Fort Anderson is well sign posted despite it being abandoned and unoccupied, but don't worry it's secure and there's a new power cable too. So at least you'll have a light for company."

Orr removed the car keys from his top drawer and held them out for Iko to take. "Just return it when you're settled in. There's no rush, in a day or two is fine. The Marine Observation Team has also provided you with a Dory speed boat. It's not exceptionally fast, but you'll find her reliable and stable. Should suit your needs perfectly."

Iko picked up his kit bag and headed for the door, with Orr running after him. "You'll need this," he said holding up a large, black, iron key. "It's to unlock the front door of the fort. Sorry about the size. Still, at least you won't lose it." He quickly stepped in front of Iko and unbolted the museum door.

"The Land Rover's just parked up at the rear, just follow the path around to the left." Before parting, Orr checked that Iko had understood. "Do you have any questions?"

Iko pocketed the keys and reflected for a moment as he stared through Orr's hollow, empty eyes. Then he looked away again, in the instant that Orr recognised in Iko a hidden look of innocence about him.

"Just one." said Iko. "Is there a refrigerator?"

Afternoons were normally our quiet time at Bar Amigo's. It was usually iced mambo's and tall, cool, drinks and the regular deliveries: like the one which arrived in an old, beat up, pickup truck, from the Antigua Brewing Company over on Crabbs Peninsula. We wanted to offer an alternative to the local brew which had quite an unusual flavour all of it's own and wasn't to everyone's liking, especially the fussy English. So we requested a weekly supply of the fashionable Red Stripe Lager from Jamaica - if it was good enough for Mister Marley, it was good enough for us.

Even when there were only a handful of drinkers sat at our veranda tables, there were always plenty of odd jobs to take care of. I routinely did a few laps of all our buildings, armed with a bag of nails and my trusty hammer, to check if anything had worked loose in the breeze. There was nothing more annoying than being woken up by random tapping and flapping noises in the middle of the night.

The sea was looking particularly inviting, becalmed and gently caressing the shore. The first high tide of the day had just peaked and was starting to recede. Not that there was a great, noticeable difference in height between the two tides. It was more about which direction the dominant current was moving in. There could be all manner of flotsam and jetsam, waiting on the high tide mark along the beach for the early strollers. In the days before our bar opened at Amigo's, Fionn and I had often taken a morning promenade, along the short beach in front of the veranda. We'd find the usual driftwood and coconut husks, bits of old rope and the occasional punctured flip flop - nothing to write home about.

Whilst the initial work was being done on the veranda Fionn had the idea of cutting a hatch in the front wall, so that we could serve drinks directly, without our clients having to queue up inside. It's strange how at first we were nervous about making changes and improvements to the buildings. It was as if we were being eyeballed, or that we were trespassing on someone else's land. We had to pinch ourselves daily that it actually all belonged to us.

Leyda Friday, who had helped us to secure the purchase of Amigo's, was a regular late afternoon visitor. She'd drop by after finishing work for a cool, island rum, having walked the short distance from the nearest car park outside the chandlery shops in Cross Green. Besides enquiring about how our business was shaping up, she was also a well-informed source of local gossip. She sat at the same table that Pug occupied each morning before breakfast.

"I've a new neighbour," she announced, as she removed her purse from her handbag to pay for her drink. "Some young boy from Grenada. My office has also been notified. He's got a job on the Marine Observation Team."

Fionn handed her a few coins in change from her bum belt. "I didn't know you had any houses near you." She replied.

"Well, it's one of the old forts. You can't actually see it from my house. Fort Anderson is just the other side of the mangroves. It'll be lovely to make a new acquaintance, he'll probably walk right past my home, if ever he takes the path this way into town."

I returned to the busy end of the bar, after stacking up the empty crates around the back. Leyda and Fionn were still chatting together as some of our clients began trundling back to their rooms from their daily excursions: the beach and perhaps the ruins on top of Shirley Heights. It was a popular vantage point and much easier to access than the summit of Arawak hill.

The sun was making a slow descent and setting fire to the horizon. It occurred at more or less the same time everyday, around six p.m. It was a view you never tired of, but then, as I was about to step back inside the bar, I noticed a seagull, about twenty-five yards out at sea, standing on the water; or rather standing on something which was partially submerged in the water. I moved forward and stood next to Leyda's table, to get a clearer view. Fionn, who'd been facing the sea, had noticed it too; the seagull had begun pecking on the object directly beneath it's feet.

"What's it eating?" She asked, casually.

Leyda turned around also, to face the strange looking phenomenon.

"I'll go and take a closer look," I volunteered. "Perhaps it's a dead fish, or something."

I walked down the gently, sloping, sandy beach until I reached the water's edge. I flapped my arms and shouted a few 'shoos', but the defiant seagull was having none of it. I slipped off my trainers and paddled out the short distance. When I got to within five feet, the lone seagull reluctantly took off, with a squawk of complaint. Stepping to within an arms length and waist high in the sea, I suddenly lost my footing at the shock of what I was seeing and began to panic, breathing frantically. I could hear Fionn shouting from the edge of the shore.

"What it is, Byrney? What have you found?"

I turned around in line with her voice and saw her expression change rapidly, when she caught the look on my startled face. Behind her, I could see some of the other guests were moving down from the veranda. Eventually, I found my own voice again.

"You'd better go back and stop the others from getting any closer."

"Oh my god, what is it?" She answered nervously.

"It's a dead body. The body of a woman."

I gently held one of the cadaver's ankles and began to ease her closer to the shore. As she rolled sideways, with the movement of the rising sea, a wave flipped her body over to reveal her naked torso. Her head was missing and there was a large gash across her stomach. The whole of her skin was white and pock marked like a sponge. I turned away and dragged her along behind me.

Fionn had succeeded in preventing anyone else from rushing into the sea, but they were all now stood around her like a gallery of ghouls. There was only one of our guests remaining on the veranda. She was standing against the handrail, taking photographs. I felt myself cursing her.

When the body was almost completely out of the water, Leyda stepped forward from behind Fionn and covered it up with a tablecloth.

"Fi, I'll stay here." I said, shielding her from the worst of it. "You'd better call the Police at Charlestown." As she left, the crowd began to pull back too.

Leyda touched my shoulder and asked if I was okay. Then she said, "That's the third body that I know of to wash up on our shores in the last two weeks. I don't understand it. Where are they coming from?"

In the fading light, I'd not seen the stranger with the camera creep up next to us.

"It's one of the disappeared," she said solemnly, with a French accent.

Chapter Three
On Death's Trail

It had not been a comfortable day for flying. Ben Hansen had mixed feelings about taking this trip. His thoughts were caught between his current assignment and his previous mission in this part of the Caribbean, when he'd come closer to death than he cared to recall. The six-hour flight from Phoenix to Puerto Rico, in one of American Airlines DC-10's, had been just about bearable. His seat at the rear of the plane, just below the noisy air intake duct for the big tail engine, had left him with a throbbing headache. Then came the unscheduled delay at Luis Muñoz Marín International Airport, testing Ben's patience to the point of anger. The pilot of the tiny, six-seater Cessna 206 had refused to take off until all six seats were filled - 'It's not my fault man, it's company policy'.

In the end, Ben agreed to pay for two seats, just so that all five paying passengers could finally get on their way. He made a note in his diary never to use Kahbuna Island Air ever again. But perhaps he should've shown a little more tact when speaking to the pilot prior to take off. It was not like him to abandon his professional cool. As a result he was now experiencing the bumpiest flight he'd ever had the misfortune to endure. Ben was convinced that the pilot was deliberately flying out of his way to find pockets of turbulence. And hearing him laugh and holla 'Oh my, that's a big one' had Ben and the others belching into their sick bags.

Not only was it the bumpiest, it was also the longest two hour flight imaginable. As the flimsy aircraft began it's decent into Antigua, Ben could at last heave a small sigh of relief. The view from his window was captivating. The beautiful Caribbean islands below were as near to any paradise as he could think of and his mood lifted immediately. Suddenly, the memories came flooding back: two years ago, he had made the most important drug arrests of his entire career to date - taking down drugs lords and seizing a record quantity of cocaine and marijuana.

He'd been highly respected ever since, along with his dear old friend and partner Chuck. It was also true that they'd had a helping hand from the two English guys aboard their charter yacht, but let's not get carried away with all that. Things were going to be very different this time around. For a start he knew he faced far fewer dangers. The only pressure he truly felt was having such little time to track down this so called 'photojournalist traitor'.

Ben took out his wallet and looked at the business card he'd been given back in Santa Barbara as his point of contact.

John Arfield
Director General

The Fairplay Corporation

14a University Ave. Sunnydale, Silicone Valley, California 95305
Telex: 67-4774 Telephone: (805) 283-9485

He focussed in on the irony of the name - Fairplay. From the onset of that meeting yesterday morning, he'd come away with the gut feeling that it might only be a few rolls of film this time around, but what happens next? Once you're in, you're in for keeps. It wasn't as if Arfield had any hold over him. He just made such a big play about patriotism and putting the defence of the good people of America first.

The lightweight aircraft banked sharply his way as if controlled by a strong breeze instead of the guiding hand of the pilot. He was so close to the sea he could almost feel and taste its solid, rippled surface, like the world was coated in coloured sugared icing. And then almost immediately, coming into view he saw the safety of the grey tarmac strip just a short distance ahead.

"Business or pleasure, sir?" Asked a slender slip of a girl in a white uniform as she paused with the official Island stamp, hovering above Ben's passport.

"Pleasure," lied Ben with a fake smile.

The stamp touched down onto the open page and clicked as it left behind its inky mark. "Well, have a nice time, Sir. Welcome to Antigua," she said, with an equally tired smile.

Out on the concrete drive, on the furnace side of the arrivals exit doors, Ben was, instantly, struck, by a wall of heat. 'Jesus, I'd forgotten how hot it get's down here', he thought and automatically peeled away the wet, sticky shirt from his back. 'I'm going to have to get used to it again, and quickly'.

He opened the door of the first available taxi waiting in line and instructed the driver to take him to the nearest, large, air-conditioned building, with lots of rooms. This turned out to be the Ocean Edge Hotel and Spa.

It was definitely not somewhere Ben would have chosen for a holiday. From the moment he stepped inside, he recognised its old imperial style and formalities. It was the kind of place where an American tourist could order their favourite cocktail twenty-four hours a day, to the live accompaniment of a Burt Bacharach tune. And apart from the hotel manager and his deputy, the remainder of the subservient roles were taken up by local inhabitants. Not only did your average American millionaire want to be indulged, he also wanted to feel superior. There was no disguising the fact: old colonial hierarchy of master and servant, of white versus black, was still, sadly, very much in evidence.

Once inside his room, he closed the large, sliding door, turned the fan up to full speed and the temperature control down to zero. He even closed the curtains to block out the view of the bathers on the sun soaked beach. He wriggled out of his shoes and stripped down to his 'y' fronts.

He grabbed himself a bottle of Red Stripe from the cooler and spilled the contents of his briefcase onto the bedspread. And before taking a large swig of the amber, fluid he rolled the ice-cold bottle across his forehead. 'Now, where's that folder again?'

Right at the last minute, before boarding his American Airlines flight in Phoenix, Ben had been held up momentarily, by one of Arfield's lackies. He had been called to the information desk where he was greeted by a pot faced, middle-age guy, wearing a typical, dark, G-man suit. He looked vaguely familiar, but he'd not come across his name before - Bob Fagg.

Bob was sweating rather profusely; he'd obviously been running a while, maybe he'd even got lost. All he had to do that morning was hand over some very useful documents that Ben had requested from Arfield to help in his search for Miss Romero. And now it was his turn to run, straight to the waiting aeroplane. 'Thanks Bob, not exactly the best start to a day'.

Yet, here he was, ten hours later, slumped in an armchair and feeling cooler by the minute.

The documents that Fagg had handed to him turned out to be very useful. There was more background information on Ilena Romero which he'd had time to read earlier, during his flight to Puerto Rico. He stretched across to his bed and picked up his map. Then he began by drawing circles at two-mile intervals away from the airport. If Miss Romero was planning on making a quick escape back to the U.S, then perhaps she was holed up close by. It seemed as good a place to start his search as any.

She had won Ben's respect with what he had read about her in his latest report. Although she was still only in her mid-twenties, she had already assembled an impressive portfolio of photos from some very dangerous assignments. She not only focussed on the destruction and death, which these conflicts produced, but also on how the victim's lives were affected. Ben surmised rightly or wrongly that Miss Romero regarded herself as a vanguard to their plight. If she could change their lives for the better then her efforts were justified. Her most notable triumph to date had been alerting the world to the apartheid struggles in South Africa.

Prior to her initiation in Soweto, she had studied at the Penninghen School of Art in Paris, where she'd dropped her ambition of becoming an artist after discovering a love for photography. Ilena was further influenced and encouraged to make a career for herself by Philippe Cartier, a fellow student who was ten years her senior. She greatly admired his ground breaking 'photo realism' shots, taken amongst the fury of batons and bricks during the student riots of '68.

Later, as the protest marches were taking place in most European cities highlighting the obscene nature of suppression against the majority of ordinary people in South Africa, they chose to take a more direct approach. And so, together, they abandoned their studies in the French capital and flew down to Johannesburg, at the end of 1975, just before her twentieth birthday, to witness the deteriorating situation between the Government and the High Schools and Universities in the south of the city.

The morning of 16th June 1976 saw the start of what has been called the 'Soweto Rebellion'. According to official figures released by the government, one hundred and seventy six people died. But when Romero and Cartier gained access to Pheleni Clinic where some of the dead and dying were hurriedly taken, it soon became obvious to them that the excessively brutal and indiscriminate force used to break up the demonstrations had resulted in many more hundreds of casualties and deaths.

The immediate, worldwide publication of their material, together with other international reporting was the catalyst for a global condemnation of the Afrikaans government. In its aftermath, all foreign members of the press in South Africa became subject to police harassment. When Phillipe Cartier was beaten and hospitalised, Ilena Romero, fearing for her life, was forced to flee to Ghana, with a handful of the student leaders who had so far escaped reprisals. There, she was contacted by The Washington Chronicle and Herald, whose African office was based in the capital, Accra.

The WCH was and still is renowned for it's aggressive style of reporting and its actions enabled the start of a new era for

Romero and Cartier who, seven weeks later, had recovered from his wounds and renewed their partnership.

In a foot note on the last page of the report, Ben noted that Cartier had been killed in a car accident, two years ago in Argentina, whilst Romero and he were both on the trail of exiled members of the Nazi Party.

Ben studied the photo of her portrait again. She had a very short cropped head of hair. Maybe she had tried to hide her own natural beauty by appearing more boyish. Photojournalism was a tough occupation for a girl. It was a measure of her courage and determination that she'd been as successful as her dossier gave evidence to.

He scribbled down a few notes on the reverse of the photo and once again picked up his National Geographic map of Antigua. There were only a handful of hotels within the first two-mile radius. If he started his search right away, he'd have them all done by midnight. Right on cue, the internal telephone rang inside his room. It was the reception desk informing him that his hire car was ready to collect from the hotel car park.

Having quickly changed into a clean set of clothes, he divided the pile of cash from his briefcase into three equal stacks. He stuffed one into the back pocket of his Italian shorts and the other two in separate hiding places, inside his wardrobe. Although he knew he had a lot of ground to cover, Ben was confident he was fitter than the opposition, or anyone else on his own team for that matter. He worked out everyday and only ever missed his morning jog whenever he stayed within earshot of the ocean. He was already looking forward to a refreshing plunge the following morning.

He replaced his Smith and Wesson, model nineteen back inside his briefcase, rotated the tumbler locks and slid it under the wardrobe too. He figured his favoured pistol wouldn't be required just yet. Looking back at the remaining notes of paper strewn across his bed, one in particular caught his eye. It was the address of Bar Amigo's in Cross Green. If his own searches over the next twenty-four hours were to prove fruitless, then he at least had a Plan B to fall back on. He knew Mark Byrne and his accomplice friend at the Barracuda dive shop would no doubt hear and see all the new faces on the south-eastern side of the island. They were more than capable of assisting him in a simple, missing persons case.

Charlestown, Antigua was one of those sleepy hillside places which tourists tended to avoid for a couple of reasons. One, it was five miles from any beach and two it was uphill all the way. The highlight of any unlikely tour around its streets would have only included the prudently constructed wooden church of Saint Michael's and the half a dozen shops, which tended to cater for the needs of the locals. On a roughly surfaced side street, opposite the cemetery, was the solid stone jailhouse, a throwback from colonial times. There were two rooms inside, one of which was a caged cell. Down in the cool, vaulted cellar was a makeshift morgue and a single water closet. To all intents and purposes, the old building was literally situated in the dead centre of town.
But this was also home to the most reliable government paid official east of the capital - Sergeant Fred 'Hawkeye' Hawkins. He was comfortably sat behind his polished oak desk as usual, gripped by the weekly comings and goings in the local newspaper. It was one of his main sources of information. And right at this moment, his face bore a permanent, satisfied grin as he studied a photograph of himself, handing out the book tokens at the last end of term at St. Michael's school, just over a month ago. He took a pride in his neat and shiny appearance. He could sit around all day and never get a single crease in his trousers. Although he possessed a rakish figure, it didn't necessary lend itself to speed and fast reaction. Even on the warmest days, he always wore a white vest underneath his khaki, uniformed, shirt jacket. He had a row of colourful medal ribbons above his breast pocket, which were more of an indication of his length of service rather than acts of valour. On his left arm, above the three gold braided chevrons denoting his rank was the cloth patch of the Antiguan flag, symbolising the sun, sea and sand, the three elements Hawkeye avoided at all costs. It was a mystery to everyone how he'd acquired his

nickname. Most assumed it was some ironic joke, which he'd been tarred with many years earlier.

Now, there were only a couple of years left until he could retire and he fully intended on seeing it through with the least amount of fuss as possible. Luckily for Fred, his workload had been watered down in recent times, since the creation of several new law enforcement agencies on the island. These had been gradually introduced, in the aftermath of the big drugs seizure two years ago, when the government first established the DDS, the Drug Detection Squad. Then came FACIT, the Fraud and Corruption Investigation Team and in the last three months came the introduction of the MOT, Marine Observation Team. It all added up to Fred having more time to concentrate on what he loved best, his collection of novels by Agatha Christie.

Apart from missing cats, domestic arguments, petty pilfering and a craze for playing loud music, life in Charlestown was rather dull, which suited Fred's personality perfectly. Dull meant going home every evening at six p.m. so, after checking his wristwatch, he turned off the overhead fan, returned his newspaper to his drawer and double-checked that it was locked tight. He'd almost reached the door when the phone began to ring - 'oh blinking bumbo'.

It had been over two years since he'd last fished a body out of the sea. That had been what looked, at first glance, like an unfortunate boating accident. It later turned out to be something much more sinister and it was largely down to his administrative house keeping skills that he had been able to gain a conviction. He was always very particular about labelling and storing items found at a crime scene. The torn shirt he'd kept inside a sealed bag in the station evidence locker had won the day, back then.

When he arrived at the dusk lit beach below Bar Amigo's, the body he was examining on this occasion did not look at all like it had arrived there as a result of an accident.

"I might have known you'd have something to do with this, Byrney," he commented in his favourite tone, the natural tone he'd perfected, which suggested he was attempting to flush out a truth. His theory was that by adopting a sinister tone any guilt would rush to the surface and possibly lead to a confession. This always saved a lot of time, according to Agatha Christie's Inspector Craddock.

'One of Hawkeye's typical comments', I thought, before replying truthfully that I'd only been responsible for finding the body. "I almost leapt out of my skin when I saw the state of her."

Before ambling out of the station, Hawkeye had managed to summon the help of his off duty constable, young Clarence Throup. He was now busily engaged taking witness statements from Leyda and Fionn. The other guests at the bar had returned to their drinks, not wanting to get involved with the local police.

"Have you heard of the disappeared?" I asked.

Hawkeye replaced the table-cloth over the body and stood to his feet again.

"Disappeared? What's that, a Sherlock Holmes story?"

I frowned at Hawkeye, wondering if he really knew something, but wasn't letting on. "It was just something I heard earlier: that a few bodies had been washed up here recently."

Not wanting to get any more deeply involved, Hawkeye rubbed his chin and called for young Throup. "Get the stretcher out of the back of the Land Rover. We'd better get this mess over to the morgue and let Doctor Roberts take a look at it in the morning."

"Aren't you going to take her fingerprints or something?" I asked, thinking that we should at least try to identify who this body belongs to.

The young constable had returned with the stretcher and had laid it out on the sand. "It'll be impossible to take a sample from her," he said confidently. "Her body is too decomposed. If you ask me, I'd say she's been in the water for several days."

"Well we're not asking you Throup," replied Hawkeye, slightly annoyed. "Let's just concentrate on getting her out of the way."

"Is there nothing else we can do?" asked Fionn in response to Hawkeye's last comment.

"Well, it's going to be tricky without any clothing or documents, but please let us know if her head turns up."

Fionn looked at me in bewilderment and I could only shrug my shoulders as we turned to watch Hawkeye and Throup bungle the stretcher into the back of the police vehicle.

"Take no notice of him," said Leyda. "It's a bit of an act he likes to put on. You know, pretending to be dumber than he really is."

"Well he had me convinced." I replied laughing.

"Don't be fooled, Byrney. He's a wily old fox."

Chapter Four
A Grey Day

The plastic trimphone was chippy-chirping away at seven a.m. Atlantic Standard Time. Ben was just drying his hair with his bath towel, having exited the bathroom. His wet shorts were slumped over the back of a chair, from whence he'd taken his early morning swim. Ben dried his right ear again and picked up the phone.

"We have a long distance call for you, Mister Hansen."

Ben dropped the towel and spun around on the bed, to face the map that was laid out in front of him. "Okay, I'll take it."

"Go right ahead caller," announced the hotel receptionist.

"Hansen? It's John Arfield."

"How are you, sir?" replied Ben, inquisitively

"What the hell are you playing at, Hansen? Where's my progress report?" Arfield was in a foul mood, having had a poor nights sleep. His voice grew even more demanding. "When I said seven a.m. Goddamit, I meant precisely that."

Ben looked across at his bedside cabinet as the minute window on the mechanical clock flipped over from a two to a three, meaning it was precisely seven o' three.

"Good morning to you too, John. I was just about to call you, right after my shower."

Arfield's voice simmered down a tone, but he rattled off several sentences without a pause, dominating the conversation. "Well, have you found that bitch, or do I have to come down there and find her for myself? It's been twenty-four hours since our meeting yesterday and I thought I'd made myself plain. Locate the girl." Arfield quickly placed the palm of his hand over the mouthpiece as he stifled a belly cough. Although, over the years, he should have taken heed of his wife's nagging at him to quit smoking, he couldn't start the day without a couple of drags on one of his favourite Garcia and Vega cigars. The embers were still slowly suffusing in the ashtray that sat on top of his home desk.

"We had some bad delays getting down here," replied Ben. "But, I was out until the early hours of the morning, covering every hotel within a five mile radius of the airport. Either Miss Romero's holed up elsewhere on the island, or she's hopped off back to the mainland. I intend to cover the southern half today Sir and if needs be, muster up some help from a few trustworthy locals."

"Well get on with it boy. My sources tell me she hasn't made her move yet. I want to hear from you the minute you locate her, or if not I'll be waiting for your call at seven p.m. this evening. Not seven o' one or seven o' two, but seven on the dot. Do you read me?"

When Arfield put down the phone he opened the top drawer of his desk and took out his telephone contact holder. He began to grimace, muttering a few words of annoyance. "If I need a job doing well, must I always have to do it myself?" He shifted the plastic dial down to the letter R and flipped open the index card. The first name on the list was Removals. He dialled up the number and spoke to Felix Schwarzkopf, to enquire as to whom amongst the 'Dustcoats' was immediately available. Schwarzkopf's reply wasn't exactly music to Arfield's ears. They were all currently out on assignment. The only one who could meet his requirements, at such short notice, was Bob Fagg.

"Bob the bungler. Are you absolutely certain there's no one else?" Arfield had had a few, memorably bad experiences in the past, when he'd had to rely on Fagg. He had a habit of going off at half cock, or worse. To Arfield, Fagg was a trigger-happy lack-wit: the sort to shoot first and then ask the questions afterwards. But then he was too dumb to know what questions to ask. How could Arfield ever forget the part Fagg played in the failed coup in Bongo Bongo, when a group of partisans he was leading opened fire on their own allied forces, killing the leader of the U.S team.

"Well, God save us, I'll have to take him," agreed Arfield with mounting reservations. "Here's what needs to happen. Get on the phone and get to it. Get him prepped and ready to go and for heaven's sake don't breathe a word of this to anyone."

I'd always remembered this place as being a bit of a dump, in the days when we used to congregate in it, before the doors and windows of Bijoe's bar were boarded over and nailed shut indefinitely. Having said that, it'd had a character all of it's own and we'd kind of grown accustomed to it's state of dilapidation, happily engrossed, inside the dimly lit atmosphere, drinking our Caribbean cocktails with other members of our ships crew. And despite the patched up, unwelcoming, outdoor appearance, we'd always felt accepted and safe. It never occurred to us that we probably stood out like polo mint chips in a bar of Cadbury's. A dungeon of immoral activities it may have been, but Fionn judged it perfectly. She had looked beyond the obvious, by alluding to its unique location and potential and in the two years since Bijoe's had been renamed Bar Amigo's, we'd practically reinvented it, making several improvements by reinvesting our profits. We'd truly stamped our mark on the decoration and structure and in doing so we had changed its personality completely.

The only item that we'd decided to keep was the old jukebox, which still scooped up dimes and nickels from a music loving clientele. Most of the popular songs remained on the menu, the ones normally selected by the old faithful: the Marleys, the Maytals, and Millie. But we'd also added some new, vinyl forty-fives too, which had been sent over to us by my brother Anthony: Queen for Fionn and Fleetwood Mac for me and two Stranglers songs, which no one else played apart from myself.

The internal walls of the bar were now lovingly adorned with bits of old fishing equipment that Sly, at the Barracuda dive shop, had been throwing away: old fishing nets and cork floats, a few rope fenders and broken wooden oars. Behind the bar itself were lots of mirrors and glass shelves and next to the bottles of rum and bourbon, were hand carved wooden sculptures of dolphins and blue fin marlins. And then, partly hidden away on the top shelf at the back of the bar, were two voodoo masks, which Pug had donated. Fionn hated the sight of them. She said they always give her the heebie-jeebies. She'd threatened to return them on numerous occasions, but they were still hung in the same spot, casting their spells and keeping the demons at bay.

A few months ago, along with most other hospitality businesses on the island, we'd signed up to be members of the recently formed tourist's association. It was a government-sponsored initiative to bring all the hotels, lodges and bed and breakfast establishments under the stewardship of one organisation. Each enterprise had to be assessed against a range of criteria: size, menu, bedrooms, hygiene, location and customer satisfaction, etcetera, in order to receive a star rating. Okay, so we had only been allocated a one star rating, but it meant that we were now being listed and promoted throughout the Caribbean and with international travel agencies. As a result, all of our rooms were fully booked for most nights.

To begin with, our clientele was still, for the most part, dominated by 'would be' treasure hunters. When anyone ever enquired about local accommodation at the Barracuda dive shop, Sly and Raoul would always loyally point them in our direction.

When the news circulated around the Caribbean that a vast haul of treasure from the wreck of the 'Nuestra Señora de la Concepción' had been rediscovered, on 26th November 1978, the treasure hunting scene began to drop off. I remember thinking about Kris and Karen Eidelberg and their own dreams of finding this incredibly rich treasure. Although they'd been wrong about exactly where to find it, they were right about the size of the haul. The successful team, led by fellow Americans Burt Webber and Jim Nace, had managed to raise over a ton of gold and silver treasure, valued at over thirteen million U.S dollars.

But, they'd not found anything as grand, or as beautiful, as the Pitosi Cross. Which reminded me that I should ask Leyda again how the islands bid for independence was progressing. I was already looking forward to the day when we could take it out of the bank vault in St. Johns and put it on display. It was going to be a star attraction for the island for many years to come. 'Something wonderful to be a part of and remembered for,' I thought. 'They might even let us stay in Antigua for good'.

I could hear Fionn closing the doors to the rooms at the rear of the bar as she finished off the morning routines. There were only six guest bedrooms in total. True, we could have squeezed a few more in when we demolished some of the internal walls, but we both felt that each room must have at least one window. And with the removal of the low ceilings, which allowed the roof rafters to be permanently in view, this gave these rooms an additional, airy feel to them.

I was serving drinks behind the bar, keeping an eye on our veranda and checking the beach and the waves in the background too. We were practically the last property on the dead-end road, at the point where its dusty, yellow surface disappeared into the white sand. Beyond us lay White House Bay and the old colonial outpost where Leyda Friday lived. Since Amigo's had gradually increased in popularity, Leyda had agreed to give up part of her private beach, to allow our guests to bathe there. She always said that she loved having a few holiday makers around, but I sometimes wondered if she regretted how it used to be: quiet and relaxed in her own unspoilt haven.

There were currently three people sitting inside the bar, including a middle-aged couple from San Diego who were on their Honeymoon of sorts. They'd just been married four days ago, right here on the beach in front of our veranda. The ceremony had actually taken place in the sea. The two of them, Louise and Rory had stood, knee deep in the water, together with the pastor from Cross Green church. They'd both been dressed appropriately, in fine wedding attire. Denise had worn a white satin dress and the groom a morning jacket with a white shirt and a dickie-bow tie. Both their outfits ended at the waist and just below they'd each worn swimming shorts. When the pastor closed his bible, at the conclusion of the marriage blessing, Fionn paddled out to the happy couple with a bottle of champagne. Long after the ceremony was over, when dusk had begun to fall, they were still sat, beyond our veranda, waist deep in each other's arms, watching the sunset.

One thing I did know for sure about romance is that it was very infectious.

"Maybe we'll do that one day." Fionn had commented and I was thinking the same too, 'how nice would that be'.

But alas there was not a soul on the beach today. For once, the sky was overcast and grey - an opportune fishing day for the pelicans. They swooped down upon the sweeping waves and plundered the depths freely. They had it all to themselves.

I noticed our other, mysterious guest with the camera, sitting by herself. She was sat at the very end of the bar, with her back next to the jukebox. She was idly stirring her cup of coffee. She looked up at me watching her and I immediately recognised the sort of look in someone when they're about to make a complaint.

"Where are you from, Byrney?" she asked politely.

Her question, when it came, took me by surprise, as did the way she gently smiled afterwards. I moved more closely towards her and thought how her naturally wavy, dark hair really suited her delicate features. She had an interesting face, a face that I imagined would inspire an artist to create a bronze cast of.

"Actually, I'm from West Lancashire, England, the North," I replied cheerily and grabbed myself a bottle of Red Stripe beer, as I sometimes did when I had the bar to myself. It was going to be a long, quiet day; the weather had seen to that. So, despite the earliness of the hour, it still wasn't quite midday yet, I thought 'sod it, why not?' "Would you like one of these too?" I offered.

I filled both glasses as she continued with our conversation.

"That's a very long way. How is it that you are here, if you don't mind my asking?"

Her long lashes fluttered in front of her dark brown eyes and for a second I wasn't sure if I was either being chatted up, or just harmlessly interrogated. Her French accent gave away her origin and although I could speak her language competently, I reckoned it would be wise to keep this to myself, for the time being.

"No, erm, it's okay. I arrived here about two years ago, aboard a charter yacht, called Liberty Angel. I was one of the crew until one of its engines flew into bits," I replied, and then quickly took a swig of my beer. I wished I'd not mentioned that part.

"Was it your fault?" She smiled, "or the engine's?"

"Well, the tired old machine was over forty years old. They used to put the same ones in German U-boats." I commented, smiling at my own authority of knowledge, thinking she'd probably soon get bored with me.

"Sounds like a very interesting lifestyle. How long were you onboard this Liberty Girl? I suppose you visited some nice places?"

"Only about fifteen months, but long enough to get to know the Mediterranean quite well."

I noticed her eyes widen. "It's my favourite place, the Côte d'Azur, Villefranche sur Mer and Antibes in the sixties, before it became commercialised. We used to spend our holidays there."

"I can't imagine that part of the French Riviera was ever that quiet?"

"If you know how to find the right places, it is."

It felt like she'd been digging into my background with so many questions. Of course it could be that she was just being polite. I'd forgotten how forward the French could be with their conversation. Then there's also something strangely different about a dull day in a hot climate, more so than the ones I knew all too well, which occurred regularly back home, where I'd grown up. Here, it stopped you in your tracks, or spoilt your plans and it felt like you had to fight against the boredom of it, not that I found answering our guest's questions boring. But up until now, the only thing I knew about my inquisitor was her name, Ilena Martini and the fact that she'd arrived here by taxi the day after the beach wedding. After making her booking by telephone, she'd asked to speak to Miss Terry. We both thought at the time that this was a little odd, but we put it down to the possibility that she'd seen the Island Tourist Association brochure. For all we knew, they could be readily available at the international airport in St. Johns.

"So what do you do for a living?" I asked.

"Would it surprise you if I said I was a photojournalist?" She bent down to remove her camera from her shoulder bag. "Do you mind if I take your picture?"

"No, not at all," I replied as I quickly rubbed my fingers through my hair.

She held her Nikon camera to her right eye. "Say blue," she teased. The flash on her camera blinded me for a moment and suddenly I was reminded of the blue flashing lights from the previous night, when Hawkeye and his deputy had arrived to collect the body I'd fished out from the sea.

Ever since that event, I'd had a gnawing feeling about something, which I needed explaining to me.

"Ilena, last night, that dead body, you said she was one of the disappeared. What does that mean?"

Suddenly, she looked serious. Tiny 'worry lines' appeared on her forehead, registering the fact she'd perhaps experienced pain and suffering, despite her youthful appearance. I was also aware that she was older than Fionn and me. I guessed her age to be around thirty years old.

"Well, to be very blunt," she said plainly, "she fell out of the sky."

"From an aeroplane? By accident?" Now I was visualising all kinds of things. "Was she in a plane crash, or was the plane door loose or something?"

"No, nothing like that. It's an act of will, which has been happening for a long time, especially in South America, in Chile and Argentina and now in San Albarra." Ilena lifted her glass and downed what remained of her beer in one. "Let's have another one of these," she said.

I took another bottle for myself too and refilled our glasses.

"The men in charge of those countries I mentioned are not nice people, Byrney," she continued. "If someone complains, or makes trouble, or challenges them, then, they are made to disappear. It's happening all the time, even right now, as we speak. And the leaders of those groups who oppose these governments are quickly arrested and tortured. And then, one night they are put on a plane. They are flown over the ocean and after it has flown a safe distance from the shore, they are simply thrown out. Those who are responsible don't care if they are already dead or not. As an extra precaution they slit there stomachs open." Ilena demonstrated the action across her own bare skin with her right thumb mimicking the action of a blade. "This is so they will sink as soon as they hit the water. The woman that you found was one of those. She must have somehow stayed afloat."

"Jesus, fuck, is that true?" I could feel the knots tightening in the pit of my own stomach.

"I tell you, Byrney, some of the things I've learnt and witnessed for myself, confirm exactly what I know to be true, that it's not a nice world we live in today. And, I also believe things will get much worse before they get better. I've learnt that you can't trust anyone these days, especially those who have the power to change things."

I looked away, to peer out of the open hatch at the other end of our bar. What Ilena had just spoken of seemed impossible to believe. Was I wrong to feel safe and secure in our island home now that evil was starting to wash up here on these idyllic shores?

My thoughts were interrupted by a speed-boat, making a dash across the bay towards the shoreline. As it approached, the engine cut out at the last minute and it's bow dropped as it levelled off, coasting up to the beach. The pilot tilted the outboard motor and locked it in its horizontal position, just as the boat grounded to a standstill. The slim figure leapt over the side rail and landed with both feet expertly together. 'He's done that before', I thought. I watched him for a few seconds more. He was heading straight for our bar.

True to Orr's spoken directions, Fort Anderson had been easy enough to find by following the road signs. It's presence hadn't been recorded at all on the old map of the island which Iko had been given, along with his other documents and instructions, at Station Z in Grenada. He parked the museum Land Rover, right beside the large pair of oak doors. The big, cast iron key slid in neatly and the old lock turned with no effort at all.

The fort itself was mostly made up from large, rough cut boulders of stone and planks of wood, nailed together in butt joints, like the ones used on the hull of a ship. The stone wall began at ground level and rose as far as the first window lintel, which also supported two oak beams that ran the full width of the ground floor. These, in turn, supported a planked floor to the upper level. The floor planks had been hand cut in large, irregular widths. It was in this shady, upper room that Iko discovered his bed and a stone sink with a soak away waste pipe. There was no toilet, just an earth closet in one of the alcoves on the ground floor.

It was late afternoon when Iko eventually settled into his new surroundings, having completed his search of every square inch of the old fort. He switched on the overhead light and studied the items he'd tipped out of his kit bag onto the bare mattress. Together with a set of spare clothes and a couple of tins of food, were several pieces of military hardware: a Soviet made polaroid camera with a three hundred millimetre, telescopic lens; three packs of instant film; a Soviet .38 calibre Makarov pistol, with two detachable magazines and a box of ammunition; a small brown case, containing a pair of East German, Hendsoldt and Wetzler, eight by thirty field glasses and two fat rolls of American and Caribbean dollars; as well as his book of travellers' cheques and the drivers licence and passport in the name of Eldridge Delgado. His Cuban passport, the one in his own name, was locked away in the top drawer, back at the travel agents in Grenada.

His favoured item amongst all of his kit was undoubtedly his lightweight sleeping bag. Even in the darkness of the early hours, when returning from sorties back in Ambundu, every soldier had known how to find his own place of rest - by it's own peculiar odour and Iko's tatty old sleeping bag was no exception. He quickly surveyed his combative possessions that were spread before him and reached down picking up the sulky, cold-steel, firearm. It had a familiar comfortable balance in his right hand. He released the ammunition clip and examined its contents despite knowing he'd find it already fully loaded.

It had been several weeks since he'd last fired a weapon and even then it had only been at a paper target. Across the length and breadth of Grenada he'd only ever encountered warm hearted people. Only once had he seen a man having a set to with another inside one of the back street bars in St. Georges. The quarrel between them had reached a height where violence erupted, but this had been used as a last resort, and there were certainly no weapons involved. Despite the disappointment of unfulfilling his mission, on the whole Iko had enjoyed his unaccompanied peaceful meanderings.

As he gazed down once more at the Makarov pistol he felt a change coming over him. He found himself wishing that he might have no need of it here in Antigua too. He dropped the gun back inside his empty kit bag, picked up his camera and slowly looked around.

There was no telephone anywhere in the fort, neither amongst the basic furnishings in the room nor on the upper floor. At the opposite end to his bed there was a butane gas stove and a small white fridge. Iko opened its dented, vacuum-sealed door. A single, bare bulb illuminated the shelf space. It was empty, but at least it felt very cool. First thing tomorrow he intended to fill it with his favourite beer and drink, a toast to his former sponsor, Captain Miguel.

Before the remaining daylight faded altogether, he climbed out onto the flat roof, using the external wooden steps. He lifted his field glasses with his right hand and surveyed his panorama. To the east lay the mangroves and just behind them he could detect the partially obscured outline of a white building, which appeared to be his only neighbour. Beyond that, the ground elevated gently towards the barren plateau of Arawak Hill. He looked down at the small, private jetty in front of him, which appeared to be an extension to the fort itself as the sea wrapped itself around its stone foundations. Tied to it's mooring at the far end, was a plain, beige coloured, plastic boat. Its open quarters were protected by a canvas cover, draped across it's hull with just the outboard motor and its single propeller visible at the rear.

He raised his field glasses further, out into the Caribbean Sea. Beyond the foaming line of a coral reef, his aim focussed upon the dark outline of a sizeable island. "That's a possibility," he said to himself. With no other points of interest in the immediate vicinity, he went back inside and revisited the open cupboards in the downstairs room, where he'd noticed a few more tins of food and a glass preserve jar filled with rice.

Not surprisingly, when he turned on the single water tap it spewed out a rust coloured liquid, leaving a tide mark around the rim of the stone sink until it ran clear, dissolving the thin brown line once again. He straightened up the only chair in the room and ate the red beans cold, straight from the tin, alternating between these juicy morsels and dipping his fingers into a warm pan of boiled rice. Iko felt like a king in his own castle. He turned out the light and continued to sit in the darkness by the open window, watching the magical movement of the glowing phosphorous patterns, striking the shore to the applause of the tireless crickets and the stumbling song of the cane toads and thence to his own effortless snoring.

The young man walking up the beach towards Amigo's would not have looked out of place in one of those wartime action dramas like The Dirty Dozen. The only thing missing from his combatted appearance was a tommy gun, casually slung from his shoulder. In its place he carried some sort of new fangled camera. He looked like one tough cookie, the sort of person I wouldn't want to come to blows with. Behind him, his boat was stuck fast, half out of the water with its stern tipping and bowing with each incoming wave. It hadn't been tied up, so I guessed 'action man' was only making a temporary stop off.

He walked briskly across our veranda and straight into the bar and ordered a beer. Everyone inside suddenly stopped what they were doing and stared at the stranger. I placed a bottle of Red Stripe on the counter in front of him and flipped off the lid.

"That'll be one dollar, fifty, please." I said amicably. I was quite surprised by his shyness. He peeled a Caribbean Two Dollar bill from a roll of bank notes that he tried to hide from view, before returning it to his trouser pocket. I noticed the anchor motif on his cap with the initials M.O.T. Then I remembered Leyda telling us about her new neighbour, staying at Fort Anderson, who had begun work for the Marine Observation Team. It was a rare event to meet a fellow neighbour in our small little town, so I warmly held out my hand. "Hi, I'm Byrney. I live here with my girlfriend Fionn, welcome to Bar Amigo's."

The stranger took a long swig of his beer, straight from the neck of the bottle, emptying half of it. Then he grasped my hand and replied, "I'm Ellie, I've just moved in, the other side of the swamp." He bowed his head again and turned away to glance around at our clientele who had all since picked up their former conversations again. Then he asked me an obscure question. 'Did I know the name of that off-shore island, the one south of the coral reef?' I knew instantly which one he was referring to, having become familiar with the thin dark dash on the horizon, not that I'd seen or heard of anyone having ever been there. I remembered Pug telling me it had once been a leper colony. "I think the locals call it Monkey Island." I replied then added, "legend has it, that it used to be a leper colony, back in the day." There was no reaction in the stranger's eyes, but I could tell he was processing what I'd said.

"Do you have monkeys here?" he asked eventually.

"Not as far as I know, we've never seen one."

I looked across at Ilena who'd been listening to our conversation and smiled at my last reply. Then she walked over to our end of the bar and stopped next to the stranger.

"That's a Soviet TX 10, isn't it?" she said pointing at the camera. Ilena had seen one few years ago, during the Soweto uprising. One of the foreign journalists had used one, but she'd never before seen one fitted with a large telescopic lens.

The stranger looked a little embarrassed by her sudden confrontation. "How do you know that?" he asked.

"It's what I do," she replied. "I'm a photojournalist. By the way my name is Ilena." She lifted her hand towards the camera and asked if she could take a closer look. The stranger paused for a few seconds then handed it over. Iko was certain Ilena didn't pose any real threat. In fact it was a nice surprise to see a 'Latino lady' on his first outing. He felt an obvious attraction towards her.

"Please be careful with it," he said as he lifted the strap off his shoulder and handed it over. "It's for my new job. I'm supposed to keep a look out for any irregular activity around the bay. Perhaps I'll check over that island out there, to see if anyone has set foot on it recently."

"Well, I doubt that," I replied. "Tourists tend to be put off the idea of visiting ex-leper colonies."

The stranger wasn't at all bothered by my comments. He downed the rest of his beer then asked if he could buy a full case of them.

"Sure, I'll just go and fetch one."

When I returned, Ilena and the stranger were still talking cameras. It looked to me like a game of 'I show you mine, if you show me yours'. They looked as thick as thieves and within two minutes they both left together. I watched them walk slowly down the beach, the stranger brandishing his case of Red Stripe like it was a souvenir from the spoils of war. He helped Ilena into the speedboat and she took his picture as he pushed the bow of the boat back into the sea.

I was surprised Ilena had decided to bunk off so freely. But then, we'd seen a lot of our clientele hook up together over the past two years. People often acted differently away from home, became more adventurous than they would be normally. Some even came here specifically to have a holiday romance. Fionn was proud of the fact that our little, humble establishment had been responsible for joining several pairs of lonely hearts together.

The Dory sped off towards the horizon, bouncing across the white caps. I'd enjoyed my conversation with Ilena. I was certain she wasn't staying here by choice and for whatever reason, I couldn't yet say for sure. But one thing I did know, she just didn't fit in with someone who was here to relax. I thought that she must be waiting either for someone, or something and now that she'd gone swanning off with a stranger, I guessed it must be the latter. And what of the MOT guy? I thought he was very accomplished in the way he handled himself and yet he came across as shy and awkward. But then, I knew from my own experience, it's never easy being the new kid in town.

Chapter Five

The Ruins Of Machacaan

Ben was slowly running out of solutions as to where Miss Romero might be hiding. He knew she was no amateur with regard to choosing the most effective time to go public with her evidence. If she'd not forwarded her films already, then perhaps she was waiting to have them developed beforehand. But, unfortunately, he'd drawn a blank with all six of the registered Kodak outlets on the island.

He was now, reluctantly, heading south in his hire car, playing a Chance Card that perhaps she'd been spotted on this side of the isle. The Volkswagen Beetle that had been provided for him, at his hotel, wasn't the most comfortable car to be sat in. But, it's size and ruggedness was better equipped than the large, gas guzzling American cars for 'rough riding' the differing road surfaces.

After a sultry, dusty and disappointing morning, he was looking forward to feeling the fresh breeze along the southern coast, where the yacht-chartering world would pay him no mind at all. During his previous visit to Antigua, he'd been awoken to the rich resources available to clients with wads of money. There were any number of opportunistic captains who would gladly look the other way if their palms were filled with enough golden nuggets.

He swung into the marina at Cross Green, ratcheted up the hand brake and stared at the many, wonderful, glamorous vessels lying at rest. Their colourful flags flapped furiously at the greyness of the sea and sky, matching his own declining mood – not the welcoming vision he'd imagined. He had been depending upon finding a few familiar faces, in particular the ones who crewed the Liberty Angel, or the MV Charisma. He walked the full length of the quay, without finding either.

Eventually, he stopped a young skipper who was rushing past him, carrying a couple of buckets filled with fish bait. Ben was casually brought up to speed that the Liberty Angel was no longer seaworthy. She'd been towed to Guadeloupe and was now permanently moored as a 'liveaboard'. As for the Charisma, she'd departed a week ago, for the Azores. Amongst the clickety-knitted livelihood of yachters, almost everyone knew each other's business. Ben thanked the sea captain for his information, although it wasn't the least bit helpful - another blank, another heavily pencilled line drawn across his notebook.

He looked back to where his little car was parked and at the row of ship's chandlery shops just beyond. One sign stood out and caught his attention immediately: Barracuda Dive Shop. He made a beeline for it, desperately trying to recall the names of the owner and his young assistant. At its entrance, above the open door, he noticed a scruffy, hand painted sign, with a name in white lettering: Proprietor Sly Rodriguez. "Of course, Sly and Raoul," he said aloud.

Sly was standing behind the long, shop counter at the far end of the store, busily opening a stack of new cardboard boxes and inspecting his latest delivery of life jackets. His eyes squinted, with a faint hint of recognition, at the customer walking towards him

"Hello Sly," said Ben jovially. "Do you remember me, from two years ago? We bought some underwater cameras from you?"

Sly didn't look all that impressed. "Yes, I remember your group. Have you come to pick up the old cannon? It's still sat rusting away in my lot where you left it."

Ben felt awkward and a little embarrassed and knew he had to offer up an excuse. It was unbelievable that no one had come to collect it, after all the trouble it'd taken to recover it from the seabed, near the Isles des Saintes.

"My apologies, I thought Jim would have had it shipped to the U.S by now. I'll give him a call when I get back to my hotel tonight and remind him it's still here. He's probably having trouble with the paperwork. You know how government offices love to throw a net of red tape around these things."

He was interrupted by the sight of Raoul, carrying another stack of boxes in through the back door. He looked much taller than he remembered. Raoul set down the boxes at the end of the counter and walked around to Ben's side and held out his hand.

"It's Chuck, isn't it? Or Ben?" He asked with a friendly smile.

"Ben Hansen. Hello Raoul, good to see you again."

"What brings you back to the Caribbean? Another drugs bust? Or come to pick up the cannon?"

"Actually I'm looking for a missing person," he replied quickly, whilst placing the photo of Ilena Romero on top of the counter. "I'm trying to locate this woman on behalf of a client."

"So you're not with the Drug Enforcement guys, anymore?" Asked Sly as he shook his head at the pretty face in the photo.

"No, I'm freelance. Here's my card. What about you Raoul? Does she look familiar at all?"

To Raoul's mind she looked much like most holiday makers in the Caribbean: beautiful, rich and spoilt. The camera she was holding was an expensive one too, he thought.

"How long has she been missing?" He asked.

"Oh, four or five days, approximately." Ben was rapidly counting the days since she was last seen at the Spanish Embassy in San Albarra. "A week at the most," he said revising his first estimate.

"In that case, she could be the dead woman who was dragged out of the water last night, near White House Bay,"

"Really, what woman?" Asked Ben enthusiastically.

"They took her body to the police station up in Charlestown. I think they're trying to identify it. Maybe she's the one you're missing," said Sly in his deep, serious voice.

"Great, thanks for the tip off. I'll catch you both later."

Ben rushed back to his car. He fished a cold bottle of Coke from his plastic icebox and hungrily gulped most of it back. At last a promising lead; he was feeling very pleased with himself.

As he navigated the five miles up to Charlestown, thoughts and memories stirred around his mind, moving backwards and forwards. If this dead woman was Ilena Romero, then someone else must have got to her first. He wouldn't have put it past Arfield to have more than one freelance looking for her. Or perhaps one of his controls in the intelligence departments had rubbed her out already. As he drew closer to the outskirts of the small hillside town he began having tingling bouts of Deja vu. He'd been here many times before when he and Chuck had used the basement of the police station as their Ops Centre, during their covert drugs assignment back in '78. Maybe the old desk sergeant was still running things. He'd been very easy going, back then, about having a team of American strangers getting under his feet. Ben was hoping that this time around he'd be just as useful.

The station building looked more or less the same: weathered and now in even greater need of a brush or two of daub. The external paintwork, he remembered, had been flaky and peeling off in strips two years ago. Ben continued to smile to himself when he also noticed that the basement window still had the same crack in it too across one of it's corners. He took a deep breath, walked up the three, worn, wooden steps and paused at the entrance to the open door.

Inside the spacious office, there were only two uniformed policemen in attendance. A young constable was sat bent over at the desk with his nose was almost touching the ribbon as his fore fingers methodically prodded away on the keys of a large typewriter. Toward the opposite end to the office, Ben saw a familiar face staring back at him, intently. Fred instantly rose to his feet, bursting the silence by loudly dragging back his chair, abruptly causing the young assistant to cease typing and wonder whether his boss was about to have a seizure.

"Welcome, welcome," commented Hawkeye warmly to the man who'd just entered the premises. "Have you come about the dead woman?"

Ben was taken aback by Fred's awareness. It hadn't occurred to him that the police force in Charlestown had no other case currently on their books, not to mention any other cases for the last fortnight.

"Hello again," replied Ben shaking Fred's hand. "You haven't aged a day." he smiled.

"Are you alone this time, or is there an invading army of detectives waiting outside?" enquired Hawkeye, peering out into the quiet street.

"It's okay, I'm working alone these days, as a freelance detective. So what's this about a dead woman? Has anyone come forward to identify her?"

Hawkeye thought Hansen was getting a bit ahead of the situation.

"We've only had her for twelve hours. You're not in America now. Most of the dead bodies we get here tend to be the ones who have died of old age," he smiled then pointed at his assistant. "Constable Throup here is just typing up the report. All we can say for sure at the moment is that she appears to be quite young, in her twenties or thirties and has dark hair."

Ben took out his photo again. "Something like this?" He asked, expectantly.

"Well, it's difficult to say," replied Hawkeye, rocking his head slowly from side to side and pursing his lips.

It wasn't the helpful answer that Ben wanted to hear, but he was still hopeful. "Why is it difficult? Has she been in the water a long time?"

"We're not exactly sure how long she's been floating in the sea."

"I'd guess she's been in the sea at least four or five days," interrupted the constable. "Her skin's all white, pock marked, and wrinkled. Spongy like."

Ben took his photo over to the constable and held it out for him at eye level. "Surely you can tell if she looks similar to this or not?"

"I'm sorry we can't." Replied the constable and returned to punching out his report.

Ben was getting tired of the negative responses to his questions. "Why can't you, for god's sake," he asked as his frustration began to bubble to the surface.

"Because her head's missing," replied the two officers almost in unison.

Ben returned the photo back inside his pocket and asked, calmly, if he could take a look at the body for himself. Hawkeye led him down to the basement then left Ben to examine her alone.

After ten minutes, Ben headed back up the wooden stairs to find Hawkeye waiting for him with a cup of tea.

"Here you are Hansen, sit down for a few minutes. My constable has just made us both a nice hot cuppa and if you wait a minute or two longer, you can have a copy of our report. How's that for service?"

Ben sipped at his hot drink and explained to Hawkeye about his reasons for being in the Caribbean. Hawkeye had no reservations about meeting up with Hansen once more. He'd done alright the last time, taking a share in the credit for the famous drugs arrests two years ago. Since that day, Hawkeye's prestige had leapt forward immensely and it'd also swelled the size of his forthcoming pension.

When Ben began to read the report, he had to do a double take. The name of the person who'd found the woman's body was none other than Mark Byrne. The very same Byrney who'd previously helped him and Chuck in Puerto Rico to arrest several members of the drugs gang and whose help he was hoping to enrol this time around too.

"So, just to confirm, Byrney now runs a bar in Cross Green called Amigo's.

"Yes, that's correct. Byrney and Fionn. I believe they're very well liked. I see them most mornings." Replied Hawkeye gleefully. "They're a charming young couple."

It was obvious to Ben Hansen that the unfortunate creature lying in the morgue here at Charlestown police station wasn't the girl he'd been sent to find. Clearly she'd been in the sea for several days. It was highly unlikely that if an accomplished journalist like Ilena had met her death almost a week ago, then Arfield's team would have known about it before the meeting in Santa Barbara just two days ago. He kept his conclusions to himself as he parted company with Hawkeye. The least Hawkeye knew of his plans the better. He intended to quietly carry on with his search, unhindered by police bureaucracy. Now that he had an address for Byrney, he pointed his car back in the direction of Cross Green.

John Arfield had already been busy tidying his desk inside his private office at 14a University Avenue, Sunningdale for a full hour when Bob Fagg arrived, armed with two plane tickets. His taxi was parked by the front door. The driver took full advantage of the wait by lighting up yet another cigarette and cursing the day he ever started smoking. At least he'd left his meter running.

The interior of Arfield's office was like a 'dream team's' trophy room. The four walls were lined with souvenir photos and certificates of his travels and major achievements. The large, framed one above his desk showed two men inside the Oval Office in Washington. One was of a slimmer, younger version of Arfield being congratulated by the late president, Dwight D. Eisenhower.

Arfield currently had his back to the door unaware that Fagg had entered the room. He was totally absorbed with his last minute packing. Fagg held his breath, peered over Arfield's shoulder and instantly recognised the large, dark green, leather duffle bag. The design of the United States diplomatic pouch hadn't changed for the last three decades. Over the years its illegal use had become widespread amongst certain undercover agencies.

Fagg thought he should at least cough to alert Arfield of his presence.

"Hell and damnation, Bob! How long have you been standing there?" Fagg was about to answer, but Arfield cut him off short. "Well don't just hang around empty handed, take my cases down to the car."

For someone who was going on an Ops mission for only two days, Arfield had packed enough kit to weather a siege. Fagg picked up the first large holdall and struggled to turn around with its weight dragging on his shoulders. "What have you got inside here, boss? The kitchen sink and both faucets?"

Bob glanced over the room whilst Arfield finished filling up the final case. Cramming in a pair of sturdy brown shoes with commando soles. Arfield was making sure he was equipped to deal with all types of terrain, although he would be relying on Fagg to do the majority of the leg work.

Whilst Fagg was hanging onto his load, he studied the old black and white photograph nearest the door. The same smug looking operative who had shared an audience with Eisenhower was this time wearing jungle camouflage army fatigues. He was posed at the centre of five, similarly dressed soldiers in front of what appeared to be an Aztec temple. They were armed to the teeth and their faces also displayed the same triumphant, tongue-in-cheek grin. The descriptive tab below the photo read, 'Road To Machacaan - 4th July 1952'.

It was hard for Fagg to imagine that the slightly balding, heavyweight leader who stood before him now bore any resemblance to the central figure in the photograph. Arfield sounded short of breath just buckling up the straps of his briefcase.

"Right, that's the lot. Jump to it, we've got a plane to catch."

On arrival at Sky Harbour International airport, Arfield went straight to the information desk, where one of the security guards was waiting for him. Together, they were led away bypassing the 'check in' process without the need for any queuing and the two agents were shown to their own, private suite in the departure lounge. Once inside the air conditioned, sound proofed booth they were next greeted by a plain clothes member of the security staff who handed Arfield a folded sheet of foolscap, which had just been torn from a teleprinter. It contained the latest intel on his quarry and details of Hansen's movements on the island. Miss Romero had arrived at Coolidge International Airport in Antigua on the first day of February and a woman matching her description had taken a ride in one of the Island Yellow Cab taxis to the marina in English harbour. After that there were no more reported sightings of anyone matching her description and her name hadn't so far appeared on any of the guest lists of local hostelries. Arfield's contacts in the CIA had also, in the last hour, intercepted a request from Hansen to his one time manager at the DEA, regarding information on a dead body, which had washed up the previous night. 'Well, at least we have something to go on', he thought. It's just a matter of time before we catch up with the bitch. Arfield was impressed with this latest report. He had little difficulty in obtaining this kind of information from his old boy network. Arfield was aware the intelligence agencies had listening posts everywhere around the globe and no doubt even on Antigua too. He was also grateful to the fact that the current Chiefs of Staff were firm supporters of the Republican Party candidate.

At six a.m earlier that morning, Arfield had had to deal with a tricky telephone conversation with the main man himself. He was deeply troubled that the rogue journalist was still in play and the incriminating films of the U.S backed massacre in San Albarra, which would derail his likely ascendancy to the White House, had yet to be found. The irrefutable words blasted out at the other end of the line, about putting an end to this crisis, left Arfield in no doubt that it was no longer classed as a mere request, but as a final demand for action. Nothing could stand in the way of progress. The 'United States' was feeling the heat from outside influence in Latin America and currently every General and Commander of the armed forces and the combined intelligence corps was baying for the chance to beat the crap out of any country that threatened their security, or worse still closed down the flow and wealth of their natural resources to North America. Their candidate had promised he would stop at nothing to prevent the communists from siphoning it off inside their own backyard.

Arfield never gave it a moment's thought, that news of his intentions in Antigua would fall into the wrong hands. In just seven hours from now he would be let loose in the Caribbean, and if by chance that bitch with the film had somehow managed to slip through his fingers, then Arfield was at first base, to make sure there was a scapegoat he could pin the blame on.

At the conclusion of the recent prosecution of the captured drugs cartel in the Caribbean, all assets and properties had been awarded to the successful governments involved. As a result, the British were given the land to the eastern side of English Harbour, all the way around to Indian Creek and up to half a mile inland, whilst the house and plantation that had belonged to the Padgett family for eight generations was now under the jurisdiction of the American government. The British government had already sold most of their portion of land for building development, but America had, as of yet, done nothing with their share of the gains. The grey mansion and swimming pool had not been occupied since Jericho and his wife had been thrown in jail. However, on behalf of the American government, the British had, at least, kept a watchful eye on the property and had also paid for one of their employees to see that the house and pool was aired and cleaned regularly.

With these facilities now made available to him, Arfield knew he could come and go as he pleased. And he'd also been given the verbal authority to do just that. On their arrival in Antigua, Arfield and Fagg headed down to the old colonial villa on the eastern side of English Harbour, where they'd find a caretaker waiting to meet them.

Norman Orr had been kept busy all day at the Dockyard museum. He had his hands full at last, unpacking some of the stored artefacts and was in his element, making constant adjustments on how best to display them, until he was completely satisfied with how the new gallery on the upper floor was being laid out. Amongst the many eighteenth century naval items were: uniforms, flintlocks, swords and sabres, models and drawings and paintings of naval warships, a globe clock and sextant and his prize possession, the original ships bell from HMS Winmarleigh. He was working meticulously in order to have every single exhibit looking at it's best and in the most captivating position, so as to retell the story of the Royal Navy, ruling the high seas in the eighteenth century. And of course it all had to be fixed in place and ready for the grand opening, on the seventeenth of April, the two hundredth anniversary of the Battle of Saintes, when Admiral Rodney famously breached the French line of attack and captured their prized ships and cargos.

Thirty-five years ago, in his student days, Orr had studied classics at Jesus College, Oxford, during the opportune years of the post war era. He was especially drawn to history and archaeology under the enthusiastic and charismatic tutorage of Professor Arthur Hodgkinson. After graduation, he was invited to join Hodgkinson's ill fated, British led expedition to locate the ruins of the lost city of Machacaan, deep inside the Lacandon jungle. The expedition had initially been awarded just a meagre budget, which only allowed for a preliminary survey, with the bulk of the heavy work involved in accessing and clearing the site being carried out by a crew of local Mayan volunteers. Orr had a strong respect and fondness for these adaptable and astute tribesmen. He had a great admiration for their tenacity and their commitment to the task ahead of them. He understood that the ancient site, which had been buried beneath centuries of neglect and left at the mercy of the natural world, held a deeply significant, spiritual and sacred attachment to them.

However the expedition came to a sudden and tragic conclusion in the summer of 1952, when work on the site was interrupted by civil war. Orr was one of the lucky few who managed to make a miraculous escape from the fighting, for which he still bore the scars, although most were now only emotional ones. He'd always planned to return to San Albarra, but somehow, everyday life had got in the way of his plans. The only physical reminder he kept of those delightful days of discovery were the ones held in a scrapbook of photographs and sketches he'd made, all those years ago.

He looked up at the oversize, Bakelite Smiths Sectric clock, which hung on the wall above the entrance door. It was time to lock up and leave. He had hoped that young Delgado would've returned his Land Rover that afternoon, but it had only been just over twenty-four hours since he'd borrowed it. Instead, he trotted outside and hopped onto his naval regulation bicycle and pedalled over towards the old villa, on the eastern side of English harbour. For the past six months, he'd been handed the keys to this splendid, colonial mansion with the thankless task of ensuring it remained intact, by organising and supervising repairs as and when they were required in the aftermath of the occasional storm. Today's task was going to be very different. He'd been instructed by the cultural commissioner in St. Johns (who was in overall charge of the historic dockyard) to open up all the outer shutters and let the light flood into the rooms. This would allow him to check for any unwanted house guests, such as the hairy horse spiders and/or scary centipedes.

Orr was more than happy to be the custodian of such a fine old building, one that had an accrued history all of it's own, even if that history was a tainted one, be it from centuries ago, or more recent times. The reason for this unexpected request to open up the house, he'd been informed, was because of the imminent arrival of a diplomatic guest, from California. It was fast becoming an interesting week, Orr thought to himself. He'd gone for years without being burdened with having to look after anyone else but himself, and in the spate of a day and a half, two VIP's had turned up out of the blue.

After a thirty-minute cycle ride, Orr was counting his blessings that the day was cooler and cloudier than normal. Once inside this sleeping, sprawling house, he found himself fumbling around inside the vaulted cellar, checking the fuses, one by one, before he was able to turn on the power. He'd arranged to meet Annette beforehand. She cleaned the floors at the museum and for an additional twenty dollars she'd agreed to drop in and dust these rooms and make up a bed with fresh linen. She performed her work quietly and competently as ever and had been gone for some time before Arfield jostled his way up the front steps and in through the entrance door.

It was a very uncomfortable exchange when the two men greeted one another. Arfield was blustering and complaining about the state of the facilities. He was desperate to get freshened up, after making the mistake of walking the length of the driveway. Fagg had let him out earlier, so that he could return to St. Johns to pick up a few essential provisions.

It had only taken one look for Orr to recognise the aggressive and hateful persona delineated by Arfield's most wrinkled characteristics. But there was something else bothering Orr too, about his temporary visitor. His inner body began to tremble nervously at the thought that here, standing before him, was an enemy from his past - the monster who'd been responsible for suffocating his beliefs in religion, justice, loyalty and love. Orr made his excuses to leave, not that Arfield objected. He'd already stated his objections, repeatedly, at the prospect of being patronised and molly-coddled. He was more than capable of finding his own way around. Orr suggested to Arfield he would check in on him again tomorrow morning.

He was still shaking with anger when he returned to the museum. He opened the old iron safe in the storeroom behind the desk and gently took out his scrapbook from the archaeological dig at Machacaan. He flicked through the pages, sometimes pausing to trace the outline of a figure with his hand. Buried alongside these ghosts from his past, Orr knew he possessed one, clear photograph of the leader of the mercenaries, who had put a stop to the college expedition back in 1952. It was a good photo, despite the scary circumstances in which he'd taken it. The uniformed soldier could easily have passed for the son of the man currently staying at Padgett House. He was younger, had a full head of dark hair and a dark unwashed shadow on his face, but there could be no disputing the fact it was undoubtedly the very same person. The label above his right breast pocket confirmed it, in black capital letters - ARFIELD

As Orr studied the photo the memories of that day began to resurrect themselves. He'd actually met Arfield on two occasions, amongst the ruins of Machacaan. When the American soldiers first arrived it soon became obvious that they had intentions of closing down the dig and using the site for their own purposes. He and the professor had stood in silence as they watched the American agents measuring up the long clearing, which had been cut to provide access to the whole site. The clearing was indeed large enough to land a squadron of helicopters. Professor Hodgkinson made his protests clear when he informed them they had no authority to end the excavation work. As a precaution, he decided to obtain reassurances from the representatives of the International Council of Antiquities at their offices in San Albarra city. Whilst he was still indisposed the American agents returned.

Orr cursed the missed opportunity of being able to capture Arfield and his crew, on camera, actually in the act of their merciless killings. He'd run away and taken cover at the sound of the first volley of gunfire. After their first visit, Orr had expected a further confrontation, but never in a million years did he think it would end with him having to flee from a sadistic massacre.

Orr had only been gone from Padgett House for less than ten minutes when Fagg returned, with several boxes of food and beverages.

"This should keep us going a couple of days," Fagg happily exclaimed as he rested down a full crate of beer. He lifted out one of the bottles and slammed it down against the corner of the crate, flipping off the metal crown-shaped cap.

"Yes, well, I'll leave it all in your hands Bob, to unpack everything. Make sure the refrigerators are switched on first, won't you. I'm going to get my head down. We've an early start in the morning, so don't stay up drinking half the night." Arfield wearily climbed the wide staircase, carrying his briefcase. Fagg watched him until he disappeared along the upper corridor. Once he was out of sight, Fagg leant back in one of the dining room chairs. He had a self-satisfied grin on his face. It was an ideal moment to take a peak inside Arfield's diplomatic pouch, which was still where it had been dumped, together with his oversize holdall on the dining room floor.

He rotated the tumbler locks to match the number he'd seen Arfield set back at his office, when he'd secretly been watching from behind. The combination was 21769. Its significance was not lost on Fagg, who was a lot brighter than Arfield gave him credit for. The twenty-first day of July 1969 was the day of the inaugural lunar landing by Apollo 11. The live footage, beamed down from the moon that day, was possibly seen by every living soul on earth. Fagg remembered it too. He'd actually been on duty at the space centre, as part of the large security team responsible for guarding the whole launch complex at Cape Kennedy.

Inside the pouch, Fagg found a copy of the red folder marked 'Foreign News'. It contained a series of time motion, black and white, still photographs of a fire, taken outside the Spanish Embassy. Fagg guessed the photo's had obviously been lifted from a newsreel camera. The back of each photo gave the date and place of the action - 1/30/80 San Albarra. There was also a portrait photo of a girl holding a Nikon F2 camera. On the reverse was a brief description of Ilena Romero's recent activities. Fagg was already familiar with her bio, having fully read the special report yesterday, before he'd handed it over to Ben Hansen at the airport in Phoenix.

Reaching further into the leather pouch, Fagg also found a small, white, plastic bottle of pills. The label read; Tenormin Atenolol. 'So, Arfield also suffers from high blood pressure, as well as delusions of grandeur'. Fagg scoffed at the thought. In the bottom of the pouch lay what Fagg was looking for all along. He was certain Arfield would not have come all this way without a weapon. He lifted the pistol out and gave a short, appreciative whistle. It was an old army issue Smith and Wesson model thirty-nine, most probably the same gun which had been issued to Arfield back in the day. Fagg expertly removed the magazine and checked the firing action. Then replaced everything back inside the pouch, exactly as he'd found it.

'So the old rascal hung on to his military pistol too', thought Fagg. He'd a pretty clear idea about what Arfield was intending to do in Antigua, let Hansen do the donkey work then he alone would deal with the girl. However, Fagg was still trying to figure out why Arfield had chosen to jump on a plane and make this trip for himself. He wasn't in the best of shape, but that would hardly enter the mind of someone as fanatical as Arfield. Perhaps he saw this as his one last chance to see some action, out in the field. What Fagg knew of Arfield's recent activities suggested that he had been stuck behind his desk for the last decade. Arfield's oversized ego meant that he wasn't about to pass up one more golden opportunity to experience that addictive rush of adrenalin and the sweet smell of success.

On the other side of Cross Green that evening there was quite a lively atmosphere underneath the candlelit veranda at Bar Amigo's. This was what being in the hospitality business was all about. Fionn had the idea of giving Leyda a surprise party for her fiftieth birthday. We had joined two tables together and decorated them with our finest wine glasses and cutlery. Leyda herself was positioned at the head of the table and sharing in the celebrations were: Pug Walker, Raoul and his girlfriend Rosie, Sly Rodriguez and his wife Rita, whom Fionn and myself had never met before. Fionn and myself were taking it in turns to sit at the table whilst at the same time looking after our other residential guests. I think the dull, wet weather had put off most of our regulars from venturing out.

Raoul was telling me that they'd had a visit at the dive shop, earlier in the day, from an old acquaintance of ours.

"Who was that, then?" I asked casually.

"Remember the American Drug Enforcement guys from two years ago," he replied.

"How could I ever forget? Chuck and Ben, right?"

"There was only one of them this time. It was Ben. He says he's a detective now."

"Wow, I'm impressed. Is he here on holiday doing some diving?" I enquired.

"No, actually, he's looking for a missing person, some woman from San Albarra. Sly told him about the girl you found on your beach last night, so he dashed off to see Hawkeye."

"That'll slow him down a bit," I joked.

I stepped back inside the bar to let Fionn spend some time with Leyda. No sooner had she walked out onto the veranda, but speak of the devil, who should stroll into our bar none other than Ben Hansen himself. We both recognised one another immediately as he strode over and gave me a manly hug and a few, friendly slaps across my shoulders.

"We've just been talking about you," I said. "Raoul mentioned you'd called in at the dive shop earlier today." Ben still had the sort of smooth American charm of a film star, or a college quarterback, which always made me wary that he could probably run off with my girlfriend, or anyone else's, at any moment.

"So you're not with the Liberty Angel any longer, then?"

"No, sadly. She blew an engine and it wasn't economical to have her repaired, so the company sold her off." Ben nodded knowingly as I continued. "To be honest I'd had enough of working in that smelly old vessel. So Fionn and me are running this place for Leyda." I thought it would be easier for Ben to accept that Leyda owned the bar without divulging the truth about finding the Potosi Cross. It was still under wraps and the Antiguan government wanted to keep it that way, until after the British had handed them the power and authority to manage their own affairs. "What would you like to drink, Ben?"

"I could kill a beer."

He slowly looked around the bar whilst I did the honours with his bottle of Red Stripe.

"Tell me, do you have any overnight guests staying here too?"

"Yer we do. But, sorry we're full up at the moment. All six bedrooms are taken."

"Well done you two," he replied in admiration.

I guessed Ben hadn't just popped in here by accident, but I wouldn't imagine the quality of our rooms were his cup of tea. And I wasn't sure having a private detective staying with us was a good idea either. They have a tendency to snoop and spy and ask a lot of awkward questions. Not the type of occupation that is good for our business. But there was no point in being unfriendly towards him.

"Raoul says you're looking for a missing person. Had any luck?"

Ben reached into his breast pocket and pulled out a photo. I recognised it was Ilena Martini immediately and began to wonder why Ben was looking for a photojournalist here in Antigua. She wasn't missing as far as I was aware from our conversations.

"This is Ilena Romero," he said. "I don't suppose you've seen this woman recently?"

I tried my best not to let on to Ben that I knew her by a different name and that she was currently staying at Bar Amigo's. A few of Ilena's outspoken words were beginning to ring a few alarm bells. She'd made a point after explaining about the disappeared, 'Don't trust anyone in authority'.

As Ben watched me studying the face in the photo and stalling with my reply, he continued to fill in a few more details as to his presence here in Antigua. "I'm working for a client who's anxious to locate her."

Just at that moment, Fionn glided in from the veranda and walked back around to my side of the bar. She spotted Ben's photo lying in front of me.

"Hey, that looks like one of our guests Byrney. Ilena Martini."

Ben looked at me and frowned.

"Oh do you think so," I said, quickly picking up the photo, to get a closer look. "It could be anybody… dark hair, dark eyes, typically Spanish…we get a lot of them over here."

Fionn grabbed the photo out of my hand then placed it back down on the bar again. "No, it's definitely her." Fionn picked up two bottles of beer and went back out onto the veranda again.

"Now that Fionn's thinks it's her, come to mention it, she does look very similar. Unfortunately, she checked out suddenly this afternoon."

"Oh, did she say where she was heading?" Asked Ben suspiciously.

"No, but she left with a guy called Eldridge. They left in a boat together."

"What sort of boat?"

"Just your average speed boat, beige coloured, looked a bit like a Dory." And that's all you're getting from me for now, I thought as I crossed my fingers that Fionn wouldn't return to spill the beans again. Ben departed pretty soon afterwards wishing me luck with our business. I was worried that he'd lost faith in me as it was obvious I'd chosen whose side I was on. I was just hoping I'd picked the right one.

Chapter Six
Dead In A Ditch

Ben slammed down the payphone, in a temper. He'd hurriedly found the old public telephone box, outside the Dockyard Museum in English Harbour, just in time to make his seven p.m call to Arfield. But Ben's gut feeling told him he was being given the run around. His current employer had made a big deal about checking in at the exact appointed time and as it turned out, he wasn't even there to answer it. He walked back to his car, feeling more sorry for Arfield's wife who'd taken his call. With a timid voice, she had apologised constantly for being unable to supply Ben with her husband's current whereabouts. All she could say was that he'd gone fishing with a colleague and wouldn't be returning until the day after tomorrow.

Ben decided to head back to Byrney's bar and do a little more digging around. He'd sensed Byrney probably had more information about Miss Romero and for whatever reason, had decided to keep it to himself. He'd clearly stalled about knowing the girl in the photo when his girlfriend Fionn had easily recognised their guest as one and the same person.

Leyda's birthday party group were the only guests still occupying our tables at Amigo's, although we'd now decided to shift indoors. Fionn had bought her a Hermes scarf from the two of us and Leyda had immediately wrapped it loosely around her neck. I noticed that she kept running her fingers over it, no doubt delighted by it's silkiness and luxurious feel. The Dive Shop contingent of our group had already left when we'd vacated the veranda, so only the four of us remained: Leyda, Pug, Fionn and myself.

"So how's the push for independence progressing?" I asked and winked at Pug. He understood the significance of my question, as did Leyda herself.

"I suppose what you'd really like to know is when we'll be unveiling the Potosi Cross?" she teased.

Fionn joined in, excitedly. "Oh yes Leyda, please tell us."

"Well, since we last spoke about it, we've been able to secure a deal with the chancellor at The Island University in St. Johns." Leyda paused to raise her eyebrows in response to our animated faces. Even Pug was smiling broadly, revealing his large, crooked teeth, which always looked to me like a set of worn down tusks.

"The university has agreed to purchase the cross for a much higher figure than was first estimated by the chairman at Manners Bank."

"How much more?" I asked.

"I'd say at least twice as much, maybe more."

All four of us cheered.

"Wow that's fantastic. What do they intend to do with it? I mean, will it go on public display?" It was important to me that as many people would be allowed to see it as possible.

Before answering, Leyda put down her empty glass and let her lips wipe away the last notes of her drink.

"Well, as you know, it's still securely locked away, in the vault at Manners Bank. But, in a few days time, they're proposing to do some research into it's background. It's very hush-hush and the cross will remain where it is of course. But the Caribbean Historical Studies department at the university are going to try to determine it's age and origin, by taking tiny shavings of the gold and silver from it's structure. And at the same time they will make a thorough examination of the precious gemstones. Then, it should be possible to obtain an accurate date as to when it was originally assembled. The University has already stated it will put a cap on any pay out if the valuation exceeds one million dollars. But whatever they discover the outcome as I've already said is likely to render a much larger reward for you all. Perhaps as much as…"

I suddenly rose to my feet and quickly held out the palm of my hand towards Leyda's mouth, to prevent her from finishing what she was about to say. "I think there's someone at the door."

The three of them watched me walk over to the front entrance and when I opened it, Ben Hansen was standing there with his back to me.

"Sorry Byrney," he said as he turned to face me. "I didn't realise you were closed."

"We're not really. No, please, come on in. I only had the door closed to keep out the breeze. I thought we might be in for a bit of a storm."

"Gee thanks. In that case, can I have another of those beers I tried earlier?"

"Sure. Why don't you join us?" I replied, pointing towards the party table.

I re-introduced Ben to everyone. The only person he'd not previously met was Leyda. Pug, of course, had worked closely with Ben two years ago. I'd almost forgotten that Pug was one of the lookouts helping him to monitor the comings and goings at Padgett House, prior to the big drugs bust. Back then, before I was eventually put straight by Leyda, I used to think Pug was one of Padgett's thugs - Pug the thug, how wrong can you be.

Ben twirled a chair across the floor until it rested with it's back to the table and instead of sitting down normally, he straddled it and sat with his arms resting across the top. Before speaking he deliberately made eye contact with each of us. "So, what are you all talking about then?"

In the short, nervous silence that followed, we looked at one another shyly as if we'd all been caught smoking round the back of the bicycle sheds at school. I was wondering just how good a detective Ben Hansen would turn out to be. We hadn't exactly been speaking in whispers leading up to the time when I'd realised someone was actually standing outside at our front door.

The hour before the dawn is often the loneliest, watching the light emerge, ever so slowly, that half imagined, unfathomable, ungloaming of the night. The light, which Norman Orr was standing waiting for, was the one behind the first floor window of the west wing, the room in which Arfield would awaken.

Orr had always played the long game, making sure he had checked and double-checked every infinite detail. He had lived his whole life in dedicated endeavours, in restraint and in hope, with no allegiance to any political or religious party in particular. But after the events in San Albarra, his view of the world had changed. He hated the American government for their skewered and biased reasons for inflicting a civil war upon a democratically run country. Most of all he hated the men responsible, for their reckless destruction and murderous interference. He knew there was zero chance of bringing these government sponsored killers to justice. In recompense he'd decided he would act in whatever small way he could against the United States of America, by aiding those who opposed them. He recognised he was only a tiny cog in the mechanisms of this combined struggle and that the marks he'd forged in life only amounted to less than ineffectual dents. So, now, for the first time, he was acting on an impulse. He intended to confront the demon of his delusions. And if that devil couldn't be brought to a public trial then Orr intended to confront him with his own evidence and pass judgement over him.

As he waited in the eerie half-light, he felt the confinement of his inner feelings, beating against his bones like tormented hands on the bars of a prison cell. In his own right hand he held onto a photograph, for reassurance and for strength. It had been carefully lifted from his scrapbook, which was now safely locked away again, but with one page incomplete. Outlining it's loss, four, gold coloured, paper corner clasps formed a small empty square.

To keep his nerves from running out of control, he thought about his slumbering museum, on the opposite side of the harbour, the stillness of the air inside the white painted walls disturbed only by the memories of those who had once owned, or had worn, the ancient artefacts, which Orr had diligently restored to life. He closed his eyes for a second and pictured the new layout, as it stood, right at that very moment, his labour of love, with its meticulously recorded details paving a way around the gallery, every single item on display resting, impeccably, beside its own, moonlit shadow; all except one. Beneath a glass lidded showcase, lay a foreshadowing, empty space, which, according to it's hand written label, should have housed: A Royal Navy Sea Service Flintlock Pistol - Dated 1792. Mahogany Stock, Brass Trigger Guard and Nine-Inch Barrel (Safe to Use).

When the bedroom light finally illuminated the window of Arfield's room, Orr took quick, purposeful strides to the front entrance door and let himself in with his spare key. As he passed through the grand, open plan hallway he paused by the foot of the staircase and listened to Arfield, mumbling to himself in the upper corridor. Orr calmly walked through into the kitchen, switched on the light then hid behind the door.

Within minutes, Arfield followed into the kitchen and withdrew a water bottle from the fridge. Then, sensing someone was standing behind him, he turned his head slowly to find the caretaker from the museum pointing an antique pistol at his face. By the look of the caretaker's expression, it was clear that he hadn't come to do the dishes. Arfield was more annoyed by the intruder's presence than by any threat he might pose.

"What the hell do you think you're doing, here?" he demanded. "And put that stupid thing down before it accidentally goes off."

Orr stood his ground defiantly, taking a closer aim at the deep furrow in Arfield's frown. "Sit down," said Orr in a deliberate, dry voice.

Arfield noisily dragged a chair out from under the table and slowly took his seat, whilst maintaining eye contact with the intruder.

"You don't remember me, do you?" continued the intruder.

"Should I?" replied Arfield, raising his voice in anger.

"Perhaps this will jog your memory?" Orr removed the photograph from his pocket and put it down, at the edge of the table closest to him. "Pick it up," he said.

Arfield stared at the little black and white photograph and grunted dismissively, then slid it back across the table.

"That was the day you slaughtered twenty five innocent people. They were my friends, fellow enthusiasts working at the Machacaan excavation site. I watched you and your henchmen gun them down, as if their lives had no meaning at all."

Arfield began to nod his head and smile. "Hah. Now I remember. You're the faggot that ran away." Arfield pointed mockingly at the antique weapon in Orr's hand. "So, what's all this? Stand and deliver? Who do you think you are now, Dick Whittington?"

Orr jabbed the flintlock even closer to Arfield's smug face, at the same time making sure he kept a safe distance to prevent Arfield from making a grab for it.

"This Royal Navy Service pistol," argued Orr, "is as powerful as a point forty-four Magnum. And a musket ball, when fired, travels at eight hundred feet per second." It was Orr's turn to look smug. "And by the way, it was Dick Turpin who said stand and deliver."

Arfield was still smiling. "Well as I remember it in Machacaan, it was you who got his dicks mixed up."

Orr felt the cold, hard trigger against his finger. "You bastard," he cried.

A loud pistol shot rang out and Orr was dead before he hit the kitchen floor. The flintlock fell from his hand and struck the floor beside him. In doing so, its decorative hammer snapped close against the frizzen and ignited the powder. With a smoky, flash of light, a musket ball flew across the kitchen and hit the left hand, upright, wooden frame of the door, splitting it in two. In the doorway itself, Bob Fagg stood, looking slightly bemused, but neither he nor Arfield displayed any remorse for taking the life of the museum guide.

"Where the hell did you get that firearm from, Fagg?" demanded Arfield, as he calmly rose from his seat.

"It's not mine boss, it's yours," replied Fagg nonchalantly.

"How the..." Arfield was momentarily lost for words. He looked down at Orr. Blood was rapidly leaking from the hole in the back of his head and forming a pool on the tiled floor.

"I saw the gun in your diplomatic pouch last night," explained Fagg.

"But, the damn pouch was locked when I turned in."

"No, you left it open, Sir."

"Well never mind that now. For god's sake go and dump this dead body somewhere discreet, before the whole island wakes up." Arfield glanced out of the small window to see if there was still a little of the night left in the sky. Satisfied there was just enough darkness to cloak their actions he turned to Fagg again and said, "hand me that photograph."

Fagg also handed back the firearm whilst quickly glancing at the men in the photo. He recognised they were the exact same as the ones from the wall mounted frame, back at Arfield's Office in California. Fagg fetched a blanket from the linen cupboard and rolled Orr's body into it. "I'll bring the car around," he added solemnly. In the meantime, Arfield found one of his cigars, lit it and drew in deeply. The first drag always made him cough.

"Byrney…Wake up." I could feel someone roughly shaking my shoulders. I opened an eye and saw it was only Fionn. "You're late, It's gone seven o'clock, already." Suddenly, I was awake. I realised it was my turn to do the morning bakery run. But I really didn't feel like moving. I'd a humdinger of a thick head, which was mainly the result of Leyda's late night birthday party. That last bottle of rum hadn't been such a good idea after all, even if it had been shared with four others. I also had this vague recollection of unlocking the front door for Ben Hansen in the early hours. I'd no idea how he'd managed to drive back to St. Johns. I knew the rest of us were in no fit state. Then another, vague recollection surfaced. It was Pug telling me about a motorbike, which had gone missing five years ago. It had been owned by the late, Doctor Singh, who had been the previous owner of Leyda's house. Pug had been trying to explain that it would suit me better than the old step-through I was currently using. The old doctor had been somewhat of an eccentric, with a love of antiques and items from the past. And being an Indian doctor he'd wanted an Indian motorbike. I wasn't aware they made motorbikes in India. To which Pug had replied sternly, "actually Byrney, I think they're made in

America." I was still none the wiser, but Pug said he would ask around, to see if it could be found.

Ten minutes after Fionn had shoved me out of our bed, I had our shopping basket strapped to the back of our little, trusty Honda. I'd only ridden about half a mile and was about to turn into the sweeping left hand bend at Cross Green when I wondered if my eyes were playing tricks on me. On the right hand side of the crossroads, there appeared to be four, white hooded sea hawks fighting in the nearside ditch. It was such an unusual sight that I had to pull over and stop. The four, large birds of prey were squabbling over what I imagined to be some sort of road kill, lying in the ditch. I found a dusty, dried up spine of a palm leaf and used it to scare away the rowdy sea hawks. When the last of the birds departed, I saw what had held their attention.

"Jesus wept." I said to myself. The thing in the ditch was a fully clothed, grey haired figure of a man, someone I'd met on half a dozen occasions in the recent past. It was obvious, by the evidence of the merry dance which the sea hawks had been doing to his neck, that he was definitely dead. I looked around to find help, but there was no one else in sight. I rushed back to my bike and continued with my journey, feeling unnerved by what I'd just seen. I knew there was a good chance of bumping into Police Sergeant Hawkins, as usual, at the bakery in Charlestown. And, if he wasn't there, then the police station itself was only a couple of streets away. 'What was happening to our peaceful little paradise?' I thought.

After picking up our order from the bakery, I found Hawkeye at his desk at the police station. He began by boasting how he'd beaten me to the croissants this morning. But his chipper contentment was soon dashed, when I explained about Norman Orr, lying dead and being devoured by a gang of scavenging birds. He grabbed the keys to his Land Rover and left a note for his constable to make his own way to the crime scene, as quickly as possible.

Hawkeye followed me down to the crossroads and I watched him awkwardly scramble down into the ditch to make a quick examination, to confirm the dead body was who I'd claimed it to be. After a few words from Hawkeye about how a policeman's lot is not always a happy one, I left him, rolling out his cordon tape. Then, with one of his typical, witty remarks he asked me not to leave the island, before adding young PC Throup would be calling on me later to take my statement.

By the time I returned to Amigo's, it was a full hour later than normal. I sensed Fionn hadn't needed an excuse to say 'I told you so' in reference to her disapproval of last night's final bottle of rum. I apologised for my lateness. "But you'll never guess what I've just seen," I said to her, nervously. "I've just found another dead body. I saw it on my way to the bakery. He was lying by the side of the crossroads, at Cross Green."

"My god, who is it? Anyone we know?" She replied gravely. I noticed the colour drain from her face.

"Yer, it's Norman Orr, the museum guy."

"Oh, how awful. Poor Norman. He was such a sensitive, sweet person. Had he been knocked down or something?"

I thought I'd spare Fionn the details about him being eaten. "I'm not sure. I left Hawkeye investigating. I reported it to him after picking up our bread order."

"Well at least you did the right thing." I gave Fionn a hug. "I can't stop thinking about him now," she said softly.

"I know," I replied, thinking about the odds of what had recently occurred. "That's the second dead body I've found in as many days."

"You're going to have to be more careful," said Fionn, as a strange thought entered her mind. "You know what they say, to find one dead body is a misfortune, but to find two looks like carelessness." She wasn't joking.

It was two minutes to nine, exactly, when Ben Hansen pulled into the driveway on the eastern side of English Harbour. An old, rickety sign was squeaking drily in the fresh salty breeze. The faded black and gold lettering read 'Nazareth Padgett Plantation - Established 1740. Ben also noticed that some graffiti artist had recently added: a skull and crossbones, in white spray paint. Ben realised this was actually the first time he'd set foot inside the Padgett family home. He took a moment to admire the front of the spectacular looking, grand old mansion. As he looked around he smiled to himself. 'All this, and yet you still turn to crime. 'There's no explanation for single-minded greed', he thought.

Ben had made a determined effort to arrive on time. The note from Arfield, which had been given to him at his hotel, had specified nine a.m. The last thing he needed right now was another lesson in punctuality. Ben hadn't been the least bit surprised to pick up Arfield's note. After speaking on the phone to Arfield's mystified wife, the previous night, he'd had a bet with himself that Arfield was about to show up in Antigua, sooner rather than later. The question was, why had he personally come all this way? And to do what, specifically?

When Arfield heard Hansen's car pull up outside the house, it was a signal for one, final look around the kitchen. All the furniture was back in its marked position and more importantly the floor had been thoroughly cleaned. The split in the wooden doorframe had been covered with a temporary curtain and Orr's flintlock pistol was safely hidden out of sight, in the bottom drawer of the linen cupboard, beneath a stack of towels.

Fagg suggested to Arfield that he would disappear upstairs as it'd be best if he wasn't seen when Hansen arrived. Arfield thought for a second and agreed. "Okay, but make sure you don't make a sound." Arfield secretly approved of Fagg's request to hide. Plan 'B' would be easier to set in motion if Hansen was unaware of Fagg's presence in Antigua. Before making himself scarce, Fagg had already meticulously placed a cafetière of fresh coffee and two cups and sauces on a tray and set it out on the patio table, overlooking the pool, directly under the shade of the balcony.

Arfield then went to answer the door himself, when he was satisfied everything was in order.

"Hello again, Hansen." The two men shook hands. "And apologies for the note, last minute change of plans and all that," explained Arfield, without really explaining anything at all. "Please, come out onto the patio," suggested Arfield, holding out his right arm to signal the way. "Such a fabulous morning." Arfield smiled.

Hansen wasn't taken in by Arfield's attempts at hospitality. When they were both seated, Arfield picked up the pot and began to pour. " I trust you take it black," he grinned. "Sugar?"

"No thanks." Ben watched as Arfield removed four brown sugar cubes from the bowl for his own cup and began stirring them in noisily, almost irritatingly so.

"So, please tell me, you've succeeded in locating the films?"

It was Ben's turn to appear smug. He'd made a number of important discoveries at Bar Amigo's last night, after he'd been invited to join the party table. As the four guests let their hair hang loose with the effects of rum and beer, he'd had ample opportunity to search the unoccupied rooms, including Byrney and Fionn's. The empty guest bedroom was, in fact, still being occupied, although its guest was absent all evening. From the belongings stored there, it was obviously a female guest. And the real clincher for Ben was finding a t-shirt, with a Soweto Freedom logo printed across the front. Having read the report on Miss Romero's previous assignments, the t-shirt could only have belonged to her. Inside the small, deserted room, he'd searched every drawer, pocket and potential hiding place, but the films could not be found. She must've still had them about her person. In Byrney's and Fionn's room he'd found some correspondence, inside a drawer, referring to the purchase of the former Bijoe's Bar. The letter headed notepaper had been sent from Manners Bank in St. Johns and signed on behalf of the Chairman, Mr. Gilbert Chivers. The letter specifically alluded to the collateral, which had been used to guarantee the said purchase and to the fact that it was securely kept inside a safety deposit box, in the bank vault. The number of the box was B49. Its valuation would be determined on completion of Antiguan independence. There were three claimants, each of whom had a two percent share. Each of the claimants would be issued with their own safety deposit box key. Their names were listed below as: Mark Byrne, Raoul Fernandez and James Walker.

Ben took his time in delivering his report to Arfield on where Miss Romero was staying and under what current pseudonym. He wanted Arfield to realise he'd made a thorough investigation and that he'd done so discreetly, without any other person being aware of his pretext.

"Well done, Hansen. It's a pity you don't have the films with you, but I can firmly say your mission has been a huge success. Let me go and fetch my cheque book and we'll let you be on your way."

Whilst Arfield was away inside, Ben rose to stretch his legs and walked closer toward the pool. It was fast becoming a crystal clear day and the sky was the bluest he'd ever seen it. The surface of the pool was a still as a mirror, truthfully reflecting the colour above. In its reflection, he could also see the colour of the white walls of the mansion behind him. And on the overhanging balcony, above the patio, was the figure of a man, holding onto the handrail. The face was slightly out of focus, but the shape of the figure definitely didn't belong to Arfield. When Ben turned around, the balcony was empty.

Arfield returned and handed Ben a cheque, for ten thousand dollars. It would be drawn against the campaign fund. With the size of the campaign pot already standing at six million dollars, Arfield had little doubt Hansen's pay-off wouldn't be missed. "Well, thanks again Ben, we'll take it from here."

Ben took note again from Arfield's words. That was the second time this morning he'd heard Arfield use the word, we. So the mysterious figure on the balcony must be part of Arfield's team in Antigua.

"If you don't mind," continued Arfield, "I'd like to borrow a lift into Cross Green, so that I can have a quick recce at the place where Miss Martini is staying. Just drop me anywhere near Amigo's."

Arfield could feel the adrenalin starting to build. The donkey work had all but been done. Now, it was just a case of choosing the right moment to confront the bitch and make her an offer she couldn't refuse. There was, now, no need for a Plan B. Hansen had proved he was a capable detective after all; so the scapegoat could now fly back to the U.S. unaware of his unfulfilled role and be all the richer for it.

They hadn't been travelling for more than a mile when their little Volkswagen Beetle was halted in a small queue of stationary vehicles leading to the marina at Cross Green.

"Looks like the local police department has installed a road block," confirmed Ben, having wound down his window and rubber necked through the opening. "We could be held up here for sometime. I'll go and check it out." Ben switched off the engine, removed the car keys and went to investigate. He looked back over his shoulders and noticed Arfield was still hunched up in the passenger seat and was curiously sinking further down behind the dashboard. He didn't appear to be in any hurry to follow him.

As he drew nearer, Ben recognised Hawkeye, talking to an ambulance crewman. He didn't look to be enjoying himself.

"Can I be of any assistance?" Volunteered Ben.

"It's you Hansen. Yes, good morning. Or rather it isn't. We've another grisly murder case to deal with. If I wasn't retiring in two years time I'd be seriously considering becoming a priest."

"So, what's happened here?"

"It's the Englishman who runs the dockyard museum. He's been shot in the head." Hawkeye led Ben away from the back of the ambulance, in order to continue their conversation in more private surroundings. "It's my guess he's been killed somewhere else and dumped here afterwards. There ought to have been a much larger pool of blood beneath him and from my limited experience, a single bullet to the back of the head has all the hallmarks of a professional assassin." Hawkeye remembered seeing something similar on TV a couple of years ago, in an episode of Kojak. He looked at Ben for a response to his analysis, but Ben just rubbed his chin. He was having his own preliminary thoughts as to whether there could be a possible link to the previous dead body. Whilst Hawkeye waited for Ben to answer, he asked him if he had anything to do with this. "Where were you, earlier this morning?"

Ben's jaw fell out of his hand at such an infantile line of questioning. "Seriously? I was taking a swim at the beach in front of my hotel. Look, Hawkeye, I was about to fly back to the States later today, but if you need an extra pair of hands for a few days, I'm at your disposal."

Hawkeye considered Hansen's offer in a matter of seconds. The only doubt he had was, whether he could trust Hansen, now that he had chosen to be a freelance detective. "Before I say yes, do you mind telling me why you quit the DEA?"

It seemed a reasonable question to Ben, but it wasn't a subject he enjoyed talking about. "I left shortly after I lost my colleague, Chuck, who you probably remember from my last visit here. Sadly, he was killed during a house search, which went badly wrong. I thought at the time we were being set up and hung out to dry by our chief of operations. Afterwards, I became obsessed with the idea that he wanted me out of the way too. Shot in the line of duty, covers up a lot of sins. So I decided to go freelance and like I said, I'm at a loose end, as of today."

"So you've found your missing person?" Hawkeye was much sharper than he let on.

"My job was just to locate her for a client. And yes, he was satisfied with my report."

"Okay then, just give me a minute or two to finish off here and you can come along to my next port of call."

Ben waited for Hawkeye to have a final word with the driver of the ambulance. It drove away towards the inland road, with its warning siren carving a path through the stationary traffic. In the side of the road, young Constable Throup was making his own notes and taking photographs at the spot where Orr's body had lain. Ben followed Hawkeye as he stepped forward to pass on further instructions to his deputy.

"I want photos taken of these footprints next to the road, especially the ones at right angles to the edge of the path. And when you've done that, walk down to Amigo's and take a statement from Mark Byrne and don't forget to check the tread pattern beneath his shoes.

Ben turned to Hawkeye in puzzlement at hearing Byrney named mentioned in connection to this latest murder. "What's Byrne's role in this?"

"He reported Orr's death to me this morning. He was the one who found him."

Ben couldn't help wondering; as unlikely as it sounded, had Byrney got himself mixed up in something dodgy? He'd discovered a surprising amount of mysterious correspondence in Byrney's room the night before. And two dead bodies in two days; that was some going. "Tell me; did Byrne know the victim?"

Hawkeye fumbled for his keys and jangled them inside his pocket, like a handful of loose change. "Yes, he told me he'd met Orr on several occasions in the past two years. I think Byrney has a vivid imagination, but he's not a killer. However, there are a number of locals around here who are deeply suspicious of him and Fionn, because they're so young and yet they have acquired a busy little establishment that's reputedly becoming a gold mine. But, like I said to you yesterday, they are both very charming." Hawkeye withdrew his keys and smiled. "I removed this set of keys from Orr's pocket. How would you like to take a look inside the museum with me?"

Ben walked briskly back to where he'd left his car. Unsurprisingly, Arfield was nowhere to be seen. He'd not noticed him pass by en route to Amigo's, so Ben surmised he must have hobbled back to his mansion. For the time being, he put his suspicions about Arfield and his ghostly partner to one side. He'd been invited to help solve the murder of Norman Orr and in order to do that he must first learn what sort of person he was.

Arfield had waited for Hansen to reach the front of the stationary traffic before getting out of his uncomfortable little car. He was sweating like a stuffed pig on a spit by the time he'd walked back to his accommodation. That was the second time in two days he'd had to plod the full length of the bridleway leading up to Padgett House. And after further fumbling and cursing with the old lock on the front door, he was in no fit state for anything other than to take a plunge into the pool. He didn't even bother to remove his clothes. He was in a foul mood. His temperament had spiked further when he'd seen his own hire car was missing from outside the mansion and Fagg along with it too.

Arfield's soggy clothes were now creating their own pool of water on the tiled floor of the hallway as he picked up the house phone and dialled up the number for Felix Schwarzkopf, back in the campaign office in Santa Barbara. With the incriminating films still at large, he had been given the green light, from 'King Teflon' himself, to take every necessary step to liquidate them. The commandment could not have been any clearer.

The first thing Ben noticed when he pulled up next to the red, public telephone box, outside the dockyard museum, was a bicycle, leaning up against the perimeter wall. Attached to the back of the saddle post, was a handmade trailer, about the size of a dog-cart. Its crude construction basically consisted of an old fruit box, with faded markings in red ink, which read King Cornelius Black Pineapples. This, in its turn, was suspended on a pair of old pram wheels. "Well, that thing certainly wasn't here last night," he said to himself.

The owner of the bicycle and trailer was busily at work in the front garden. The gardener had gathered and tied a bundle of his pruning's and was now walking back down the path to deposit them inside the old, empty box. The stocky, round-shouldered figure could only belong to one man - Pug Walker.

"Hello Pug," waved Hawkeye as he marched past. "Lovely day for it."

"Hi again, Pug," said Ben courteously, as he followed in the policeman's footsteps.

Pug straightened his back and turned around, resting his hands on his hips, but the two men were standing at the entrance door with their backs to him, before he'd had time to reply.

As Ben waited to enter, he listened for any signs of activity beyond the sturdy, oak door. From the outward appearance of the museum building, everything appeared as one would expect. Hawkeye used Orr's keys to unlock the main door. They nodded to one another in approval. A locked door was a good omen that all was well inside. The undisturbed, regimental layout of the gallery on the ground floor confirmed their initial judgement: that no disturbances had occurred here earlier in the day. It was typical of the man who tended over the array of relics on display that there wasn't even a speck of dust amongst them anywhere. It was as if it had been prepped for a VIP inspection. It was a similar set up on the upper gallery floor too.

"I'll check Orr's private quarters," suggested Hawkeye. "He has two rooms in the loft space overlooking the rear courtyard."

Ben nodded his head. "Okay, I'll be along in a minute or two." He was totally engrossed with all the naval paraphernalia on display, in particular, the impressive collection of old Royal Navy firearms. Ben felt like he'd stepped back into another century as his eyes rested on the polished weapons of combat: cutlasses, swords and sabre's, even an old blunderbuss. Some were more ornamental than others, but in the right hands, no doubt just as deadly.

Hawkeye stuck his head back inside the gallery. He was looking anxious again. It wasn't his best look. "You'd better come up here a minute."

The contents of Orr's compact living quarters had been turned inside out. His discarded belongings had been thrown into a pile in the centre of his room and every single item of furniture was lying on its side. Ben gave a short whistle of astonishment. "Someone's done a very thorough job." He pushed at the scattered mound of insignificant rubble in the middle of the floor with his shoe, out of curiosity. "Whatever the the intruder was looking for, it must have been quite small to have emptied all the drawers like this."

"Well, if there was an intruder he didn't break in through the windows. They're all still fastened from the inside, unless there is a secret tunnel I don't know about," replied Hawkeye. "Whoever did this must have had their own set of keys," he added.

"I'll go and check with Pug," offered Ben. "Maybe he saw or heard something?"

"Or maybe he has a set of keys too," suggested Hawkeye.

As they walked back past the cabinet of weapons, Ben noticed a gap in the display. "Hey, look at this. There's a pistol missing."

Hawkeye was standing next to Ben. "Perhaps it's the one that was used to kill Orr?" he suggested with a smug looking smile, as if pleased with his own powers of deduction.

"Well, according to the label, it's an eighteenth century flintlock. There won't be too many people who know how to use one."

"Argh, good point, Hansen. But, nevertheless, it's not like Orr to be sloppy. It's my guess if we find this missing flintlock we'll also find his killer."

"Well, we'll have to wait until the pathologist removes the bullet from the back of Orr's head before we can confirm your theory. Sounds like a bit of a long shot to me."

"Yes, and flintlocks are known for their long shots, are they not?"

"Not one of your best jokes, Hawkeye."

Ben carried on back down the stairs, closely followed by Hawkeye who was still jangling Orr's set of keys. By the lack of blood inside any of the rooms, they both agreed that Orr couldn't have been murdered here.

Ben stepped outside to speak to Pug, whilst Hawkeye turned into the ground floor galley and strode over to the counter at the end of the room. He was aware that Orr kept an old iron safe in the little storeroom whose entrance was concealed by a drawn curtain. Hawkeye scrutinised the bunch of keys and selected the longest one. It was a good guess on his part as it fitted snuggly into the lock.

"Dat am clever," he chuckled to himself as the heavy door swung open. At first glance, the contents were disappointing and looked unworthy of such precautionary measures of security. On the top shelf there was only a small stack of documents. Amongst the single pile of papers, Hawkeye found Orr's British Passport, which had expired fifteen years ago. Orr's mug shot showed him to have had dark hair and a close-cropped beard, but it could not disguise his unmistakeable, timid expression. Hawkeye flicked through the pages. It was full of visas and immigration stamps.

On top of the pile was a sheet of paper with a list of instructions to a Mr. Eldridge Delgado, relating to his position on the Marine Observation Team. He'd seen similar copies forwarded to his police station.

The remaining handful of documents mostly concerned an ancient archaeological site called Machacaan, in San Albarra. There were letters of authority, all dated prior to 1952, granting permissions to explore and excavate the ruins. However, at the bottom of the pile, Hawkeye also found what felt, at last, to be an item of value. It was an envelope containing a wad of bank notes. But, on closer inspection, these turned out to be Fifty Pesos Notes, issued by the Banco National de Cuba. Hawkeye shrugged, "Ha, Mickey Mouse money."

The bottom shelf of the safe contained an old album of small, black and white photographs. He flicked through the pages and dismissed it as having no immediate value. He quickly gathered everything together under his arm and closed the door to the safe, then locked it once more.

Outside, Hansen was standing waiting. As the two men were about to leave, an old, Mark One Land Rover, with an open rooftop, swung into the yard at the rear of the museum. They stood and watched with interest, as the young uniformed driver jumped out. There were no other passengers. He walked purposefully towards the entrance of the museum, ignoring the two men who were captivated by his timely arrival. Hawkeye stepped forward and held up his right arm, "and where do you think you're going?"

"I'm returning these keys to Mister Orr," replied the soldier.

"Let me see," demanded Hawkeye.

Iko smiled politely and handed them over. Hawkeye studied the keys. They were only small car keys and nothing remotely like the old iron key, which offered access to the museum. He pocketed the car keys for safekeeping. "Well now, young man, what's your name?" Hawkeye asked, suddenly laying on an officious tone of voice.

"Eldridge Delgado, but most people call me Ellie. I'm one of the new Marine Observation Officers."

"Do you have any identification?" Hawkeye was following the well honed steps of his policeman's manual, in order to give himself more time to learn as much as possible about this new stranger in town. You never know, he may incriminate himself, he thought. Iko withdrew his driver's licence from his shirt pocket and handed it over.

"Argh, Grenada," confirmed Hawkeye with a look of surprise. "So what is your business with Norman Orr?"

"Mister Orr lent me his Land Rover when I arrived here, the day before yesterday."

"Well, I've some bad news for you, Ellie. Mister Orr was found dead this morning." As soon as he'd finished his sentence Hawkeye studied Ellie's face, but he only saw sincere shock and puzzlement in the young man's eyes.

"How did he die?"

"He's been shot," replied Hawkeye, bluntly.

Before Iko could respond, Ben stepped forward to introduce himself; he had realised Hawkeye's questioning was heading down a blind alley. "Hello, I'm Ben Hansen. I'm helping the local police with their murder inquiry. Pleased to meet you, Ellie." Ben held out his hand, which was greeted firmly by the young man. Iko was beginning to feel uncomfortable as to why a plain-clothes American had become involved.

As Ben shook hands, he noticed the young man's upper arm was swollen. "That looks nasty. What happened there?"

"I was bitten by a spider last night."

"Oh, whereabouts are you staying?"

"Fort Anderson, just a few miles up the coast. Please, if Mister Orr isn't going to be needing his Land Rover, would it be okay for me to keep it for now?"

The two men looked at each other. Ben shrugged his shoulders to suggest he'd no objections. Then, Hawkeye reached into his pocket and reluctantly handed back the keys to Ellie.

"Take care not to smash it up," commented Hawkeye as Iko walked away towards the rear yard. Then he turned to face Ben. "What do you make of him?"

"Hard to say. He hasn't been here very long. And Grenada isn't one of the Caribbean islands I know a great deal about other than we Americans have raised a number of red flags recently about their current government. There were a lot of unhappy Republicans back home last year when that communist led coup seized hold of power."

"Well now," replied Hawkeye, returning to the subject of Orr's killer. "I don't think that young man has anything to do with it. In my opinion, it's unlikely that someone who has only just set foot on Antigua for the first time, two days ago, could be responsible for the murder of a long established public servant."

Ben remained silent. When no reply was forthcoming, Hawkeye switched his attention to Pug Walker. "Did he say anything that might be useful to our case?"

"He told me he'd arrived here at eight p.m this morning, by which time Orr had already been found dead."

"I'm surprised he was so late. He normally likes to get the job done before the day begins to heat up."

Ben smiled to himself in the knowledge that Pug had been drinking until two a.m the night before.

"Anything else?" asked Hawkeye, thinking Hansen might be keeping something from him.

"He didn't see anyone at the museum, if that's what you're thinking? Pug also mentioned he'd be working at Padgett House the day after tomorrow. So I've asked him to let me know if he spots anything suspicious. Oh, and by the way Pug doesn't have a set of keys for the museum either."

"Hmmm," murmured Hawkeye. "Let's head back to the station. I need to examine these documents, which I found in Orr's safe, more closely and I'm gasping for a cup of tea. You're welcome to join me, of course."

Ben looked down at his wristwatch. It felt like it'd been a long morning so far, but as he'd no other immediate plans, he agreed. "Okay, why not. We can also check if your constable has anything new to tell us."

Chapter Seven
Welcome To The Real World

It hadn't been the sort of morning, which I'd want to experience again in a hurry. After I'd eventually returned from my routine run (which turned out to be anything but routine) up to the bakers in Charlestown, Fionn and I had to rush around to see to our guest's breakfasts. Luckily most of them were the laid back types who weren't too fussy about being served the minute they sat down on our veranda. Our morning chores were further disrupted when Police Constable Throup came to write up my statement about how I'd discovered Orr's body. We had a slight disagreement about the birds of prey that had been dining on Orr's exposed limbs. He'd never seen a sea hawk before. But I assured him the birds were much larger than jackdaws. And jackdaws, in my experience, didn't wear white hoods, not even the ones who were members of the coo clucks clan.

    I was anxious to get back to the kitchen to help Fionn clear the tables and attend to the dirty dishes, which also included our glasses and crockery from Leyda's birthday party, from the night before. No sooner had the uniformed policeman departed with my signed statement, when Leyda herself appeared, asking if we'd heard the news? The bush telegraph had obviously been singing down the wire this morning. According to Leyda, Pug had called on her earlier, with details of some of its more gruesome aspects.

    "We were both at a loss to think of who would do such a thing," she said mournfully. "That poor man. He was such a gentle, kind person. I don't know anyone who had a bad word to say against him and to think that the person who did this could still be on our island. Keep your eyes and ears peeled," she warned.

When I repeated my version of events again, about how I'd found poor Norman, Leyda put her arm around my waist in a motherly fashion and said sincerely that if I began to have nightmares about it, she would be only to glad to discuss them with me.

As Fionn was still finishing off in the kitchen I volunteered to see to the dirty laundry, which meant changing over the towels in the guests' bedrooms. Most of our guests had by now wandered off for the day, apart from our newly weds, Rory and Denise, who were getting later and later each morning before making an appearance at breakfast. They were content to sit out on the veranda, drinking black coffee until long after midday.

Prior to crawling into bed last night, Fionn and I had spoken briefly about Ilena Martini. I mentioned that I found her a little curious after my initial conversation with her. And what about later: her sudden disappearance with the young soldier and how she hadn't returned at all yesterday evening? On top of that, Ben Hansen walks into our bar, completely out of the blue, flashing her photograph around. And why had she chosen to use a different name? Part of me wanted to believe Ilena Martini and Ilena Romero were two entirely different people. My initial curiosity was quickly turning into deep suspicion.

As I stood in the centre of her cosy, deserted room, I found myself looking around at her belongings. It was a little untidy maybe, but it all looked perfectly harmless for someone of her age and profession. A framed photograph, beside her pillow, caught my eye. It was of Ilena and a slightly older man. They had their arms around each other and they both had a camera hanging around their necks. Ilena was holding hers in her free hand and was pointing it towards whoever was taking this particular photo. Both Ilena and the man next to her looked very happy. So it was safe to presume this must be her boyfriend. Just then, the door opened and Ilena herself walked in and caught me red handed, still holding onto the photograph.

"What are you doing?" She demanded, sounding more annoyed than was necessary.

I was immediately put on the defensive by her sudden outburst. "Sorry, I've just come to change the towels over."

Luckily, the clean ones were still tucked under my arm. "I was just having a quiet look at your photo. Is this your boyfriend?"

Ilena dropped her bag onto the floor and went to open her locker. "Have you been looking inside here too?" She asked accusingly.

"No, of course not," I replied quickly, then suggested I would just swap her towels for clean ones and be out of her hair.

Ilena bent down again, picked up a t-shirt from the floor of her locker and held it out in front of me. "Well, someone's been going through my clothes too and if it wasn't you, then who else has been in here?"

"No one, as far as I'm aware." I couldn't imagine any of our other guests taking the keys from behind the bar and searching other rooms. No one else had ever complained before. I watched Ilena opening her chest of drawers and checking inside them to make sure nothing had been stolen.

"Anything missing?" I asked tentatively.

"No, everything is still here, but not as neat as I left it."

I was wondering whether now was a good time to mention about the photograph of her, which Ben Hansen had been flashing around. I thought that if she was using two names then there had to be a good reason for it. And besides, I'd already lied to Ben about not knowing her, so I reckoned she had a right to know.

When I'd finished explaining about Ben's visit here yesterday, on two separate occasions, she instantly appeared agitated and deep in her thoughts.

"Why are you using two different names? Are you wanted by the police?"

Ilena sat down on the edge of her bed and prompted me to sit next to her. "Do you, by chance, know a man called Gastin De Bourges?" She asked.

Wow. I wasn't expecting her to ask me that. Hearing Gastin's name again was a real surprise, but how did Ilena know him?

"Yes, I do," I replied with a smile. "About three years ago, we worked together, to expose a wartime collaborator in France. Have you met Gastin recently?"

"Yes, I know him quite well. We were both chasing the same Nazi criminal last year in Argentina, until I was forced to leave the country." Ilena frowned deeply, once more. "You asked if the man in that photo is my boyfriend? Well, yes and no. He was my boyfriend, right up to the moment our car had a serious accident, near San Carlos de Bariloche." Ilena picked up the photo and took a deep breath. "But it was no accident. Someone had cut the brake hoses. Philippe was at the wheel. He was killed outright, when our car left the road and struck a tree. I think he deliberately swerved to take the full impact in order to save me. Gastin helped me to cross the Chilean border and obtain a passage north to Panama City as it was no longer safe for me to remain in the foothills of the Andes. During our trek over the mountains together, he spoke of a certain brave young man whose quick thinking had saved the day, during a shoot out in the Pyrenees. He knew you were living in Antigua and said that if I ever needed a friend then you were someone I could trust. He also said I should not underestimate you. I'm not sure what he meant by that." She said with a wry grin.

I was really pleased when Ilena confirmed that Gastin was alive and well. It had been ages since I'd received a letter from him, although I did feel guilty about that too, as it had been my turn to write back to him. But, as usual, work got in the way and it wasn't so easy for me to keep in touch, being out at sea for long periods at a time.

"So, why is Ben Hansen looking for you?"

"I've no idea who Ben Hansen is. I've never heard of him, but if he's an American then it's probably related to some photographs I've taken recently." She turned to face me, staring hard into my eyes as if she was about to disclose an important secret. She had a wise and noble face and like so many girls with a Mediterranean heritage, she was majestically cool, with her dark brown eyes and long, dark lashes, naturally outlined as if marked by a velvet pencil. I think she was testing my nerve to see whether I would take my eyes away from her inquisitive gaze. "Can I really trust you, Byrney?"

I answered without stopping to think about what I might be getting into. "Yer, of course."

She bent down and pulled off her ankle boots. And from inside each one, beneath the insole, she produced a roll of thirty-five millimetre film, which had been secretly stored in a recess inside the two-inch heel. "I believe American government agents are trying to get their dirty hands on these two films."

I was a little puzzled. It was almost like being in a spy story and I imagined her taking photos of some top-secret documents. "Why are these films so important?"

"They're evidence of a massacre, which occurred last week, at the Spanish Embassy, in San Albarra City. I was helping a group of delegates, from a peaceful organisation, who were meeting with the Spanish Ambassador, to report the recent kidnappings and murders of indigenous peasants by elements of the San Albarra Army. When the local government found out about the meeting, they sent in storm troopers to secure and barricade the Embassy building, before burning it to the ground. Everyone inside was burned alive. I managed to escape, because I'd already stepped outside when the troops arrived. These two films prove that the local government was responsible."

"But what has this to do with the American government?"

"The current government in San Albarra was put in power by the American Intelligence Organisation. They removed the democratically elected president and put in their own puppet dictator many years ago. They then trained all the government soldiers and are still supplying them with arms, to ensure the socialist leaning opposition parties never regain power."

"So let me get this straight," I said. "The American government is supporting terrorists and fascism in San Albarra?"

"Got it in one. So it came as no surprise, that the state run media there proclaimed the peaceful protestors inside the Spanish Embassy were responsible for starting the fires and killing all the embassy staff, before committing self-immolation."

"Fucking hell. I can see why the Yanks would be anxious to get hold of these films. What do you intend to do with them?"

"I have a friend who's a journalist with the Chronicle and Herald, over in Washington. I'm going to take these films there myself. And if that isn't possible, then I'll hand them to someone who can do it for me."

When Bob Fagg returned to Padgett House in their hire car, Arfield had already changed into a fresh set of clothes and his temperament had cooled to normal levels. He was sitting in the shade, on the patio, sipping one of Fagg's beers and plotting his next move. He was making a concerted effort to regain his composure before the inevitable battle of wills with his incompetent colleague. Only a few minutes earlier, he'd been shocked by his own, unhealthy looking reflection in the bathroom mirror. And to remedy his flushed complexion and the ominous floaters in the whites of his eyes, he'd taken two additional Tenormin tablets. When he heard the slamming of the front door, echoing through the house, he took a large swig of beer and braced himself.

Arfield looked at Fagg's dumbstruck face, completely misinterpreting Fagg's hidden coolness. "Where the hell have you been?" he demanded.

Fagg had at least half a dozen excuses ready, but chose one that Arfield would be guaranteed to let slide. "Just had to drive into St. Johns to gas up the tanks." At least it was a half-truth.

"Never mind that. I've just had a damn narrow escape with the local police. Why in god's name did you dump that dead body so close to where we're staying? You dumb ass son-of-a-bitch?" Arfield was letting fly with both barrels. "Hell, you might as well have lit up a neon sign with our names all over it. Are you deliberately trying to get us locked up, or are you just plain stupid?"

Fagg looked down at his shoes for a moment, to allow the air to clear. Then asked, "so what's the plan boss? Are we going after the films?"

Arfield wagged his finger to settle his rage and to signal to Fagg to sit down in the next patio chair. In more controlled tones, he proceeded to explain his next course of action. "Hansen's already told me exactly where we're likely to find them; but we need to keep a low profile. So, I'm going in alone. Finish your beer then you can drop me at the marina in Cross Green and I'll make my own way to this Amigo's Bar." Arfield paused to check Fagg was still paying attention. "Give me one hour then come and meet me. And for god's sake, no funny stuff. From now on I'll be keeping my firearm where I can see it. Do I make myself understood?"

Fagg put down his empty beer bottle on the patio table, with a satisfied sigh. "You're the boss."

It was not like Fionn and me to have a heated argument. But after explaining about Ilena and that she might be in danger, Fionn said firmly I should stay well clear of her. "You've no idea what she's been doing before she came here. If Ben was looking for her, then she's probably wanted by the police."

"That's what I said to her too, but she said if that was the case, it wasn't for breaking the law. It was for attempting to tell the truth."

"What does she mean by that?"

I had decided, for now, not to mention to Fionn about the films that Ilena was hiding. I thought it would be safer for Fionn if she knew as little as possible about it. It was also a precaution on my part, in case Ben Hansen returned, asking more questions, but I thought a few basic details about her wouldn't do Fionn any harm.

"She's a journalist and sometimes she has to take necessary risks, in order to get to the facts of a story."

"Well, I don't like it Byrney. We've enough on our plate here without having to hide a fugitive from justice. So please, just drop it."

"Okay, I will. But I've promised to walk her over to Fort Anderson. She's decided to check out."

The look on Fionn's face was one of dismay, but she finally agreed, as long as I promised not to involve myself any further.

It hadn't taken long for Ilena to gather up her belongings and roll them up individually into her backpack. She settled the account with Fionn for her four nights stay. She also pocketed one of our business cards from the top of the counter. She gave Fionn a French style farewell, with a kiss on either side of her face and said she'd love to return again, in more relaxed circumstances.

It was around a twenty-minute walk from Amigo's to Fort Anderson, which lay to the northwest, on the other side of the mangroves. I asked Ilena how she had got along with Ellie on their trip to Monkey Island.

"We soon discovered why it's called Monkey Island," she commented drily. "There was no evidence of a leper colony, but it was infested by a colony of horse spiders, which the locals tend to call monkey spiders. We didn't get much sleep. One of them even bit Iko's arm. It looked very painful."

"I thought his name was Ellie. Just now you called him Iko."

"Oh merde. Sorry, please don't repeat any of this, but he told me of his real identity. He's a refugee, from Lusalgo City on the west coast of Africa. He lost his entire family there in the civil war, but was saved by a Cuban soldier, who brought him back to the Caribbean to study. He's actually on a secret mission here to find a place where ships can dock and unload their equipment. It has something to do with helping countries that are under attack in Central America. Just imagine, Byrney, what it must be like to live in a country, which is a neighbour of the United States. You would be in a very precarious position. And heaven help you if the population chose to elect a socialist government."

"But I don't understand. I thought the United States was a peace loving country, you know, like they protect us all from the bad guys."

Ilena came to a standstill and grabbed my arm. "I've got news for you, Byrney. They are the bad guys."

"So where does all this violence and the need to control their neighbours stem from? Is it hatred, greed, or just wanting something which doesn't belong to you?" I was very interested in hearing what Ilena had to say about it.

"The one thing which gnaws away at the American dream is fear," replied Ilena. "Although they would never admit to it. They fear the will of the people. They fear losing their property. They fear most that an alternative way of living could be more successful than their capitalist ideals. In other words they fear the opposite of everything they stand for. Fear leads to paranoia and that leads to irrational acts: like supporting regimes that they know have an insatiable appetite for corruption and cruelty. Even today in 1980, American government agents continue to supply weapons to these rogue organisations. It's been going on for decades and from what I've learnt, in my short life, I cannot foresee things changing for the better, not anytime soon."

"Things are obviously worse than I'd realised."

Ilena shook her head at my innocent, naïve view. "Welcome to the real world, Byrney. Remember that poor woman you fished out of the sea two nights ago? She's just the tip of the iceberg. We may never know her name, or what wrong she had committed. But she is just one of the many, anonymous victims of tyranny. As for her family and loved ones, they will have no idea what became of her. So many are seized and made to disappear. We may never know the full extent of these horrors and all we ever hear from America is a distorted truth. Well, I've got news for them. My camera doesn't lie."

We continued walking behind the old, colonial style white house, which was Leyda Friday's home. All was quiet at The Alamo. She was obviously out at work. The single track we were following began to deteriorate; its edges were overgrown by tall bushes and their roots punctured its crumbling surface. The British had built this narrow track, back in the eighteenth century, for the purpose of transporting materials to service the fort. It was one of several artillery fortifications, erected to protect their island against foreign warships. I remembered I'd learned about the historical significance of Antigua to the British Empire from Norman Orr, on one of my earlier visits to the Dockyard Museum, when I'd been researching the wreck of

HMS Winmarleigh. And now, sadly, all that specialist knowledge he possessed was lost. Perhaps it would take another half of a lifetime for someone else to discover it all over again.

Up ahead, the dark, rugged outline of Fort Anderson gradually rose into view.

"Will you be okay with Iko?" I asked.

"Yes, he's a sweet guy really. He did try to paw me once last night, but I soon put him straight," she smiled. "I think his previous experience of relationships with the opposite sex amounts to, if you like it, grab it," she laughed.

I was enjoying talking to Ilena again, now that she had put her worries aside for the moment. How she described what was happening in the world was making a lot of sense to me and I could imagine her and Gastin sharing the same values about life. How I would've loved to be sitting around a campfire with them both, listening to tales of their struggles and triumphs.

I stopped within sight of the large oak door at the front of the fort and asked Ilena what her next move might be. Her answer relied upon what her journalist friend and contact at the Herald and Chronicle in Washington, Daniel, advised her to do.

She stopped a few feet away from the entrance and found the door key hidden beneath a rock. "How are you supposed to carry this around with you," she joked as she held the key horizontally, to exaggerate its size. Against Fionn's wishes, I told Ilena that if she needed my help again then she knew where to find me.

"Thanks Byrney. Hopefully I can figure this one out for myself. Just don't tell anyone where I'm staying."

When Iko had returned earlier to the fort after the grilling from the local police, he knew it was now his responsibility to find a way of contacting Alfonso Chiquata in Cuba, to report the death of Norman Orr. He still had the contact details for Station Z in Grenada and although it could be risky, Iko made up his mind to ring Desmond Riley direct. The question was which phone to use. The public telephone box outside the museum wasn't an option, simply because he didn't have enough loose change. He walked over to the magic white machine in the corner of the room and took out a bottle of Red Stripe.

As he looked out to sea, the idea came to him that he could use the phone at the end of the bar at Amigo's. This would also give him the opportunity of bumping into Ilena again. Iko had come to realise, in the short time he'd been in Antigua, that life here in the Caribbean felt like he no longer had to fight to stay alive. And Ilena Romero was the most beautiful female creature he'd ever seen.

But the course of true love sometimes takes an unfortunate turn. Whilst Iko jumped into his Land Rover to follow the coastal road, Ilena was walking the path across White House Bay, with Byrney.

Bob Fagg deposited Arfield outside the marina and watched him lumber up the dusty track in the direction of the bar at the end of the road. Once he was out of sight, Fagg turned off the engine and walked across to the Barracuda Dive shop. He expected to find Raoul Fernandez behind the counter, but he was absent. According to the proprietor he been, 'pressganged into spending some time at his girlfriend's place in Barbuda'.

'Argh well, one down, two to go,' he thought as he jogged back to his car to consult his little black book. He had one eye on his notes and the other on the view through the windshield. He watched a young man in a military shirt and 'bump' cap park an old Land Rover on the spare ground in front of the marina. There were a handful of cars parked there. Most were, probably, owned by small boat crews. There was an old Fiat 124 Sport, covered in a thick layer of dust, with four, flat tyres suggesting a long abandonment. Perhaps the owner had gone to sea and never returned to collect it.

The young soldier strode off in Arfield's windswept footprints. Despite being handicapped with a shoulder bag, the rate at which he was walking meant that he'd soon catch up and overtake the huffing, puffing Billie. Fagg added a few more notes in his book and thought about the next couple of days and his triumphant return to the good old U.S. of A.

Iko was pleased to find only a few tables occupied on the veranda at Amigo's and even inside it was still fairly quiet. He went straight up to the bar and ordered a beer from the, English girl behind the counter. He pointed to the phone at the end of the counter and asked if it was okay to use it.

"Yes, that's fine. It's been a bit temperamental lately, but it should be working again, now. The rates are written down on the wall above the phone," said Fionn, pointing to the official looking notice. "It's fifty cents a minute for a local call and one dollar a minute for trunk calls."

Iko slid his bottle down the bar and glanced around at the contented clientele. No one paid him any attention. He lifted the receiver and dialled up the number of the Queen Conch travel agents in St. Georges. He immediately recognised the strange accent of Desmond Riley who answered it.

When Iko explained about the death of their agent at Station Y, the voice on the other end of the line went very quiet. "Do you mean Norman Orr?" Whispered Des.

"Yes," replied Iko in a similar whisper.

"Did Orr say anything to you to suggest his life was in danger?"

"No."

"Besides you, are there any newcomers in your area?"

Now it was Iko's turn to fall silent. How did he know who was new? "Maybe," he replied.

"In that case, keep your wits about you and use your camera if you see anyone who might look like a murderer, or a villain. You do know what a villain looks like?"

"Yes, like Richard Nixon," replied Iko.

"Aye he'll do. I'll inform the front desk in Havana about Orr's death. Hopefully, they can send in a replacement. Until then call me at this time, everyday. Is your phone secure?"

Iko looked over at the English girl in charge. She seemed harmless enough. "Yes, I think so."

"Okay, stay away from the museum. If you need to send me some photos of suspects use the Zerox machine at the main Post

Office in St. Johns. Ask to speak to Thomas Yule. He owes me a few favours. Have you got all that?"

Iko repeated the last instruction, word for word.

"Good. Well, good luck."

Iko put down the phone as an elderly, out of breath gentleman stepped up to the bar. The red-faced man ordered a cold beer and a glass from the girl. As she poured out half his beer, the old guy glanced behind her, searching for a guest book. However, the thick, leather bound register was way out of his reach. He thanked the girl for his drink then casually asked if Ilena Martini was still staying here. He was an old acquaintance of her parents and they'd asked him to look her up whilst he was on holiday. Iko heard every word. He waited for the American to step aside, then paid for his call. The perspiring American was still standing with his elbows resting on the counter, whilst he waited to question the girl for further information. Arfield tried the chummy approach, adopting a conversation on first name terms, but Fionn would have none of it. She had no intentions of supplying any answers about Ilena Martini. She refused to involve herself in the whole affair.

Iko diligently moved back out onto the veranda to find a partially hidden spot to take a snapshot. He retrieved the Soviet made, Polaroid camera from his bag and attached the zoom lens. He positioned himself so that he had a clear line through the hatched window at the side of the bar and held his aim until the American turned to face the cross hairs of Iko's lens.

"Te pillé! Gotcha."

Iko waited for the camera to churn out the instant photo. It was a good, clear, full-on shot of the American's face. He slipped the print into one of the bespoke, white envelopes and tucked it into his shirt pocket. Time to head off into the big town. He expertly unscrewed the lens and placed the camera back inside his bag.

Chapter Eight

The Bad Guys Know Us

Ben Hansen was perched on the prickly interviewee chair, at the opposite side of P.C Throup's desk, in Charlestown police station. The young police constable placed a fresh cup of tea in front of Ben, who had his eyes fixed upon Byrney's statement from earlier that day. There was nothing out of the ordinary in what he'd read, other than to note down the time when Orr's body had been found, seven-ten a.m. He thanked Throup for the loan of the file then turned around to face Hawkeye, who was just closing the photo album that he'd recovered from Orr's safe.

"Anything there?" enquired Ben, as he rose to his feet to allow the circulation to return to the cheeks of his bum.

"Just a lot of very boring black and white photographs of some old archaeological dig. You know how the English like to plunder ancient burial sites. Luckily, we don't have anything of value here in Antigua. No doubt if we had, it would've been secreted away back to London on the first available plane." Hawkeye leaned back in his sprung loaded chair and stared out of his window. He had other things on his mind.

"Do you mind if I take a look at them?" replied Ben.

Hawkeye swung his chair back into line and put his own fantasises aside. He picked up the loose, accompanying documents and tapped them down on his desk to gather them together. "These documents are all part of the same thing too. There's nothing here to point to who Orr's killer might be. These are all nearly thirty years old."

Reluctantly, Ben sat down again, across from Throup and began leafing through the pages. The documents and photographs were all dated from 1952 and specifically related to the ancient site of Machacaan, in San Albarra. The black and white photographs, although small in size, were of very good quality. Most were views of the old ruins and of the indigenous Indian men and boys carrying buckets and spades who had, presumably, been recruited locally to help with the manual excavation work. It occurred to Ben that Orr showed a great deal of pride in his work. He recognised the detailed descriptions, which Orr had written on the reverse of each shot. They were of a similar style and clarity to the ones Ben had seen earlier inside the museum.

Ben was wondering if Orr's photo album had any connection to the briefing he'd been invited to at the outset of his appointment to locate the incriminating films, which Ilena Romero had taken, also in San Albarra. There was something niggling away at the back of his mind: something, which had been said at that first meeting. It had been the Austrian guy. Ben thought hard to recollect his name - Felix Schwarzkopf. Ben recalled his exact words, 'the same San Albarra that we crushed in '52'. This had to be significant. Ben didn't believe in coincidences. He slowly double checked each of the photos again then paused over the one that showed a clearing, with a group of men in the distance. Were they soldiers? Ben turned around again and casually asked Hawkeye if he had a magnifying glass and a map of San Albarra, perhaps?

Hawkeye was only too happy to oblige. His personal magnifying glass was kept inside his top drawer. He'd learnt, from watching several episodes of Columbo, that it was a necessary tool of his trade. Every good detective should have one.

When the photograph was magnified in front of Ben's gaze, he could see that the men in the background were indeed wearing camouflage uniforms. Ben quickly checked through Orr's documents, making notes of the dates. There was nothing later than 1952, so presumably the excavations ended around that time. Supposing the American soldiers had taken over the site for their own purposes, it would make sense. The size of the clearing in the photograph looked a perfect location to install a temporary guerrilla encampment. Had Orr recognised Arfield as one of the American's who had landed there?

Returning to the photograph album, Ben noticed a blank space next to the photograph, which he'd been pondering over. Knowing Orr's process of cataloguing details, the missing photograph was likely to be related to the soldiers in the previous slot. Perhaps it was even a close up of Arfield himself. Ben turned to Hawkeye.

"Have you removed any of these photos?"

"No, I noticed there was one missing too," he replied, shrugging his shoulders.

"I've found a tourist map of Central America," said Throup triumphantly and handed it across his desk.

"Thanks, perhaps we can find where the archaeological site of Machacaan is located, exactly."

PC Throup moved around to Ben's side of the desk as the map was unfolded and laid out in full.

"Is that it?" Said Throup and pointed to a pyramid symbol in the centre of a jungle, roughly twenty miles from San Albarra city. Ben reached for the magnifying glass again. The name Machacaan was just legible.

That clinched it for Ben. But it still seemed like a big leap of faith, to believe that Orr could have been killed by John Arfield.

"Any news on the bullet yet?" Ben asked of the helpful police constable.

"I'll give the lab a call. Perhaps the pathologist will have written up his report by now."

By the time Ben had finished his cup of tea, young Throup was able to supply the answer. The single slug which had been removed from the back of Orr's head had been identified and cross referenced as being from a nine millimetre bullet, common to a Smith and Wesson Model thirty-nine. 'That fitted very nicely', Ben thought to himself. A pistol of that make and model had been around since the mid-fifties and had been in common use amongst the U.S intelligence corps. With this new piece of evidence, Ben's gut feeling was beginning to point to Arfield as Orr's assailant. Could Orr have met his death at Padgett House? Ben was itching to take another look inside. But, for the moment, he'd prefer to check out his theory alone, without the distracting presence of Hawkeye.

"Do you still have Orr's keys?" Ben asked, innocently.

"I do indeed," replied Hawkeye. "Why do you ask?"

"I'd like to take a more thorough look at Orr's belongings, the ones which were scattered over the floor back at the museum, just to see if we've overlooked anything?" Ben was hoping such a trivial activity wouldn't arouse Hawkeye's curiosity.

Hawkeye touched the droopy handlebars of his Mexican moustache as he contemplated Hansen's request. It was nothing more than a waste a time to him, but if the American wanted to waste his own time then all well and good. "Yes, that's fine. I wish you luck, but take Throup along with you. The experience will do him good."

It hadn't quite worked out the way Ben would have liked, but when they reached the entrance to the museum, Ben made the excuse that he'd forgotten to bring the photo album along with him.

"Why don't you go up to the top floor and make a start of sifting through Orr's things. Anything that looks out of the ordinary, just put it to one side for me to cast an eye over it, when I return."

"You mean I can check first by myself?" Throup had longed to be trusted with getting to grips with a real investigation. Normally, Hawkeye hogged the limelight, leaving Throup behind to man the desk at the station.

"Yes, fill your boots, son. Try to organise his belongings into separate piles. I'll be back soon."

After unlocking the museum door for Throup, Ben raced back down the path and jumped in behind the wheel of the borrowed, police Land Rover. He headed out down the eastern harbour road, passing scattered rows of dazzling yachts. A fair wind had set them bopping upon a foaming broth of sea. And in the same, sunny moment, the multi-coloured, fluttering flags, tied to the swaying masts, announced an enthusiastic welcome to this mariner's paradise. 'What a life.' It seemed like an ironic thought to Ben. He was stuck fast to an imaginary net, headily intoxicated by the thrill of the chase, on the trail of a murderer.

It turned out to be a good educated guess on his part that the key to the front door of Padgett house was part of the bunch that Hawkeye had found in Orr's pocket. And Ben was doubly pleased to discover that the driveway to the large mansion was empty of parked vehicles and that the interior of the house was set in a vacant slumber. When he entered by the front door, he listened intently. It was deathly quiet.

Ben methodically searched the downstairs rooms, checking the drawers and the interiors of cabinets and cupboards. When he entered the kitchen, he automatically switched on the light, as the room was unnaturally dark. Next to the light switch he noticed the door curtain, which looked oddly out of place. It had also been tied up with string. He gently drew it further aside and immediately observed a fresh split, down the centre of the doorframe. He took out his pocket penknife and dug into the hole at the epicentre of the split. With a twisting and scooping motion of the pointed, narrow blade, he was able to extract the root cause. It was a small, solid steel musket ball. It was precisely the sort of significant find he'd been hoping to stumble upon. Ben held it under the glow of the ceiling light to note that it's rough surface had hardly been damaged by the impact. He placed it inside the same pocket as his penknife then carried on with his search, with even greater scrutiny. He soon found the old flintlock firearm, clumsily hidden beneath a pile of towels, in the bottom drawer of the linen cupboard. He held the impressive antique pistol across both hands as a mark of respect. "A Royal Navy, sea service pistol, I presume," he said smiling to himself. He lifted the end of the long barrel under his nose and sniffed, quickly sensing the aroma of burnt gunpowder. "Well, well." Once he was satisfied that the person who had fired the pistol could be none other than Norman Orr, he replaced the ancient firearm and door curtain back to how he'd found them. Then he switched out the light and climbed the stairs, taking two steps at a time.

He intended to prove his theory that there had to be at least two individuals staying here. Arfield's belongings were easily identifiable. The United States diplomatic pouch lying on top of his bed was an unexpected find, and next to it, the huge suitcase which had hardly been unpacked was unmistakably Arfield's. Ben had already seen him wearing the hat, coat and gloves. They could only belong to the sixty year old American. Ben observed that the dark green leather duffle bag lay slightly open inviting him to take a peek inside, but he only found a pharmaceutical jar of pills and a box of cigars. There was plenty of room for other items which Arfield had wanted to avoid declaring; a firearm perhaps? Ben made a mental note and moved on.

Inside the bedroom opposite there were fewer clues. It almost looked unoccupied, apart from a small travel case, hidden beneath the bed. It was locked shut. Ben cautiously checked his watch. He'd already spent ten minutes inside the house. He quickly checked the wardrobe and beneath the pillows and found nothing he could put a name to. Although the bed was neatly made up, it had definitely been slept in. Unlike Arfield's bed covers, which had been left lying across the floor. For now, Ben was still none the wiser as to whose room this was; but, from the evidence he'd uncovered in the kitchen below, he could now say for sure that Orr had died inside Padgett house. When Orr had come to confront Arfield, he had only one shot to play and somehow it'd missed his intended target and struck the doorframe. He now knew, for sure, the extent of Arfield's intentions towards seizing the incriminating rolls of film: that he was willing to kill a man who stood in his way.

Ben immediately felt guilty for pointing Arfield in the direction of Amigo's Bar. He knew he must warn Byrney and Fionn. If they were mixed up in protecting Miss Romero, then their lives were in imminent danger and the only sensible thing to do was for them to tell him everything they knew.

The police Land Rover raced back towards Cross Green once more. Ben was tempted to turn on the warning siren, but there was so little traffic on the roads, it would only draw attention upon him, which he was anxious to avoid. As he dashed up the dusty road past the ship chandlery shops, he saw Arfield walking back towards the marina. "Shit, shit, shit," he said out loud, almost praying to himself that he wasn't too late to save his two, young English acquaintances. 'Please, don't tell me Arfield's shot them both already'.

When I returned to the lazy surroundings of our bar, after walking Ilena to Fort Anderson, I was not looking forward to the inevitable, confrontational conversation with Fionn about helping our estranged guest. To my surprise, I found Fionn behind the bar with a quirky smile on her face. She threw her arms into the air and gave me a big hug. I suspected she'd had a couple of Bacardis.

"I'm so glad to see you," she gasped with sheer delight and some relief. "I've had this strange old man buying me drinks and asking lots of questions. He was quite grotesque really. You know, another one of those weirdos I always seem to attract." She smiled innocently.

"What did he want exactly?"

"Well mostly he was interested in Ilena what's her name. He claimed he'd been asked to look her up. Her family are worried about her."

"I doubt that," I replied then, hastily asked, "You didn't let on where she's staying now, did you?"

"Of course not, but I'd be lying if I said I wasn't tempted to. Honestly Byrney, it's time we washed our hands of that girl."

Fionn's comments about distancing ourselves from Ilena were beginning to make sense. I was confident I could hide her from Ben Hansen, but this old guy, whoever he was, had started to make me feel nervous again.

I'd only been back at the bar for ten minutes when Ben Hansen himself walked through the open doorway. 'Of all the bars in all the world, he had to step into mine'. It was like a scene from Casablanca. How would Rick Blain react to protecting a fugitive from justice, from the hands of the law? The answer to that conundrum was that I was acting as soppy and romantic as Humphrey Bogart's character had been.

Ben had a wide-eyed, open-mouthed expression on his face, like he'd just seen a ghost. "I never thought I'd be happy to see you again Byrney," he said with a reverberation of relief in his voice.

"The same goes for me, Ben," I answered jovially, pointing towards the bottles on the shelf. "What can I get you?"

"Actually, I've come to warn you." Ben's dark brows almost touched as his eyes narrowed; alarm bells tolled at the back of my head.

" It's time to drop the act and come clean about what you know concerning Ilena Romero." His serious expression demanded an immediate answer. Gaining a few precious seconds, I evaded his question by concentrating on the task of pouring two beers.

"Look Byrney, if you have those films, please give them to me. I know all about them and I've a pretty shrewd idea you do too."

It was obviously time to stop playing games. "I don't have them and that's the truth." I replied as I handed Ben a beer. "This one's on me."

"Well, if you know where they are, you need to tell me now. The next people to come in here looking for them aren't going to ask as nicely as I have. I'm not fooling with you. They've already killed one person who stood in their way and believe me they won't think twice about killing again until they get their hands on those films." Ben continued to stare at me, ignoring the cool glass of beer in front of him. I noticed his knuckles turning white as he gripped the edge of the bar. And on the back of his hands, his angry veins protruded like the giant, thirsty roots of an oak tree. I didn't know what to say, nor could I speak. My tongue was so dry it was stuck to the side of my mouth. I reached for my glass, but Ben grabbed my hand. "I'll be at the police station up in Charlestown, if you remember where they are. And for yours and Fionn's sake, bring them to me sooner rather than later. Have you got that? And one last thing, stay away from Padgett House."

"Yer, sure Ben. I'll do that."

Fionn was carrying a tray of empties, clumsily threading her way through the tables, as Ben brushed silently past her, making a clumsy exit.

"What's the matter with Ben?" she asked, as she moved in behind the bar.

"He's still looking for Ilena." I ventured coyly.

"That girl is more trouble than she's worth. If you don't tell him where she is, then next time, I will."

I was about to confess all to Fionn: about the films, about the fire at the Spanish Embassy a week ago in San Albarra city, about Ellie whose real name is Iko, the whole shebang. But I was still under the impression I could take the flack and keep Fionn out of it. That was until Ben Hansen's last visit. If I didn't keep my guard up, then the shit really was about to hit the fan. These men whom Ben referred to had already killed a man. Did he mean Norman Orr? I was struggling to get that thought out of my head. I respected Ben's knowledge and expertise. He was used to dealing with sticky situations and he'd appeared to be genuinely concerned for our safety. It felt like a dump tide was rolling in and I was about to be swept beneath it.

Arfield and Fagg were sat inside their hire car, staring blankly at the line of Chandlery shops whilst planning their next move. Arfield was certain Ilena was holed up somewhere close by. When he'd quizzed the English girl at Amigo's bar she had acted far too coolly. And even after four Barcardi's, she'd still managed side step his line of questioning.

"Do you want me to shake it out of her, boss?" Offered Fagg.

"Hell no. We don't need another dead body lying around just yet. Let's stake out the bar for the next twenty-four hours. I'm damn sure the bitch with the films will be back before too long. In the meantime, I'll call Felix and get a warrant issued over the wire for her arrest, here in Antigua as a person wanted for questioning about a threat to the security of the United States, more specifically that she has links to a foreign power with the aim of assassinating the Republican candidates at the forthcoming New Hampshire Primaries.

Fagg drove them both back to Padgett House. As they headed around the sea front of English Harbour, Arfield couldn't help noticing that the same police Land Rover, which he'd hidden from earlier in the day, was heading straight towards them. He was still feeling slightly spooked by almost being caught up in the Police search area around Orr's body, when he'd been jammed in a line of cars. He was about to duck below the dashboard again, when he recognised the man at the wheel.

"Did you see that, Bob?" Exclaimed Arfield as the Land Rover sped past them in a cloud of dust. "That was Hansen. What's he doing driving around in one of the local police vehicles?"

Fagg listened to more of Arfield's dogmatic analysis of the current situation. He knew exactly when to nod and grunt in agreement and when to play dumb. After all, Arfield liked the sound of his own voice and he didn't take kindly to being interrupted. He'd learnt it was much easier to let Arfield think he was in charge than to prolong a one-sided discussion. Fagg's agenda was much more flexible. As a one-man hit squad he could adapt to changes, at a moments notice.

At Arfield's insistence, Fagg agreed to sit tight and watch Amigo's bar all evening until an hour after lights out and to monitor who came and went. Until then, Arfield announced he would lean on the local constabulary to request an APB on Ilena Romero, whilst at the same time finding out what Hansen was playing at and if possible discrediting his reputation.

In the end, Arfield's visit to Charlestown Police Station was a brief, but profitable one. The helpful young constable informed him that Hansen had volunteered to help catch Orr's killer and the old sweat behind the desk, masquerading as a police sergeant, was equally lackadaisical as to lending his support. Arfield had identified himself and spoken in the strictest confidence that Hansen had, in fact, been sacked by the DEA. The circumstances with regards to how Hansen's procedural negligence had led to the accidental death of his partner had been kept strictly within his department. Hawkeye and Throup were both enthused when Arfield asked for their help in apprehending a suspected terrorist, who was most likely responsible for the recent murder. The death of Norman Orr had, in Arfield's assertion, been an act of desperation. "All I need from you is to issue an All Points Bulletin to prevent our suspect from escaping. And remember this," Arfield paused for a moment, for dramatic emphasis, as he linked the fingers of both hands to crack the joints, "we have to play as dirty as the criminals if we're going to catch them."

The two uniformed officers had never been so impressed by the way Arfield was handling their affairs. "And let's take the added precaution of keeping Hansen out of this. If you take my advice, I'd make sure you deny him any further access to this ongoing investigation."

When they were alone again Hawkeye turned to Throup, his chest swollen with pride by the larger than life charisma of the man who'd just left. "There goes a true, American maverick," he announced. "My god, does he remind you of anyone, Throup?" Before Throup could answer, Hawkeye blurted it out loud, as if he was welcoming him on stage. "He's the spitting image of that ace detective, Frank Cannon."

"Frank who?" replied the sceptical young constable.

Chapter Nine
Facing Up

It was always a good feeling to get breakfast out of the way and say farewell to departing guests. Our two newlyweds, Rory and Louise, were leaving us today after their eventful week's stay. I looked into Rory's eyes as we shook hands and I thought he looked more tired now than he had when he first arrived here. We watched them trundle off, hand in hand, towards Cross Green, with their cases weaving wheel tracks in the sandy surface of the unmade road.

"Just think, they'll always remember being here. It's nice to know we played a small part in their happiness," commented Fionn wistfully. "Perhaps we should include a wedding service in our brochure?" she added with a laugh.

Whilst we were both clearing up, Leyda Friday appeared at the kitchen door looking flustered and asked if we'd seen Pug this morning. Fionn and I looked at each other. "No, he's not been here today," I replied. It wasn't like him to miss his morning ritual of Capstan full strength, black coffee. Mind you, he could have been and gone whilst I'd been away on the bakery run, but Fionn admitted she'd not seen him today either.

"Then, I'm afraid it might be true," continued Leyda.

"What is it?" Asked Fionn. I felt a flush of dread descend and dissolve from my head down to my toes. Ben's warning, that there were some nasty people about, was beginning to creep ever closer to home. First Norman and now Pug. What did Leyda know?

"The university hospital at Saint John's rang me half an hour ago to say Pug was in intensive care. He's been beaten up."

Fionn let out a muted cry. "Oh my god, poor Pug. Is he going to be alright?"

"I'm not sure. I'm on my way there right now."

"I'll come with you, Leyda," I said instinctively. Then putting my arm around Fionn, I asked if that was okay with her?

"Yes, just go. I'll be fine here. Just let me know as soon as you've seen him."

I gave Fionn a little hug and Leyda and I both promised that one of us would call from the hospital when we had some news. However, Leyda further commented that she wasn't sure if we'd be allowed onto the ICU ward.

When Ben Hansen checked in at Charlestown police station, later that morning, he found PC Throup working alone at his desk. Hawkeye had apparently been called out to a case of cat-knapping. Several cats had disappeared recently and the latest moggie to go walkabout belonged to a retired widow, whom Hawkeye had long swooned after. "Most of the cats turn up a day or two later," explained Throup.

"So what's the latest on Orr's murder?"

The young PC paused for a few seconds then put Ben in the picture, regarding their larger than life visitor the previous evening. It didn't take long for Ben to work out to whom Throup was referring and he wasn't at all surprised that Arfield had tried to sow the seeds of doubt about allowing Ben to assist them with their investigation.

"He might have fooled Sergeant Hawkins, but not me. I didn't like the way he bragged about how much power he had at his disposal. When he said we shouldn't trust you, it only made me feel like I shouldn't trust him."

"Good for you, Clarence," replied Ben.

The young PC smiled. It had been weeks since anyone in authority had called him by his first name.

Ben took the young PC into his confidence. He explained how he'd found the missing flintlock pistol at Padgett House and showed him the musket ball, which he'd dug out of the doorframe. "My theory is that Orr was shot in the kitchen and his body was moved to the cross roads at Cross Green, soon afterwards." Throup was impressed with Ben's version of events. They certainly matched the evidence, or lack of it, which had been gathered from the site around Orr's body.

"I've one more lead to follow up. I believe that Arfield has an accomplice staying with him at Padgett House," continued Ben. "When I was there yesterday morning, I could have sworn I was being spied on from the balcony."

Throup suggested they should go to the airport at St. John's and ask to see the passenger lists, to see if anyone arrived with Arfield.

"Yes, and if that doesn't work we could also try the car hire company. Good thinking, Clarence," applauded Ben.

"There's just one thing," said Throup with a worried look on his young face. "I'm not allowed to leave the station unattended."

"Well, just lock the door and leave a note pinned to the window," suggested Ben.

Two minutes later, at precisely ten-forty five in the morning, Throup locked the front door of the police station and paused to admire his note in the window above - 'Back In 5 Minutes'.

Leyda, who'd been the only person allowed in to see Pug, gave me a list of his injuries together with the fact that he was almost unrecognisable. His face was badly swollen and black and blue all over. The hospital had x-rayed his skull and found it was fractured, in two places, around his jaw and eye socket. In her humble opinion, Pug must have been set upon by professionals. All she could do, in the half hour she'd been able to spend at his bedside, was hold his hand as he drifted in and out of consciousness. She also explained that she wasn't sure if Pug knew she was actually there or not. "He only spoke two words, 'The American.'" Leyda was puzzled as to who this might be.

As Leyda drove us both back to Cross Green, it didn't take a wild guess for me to realise to whom Pug was probably referring. And when Leyda finished her story in full, about how Pug had been found by the cleaner, in the garden at Padgett House, then it had to have been the big American guy who'd been quizzing Fionn.

"Lucky for Pug that Annette, the cleaner, found him when she did and was able to stop a passing motorist at the end of the driveway." Commented Leyda finally.

After she'd dropped me at Cross Green I called in at the dive shop and let Raoul know what had happened. Something told me I should try to warn him to be on his guard, if ever an overweight, middle-aged American should start asking questions, although I was stuck for a reason as to why he'd attacked Pug.

It was around lunchtime when I eventually arrived back to the sanctuary of Bar Amigo's. 'Pug's in a very bad way', was how I described his injuries to Fionn and then I related the full story of what Leyda had told me earlier. As we sat next to each other, at one of the empty tables on our veranda, I could see Fionn was lost to her thoughts. I tried to narrow the distance between us by drawing her attention to a few of the many positives around our own situation.

"Hey, I just love this view from our veranda and sharing it all with you. We're so lucky." I put my arm around her again and Fionn's smile returned almost instantly. "Stay there, I'll go and pour us a strong drink. I think we can both use one right now."

When I returned to our table, to my surprise Iko was standing next to Fionn and they were both casually chatting away.

"Ellie want's to use our telephone again."

"Yer, sure. Do you know where it is?" Iko marched straight past me. "Of course you do," I mumbled. I put our two rum and cokes down on the table. "Doesn't say much does he?"

"I think he's just a little shy," replied Fionn. " I just asked him how Ilena was settling in. You know how trouble has a habit of following her around, but I wouldn't want her to come to any harm. There's been enough violence for one day."

Iko's routine phone call to Des Riley in Grenada was a very informative one. Iko took a pen and paper from his pocket to write down, word for word, the details of the identity of the man from the Polaroid photograph he'd sent in the day before. To Iko's astonishment, it wasn't Ben Hansen, which had been the name Ilena had mentioned with regards to who'd been asking questions about her previously. It was much more shocking and complicated. Des even had to help with the spelling in some parts of his report, which Iko at first failed to understand. And Des also made doubly sure that Iko was in no doubt as to the revised changes to his priorities. When his call ended, Iko knew that Ilena was in more danger than she realised. He returned the phone to its permanent place at the end of the bar and suddenly found he couldn't take another step. The English girl had stepped back into the bar and snapping at her heels was 'El diablo' himself. Iko had a strange feeling of Deja vu. Yesterday, at this very same time, he had seen the same, nosy, overweight, American tourist but now, armed with the knowledge of who he really was, Iko had no option other than to face up to the task ahead of him. His immediate thought was to remain exactly where he was. And when the man next to him ordered a beer for himself, Iko did the same. When Fionn quickly returned to the veranda, she left the two men standing alone at the bar.

Fionn snuggled up close to me and quickly explained that the man who'd just entered the bar was the big guy from yesterday, the one asking about Ilena.

"You mean he's 'the American'. He could also be the one who's most likely to have beaten up Pug this morning," I whispered.

"Oh come on, Byrney. There must be dozens of Americans on Antigua at the moment."

"Yer, but they're not all looking for Ilena. Did you notice if his hands were cut?" I said, shielding my words again, whilst watching the doorway for anyone stepping out onto the veranda.

"No they seemed okay, but I wasn't paying much attention to his hands. I just wanted to get back here to tell you."

"Can you see what he's doing now?" I asked, suggesting that Fionn would have a clearer view through the outer hatch, next to the bar. As Fionn levered herself up by the arms of her chair and craned her neck towards the gap in the wall, I was also trying to think of how to send him away.

"He's talking to Ellie. No, hang on. They're both heading this way."

We both ducked down behind our drinks and pretended to be having an intimate conversation, as Iko and the American walked straight past us and down the beach towards Iko's waiting speedboat.

Arfield was going along for the ride. He had nothing to lose and everything to gain. He could almost picture the rolls of film in the palm of his hand. The adrenalin was pumping through his veins as the speedboat rose and turned northward beside the impenetrable coastline. He looked at the kid who was confidently piloting them across the waves and passed him off as an opportune fisherman. And like all fisherman, he was probably just an idle dreamer, looking to make a fast buck or two. He was dressed in a mix of worn military clothes, of some insignificant organisation and it had only taken a meagre fifty dollars for the kid to sell himself, for information as to the current whereabouts of Ilena Romero. His accurate description of her was enough to convince Arfield that his prey was within his grasp. And should there be any funny business, Arfield had his trusty Smith and Wesson model thirty-nine, tucked into the back of his waist band. He casually checked it was still firmly held in place, as the boat thudded against the solid fold of a wave. Arfield was impressed with how fast the little boat was moving. According to the kid, Miss Romero should still be bathing close to the shore, next to the old fort, where she was currently keeping a low profile.

'She was only meant to stay for a day. I could lose my job if my boss finds out I've been renting her a room. I'll be glad to get rid of her,' was how Iko had hooked the American. Iko looked back to see if his captive was still going along with his spur-of-the-moment scheme. Hopefully, the constant splashes of sea spray, peppering across his dark shirt, were helping to distract him from any suspicious thoughts.

As the boat roared around the headland, Iko pointed to a lone figure, swimming in the sea. "That's her," he shouted above the noise of the outboard motor.

Arfield smiled triumphantly. "Head straight to the jetty," He commanded. He rose, unsteadily, to his feet, only to be forced back down into his seat, almost immediately, as the boat slammed through the top of a breaking wave. Iko smiled to himself as the boat veered off towards a small patch of beach, adjacent to the jetty. He quickly turned the ignition key to kill the engine and took a firm hold of the steering wheel, as the bow suddenly dug into the wet sand. In the sudden, arresting impact, Arfield was thrown to the floor, causing his firearm to slide, agonisingly, across the short deck; it was only prevented from striking the bulkhead by Iko's boot. When Arfield regained a steady, semi seated position, he found himself facing the kid who was holding a Soviet, Malarov pistol in his steady, right hand. Arfield was temporarily puzzled and stunned at his misfortune. The steely fix expression staring back at him confirm he'd been suckered into a trap. The kid's gaze wavered not-a-jot as he bent down to pick up Arfield's discarded firearm.

"Give me that," demanded Arfield.

Iko stepped forward and gave Arfield a heavy blow across the bridge of his nose, with the butt of his own weapon, snapping the thin bone like a dried twig. Arfield almost passed out. It was only the after-sting of the fierce, throbbing pain that kept him conscious.

"Do you know who you're dealing with, you mother fucker? I'll have you sliced in two." He seethed, having wiped the blood from the top of his lip.

Iko quickly stepped forward again and kicked Arfield's right kneecap, causing him to scream out in agony. "Get out of the boat."

Arfield clasped his knee, refusing to budge an inch. The kid was going to pay a heavy price for this.

Iko removed the piece of paper from his own breast pocket, the one he'd used to scribble down the information relayed to him, not half a hour ago by Des Riley at Station Z. Iko gritted his teeth then repeated his demand. This time, Arfield was shocked into standing up. The kid had used a name, which Arfield hadn't heard for almost four decades.

"Get out of the boat, Obermeister Johann Friedla."

When I saw Iko walking away from our veranda and getting into his boat with the man I believed was responsible for the murder of Norman Orr, I had a deep sense of dread for both Iko and Ilena, that their lives were about to suffer the same bloody, consequences. The time had come for me to put Fionn in the picture and tell all. I was annoyed at myself for keeping it from her for this long and her reaction to hearing the full version of Ilena's story also left me feeling guilty and ashamed. She was extremely angry that I'd not confided to her sooner and despite my best intentions of protecting her from danger, I should have trusted her. The next bit was even harder for Fionn to accept, when I said I had to go over to Fort Anderson as quickly as possible to try and warn them.

"Why don't we just call the police?" She insisted.

"Because of the films. And because, like Ilena, I too want the world to know what's happening in San Albarra City."

"But you'll be putting your life in danger too, and for what? For a bunch of people you don't even know, people who live hundreds of miles away. Please, Byrney, stay here and let the authorities deal with it."

What, hush it up, you mean? I'm sorry Fi, but I have to go over there. If anything bad happens to Iko and Ilena I'm going to regret it, for the rest of my life." I rested my hands on Fionn's shoulders to reassure her. I could see she was almost in tears. "Look, if I'm not back in an hour, then go ahead and call the police at Charlestown. Try not to worry, I'll be back before you know it." I kissed her on the lips then let go of her arms. "See you soon, I promise."

The quickest way to get over there was to use our old, step-through Honda. I'd not ridden it across a loose sandy track before, but I reckoned it was my best shot and much better than trying to run all the way. As I struggled with the handlebars, across the sluggish, sandy surface, my thoughts raced ahead of me. What if the American had already killed them or was holding them at gunpoint? With several, ominous feelings growing inside me, my nerves took temporary control, reminding me of that shoot out in the Pyrenees almost three years ago, when Patrice Arnatte had been shot in the leg and both Casson and Bryn had been wounded too. I'd held my nerve that day and I was feeling confident again now, that when it came to 'hey-lads-hey' I would overcome my fears.

As things turned out, I needn't have worried. Ilena had heard me approaching the fort and was waiting for me by the large oak entrance door. She looked as white as a sheet, but was fortunately still in one piece. "We've got the American and he's admitted to killing your friend from the museum. But he's not who you think he is," she announced nervously. I looked at her curiously.

"I'll let Iko explain," she said, as she led me through the harsh, stone surroundings of the arched doorway. We walked into the dimly lit, ground floor of the fort, which was lacking in most essential furnishings. Iko was leaning against the far wall, pointing a gun at the American, who had his hands tied with thick, heavy rope and was gagged with one of Ilena's scarves. I noticed his nose was caked in dried blood and I began to feel nervous again. Iko looked at me silently and passed me a note and as I unfolded the single white sheet of paper he began to explain the events behind his hand written facts.

"Yesterday, I sent a photograph of this man to my headquarters in Havana. And when I spoke to my comrade today, that was his reply," Iko said proudly pointing to the his hand written note.

As I read the words in front of me it seemed so incredulous, I couldn't make the facts stick to my brain.

'Obermeister Johann Friedla was captured by Colonel Antonov's 301st Rifle Division, on 29th April 1945 at the SS headquarters in Prinz-Albrecht Strasse, close to the Tiergatan in Berlin. He was taken to Sachenhausen Concentration Camp for questioning, but escaped two days later. The Soviets believed Friedla ran into advancing American forces that had entered the centre of Berlin from the west. According to the Soviet army records, Friedla had been a commanding officer in the Sicherheitspolizei, who oversaw the Nazi occupation of France, from 1940 until the liberation in 1944. It is therefore conceivable that the American Intelligence Corps had marked Friedla as a person of special interests.'

When I finished reading Iko's note, I turned to Ilena and asked if this could be true? "Mais oui, of course," she confirmed. "At the end of the second world war, it's common knowledge that the American government feared losing former Nazis to the Soviets. So they weren't too fussy about recruiting members of organisations that the Allies had deemed to be outlawed, such as the Gestapo and the SS. As well as the technical expertise which scientists and scholars possessed, even butchers and murderers could be seen as being suitable for certain purposes. Isn't that right pig?" Her last words had been directed at their captive, who wriggled tirelessly in frustration and annoyance.

"What are you going to do with him?" I asked. Then the thought came to me that if Iko was going to kill him, I wanted no part of it. A part of me was beginning to wish I'd gone along with Fionn's suggestion after all, about calling the police.

It was Ilena who answered me again, putting her case forward with the hindsight of her recent experiences.

"Byrney, Last year I survived an assassination attempt by former Nazis, who, as I told you before, killed my boyfriend. And afterwards I was hounded and hunted down, until I was forced to flee South America. It was very frightening. There's no telling how far these fanatics will go to preserve their freedom and their ideology. Even today, they still hold onto their power, protected by a large network of followers who are paid to do their bidding for them. If you should ever find yourself on their radar, like I was, then your only option is to remain one step ahead."

Once again, Ilena convinced me that every word she said had an undisputable ring of truth to it. I also remembered Gastin writing to me with almost the same explanation, about the difficulties he faced in tracking down former Nazis, in

Bolivia and Argentina. But, all that Ilena had said still didn't answer my question about the American's fate.

"So what happens now?" I asked again.

"Tomorrow, Iko and I are leaving for Grenada. And we're taking Friedla with us. Iko is going to hand him over to the Cubans." Once again the bundle on the floor began to writhe and wriggle, in defiance at his forthcoming prospects.

"Don't worry about me Byrney," continued Ilena. "I'm in safe hands. Once I get to Grenada, it should be quite easy to obtain a passage back to the south of France." Ilena moved in closer towards me and led me to the back of the room where their bags were stored. She stared at me with her bright-eyed gaze, leading me to feel as if I was being coaxed against my will. She had an easy charm and beauty about her that was hard to resist.

"There's one thing I need you to do for me," she asked, as she undid the zip in the front compartment of her rucksack and handed me a padded envelope. I knew, instantly, what it contained. "I'd like you to post this for me, please." I stared at the hand written address.

For the attention of Daniel Duhamel
The Chronicle and Herald Newspaper
1101 13th Street (North West)
Washington 20009
District of Columbia
United States of America.

"I've written a note inside too, to cover the details on the films; so all you need to do is drop them into a Royal Mail collection box." Ilena looked straight into my eyes. "I can trust you, can't I?" The way Ilena spoke made me feel as if she was testing me, like when Gastin had tested me, by saying that if I reached his office door on the fifth floor of his office block before him, then he'd agree to take me to the Col du Monde. Only this time there was no flight of stairs to climb, whilst my companion rode in the lift. Ilena's test was much easier to accept, but the consequences could be even more treacherous than climbing along a glacier, high in the Pyrenees. And when the American intelligence agencies find out about the abduction won't they send more armed nutcases to come looking for him? It seemed to me like the best end to it was to send the films to Washington and get the story published. Then at least the search for the films would be called off and we could all get back to our simple lives again.

"Okay, of course I'll post them for you."

"Wait a day or two, at the most, for us to reach Grenada and that way, whoever else is chasing me will presume I still have the films."

I nodded in agreement then added, "But how are you all going to get to Grenada?"

"Iko knows of a fishing boat which he uses for a Bateau Buss. It's due to arrive here just after midnight. Iko's assured me we'll be safe, once we get our cargo on board." Ilena glanced over at the squat figure. He'd given up his struggle and was curled up quietly for the time being. I could hardly bring myself to look at him in case I was recognised.

Iko came up to me and thanked me for coming over to warn them. "You didn't have to do that, but thanks anyway." I watched Iko gently move his hand across Ilena's back as he drifted toward the other half of the room. I had a good feeling that he would protect Ilena at all costs.

"So this is goodbye then?" I said, with a hint of sadness in my voice. Ilena smiled broadly.

"Non mon ami, just farewell. Perhaps next time I meet up with our friend Gastin, we'll have lots to talk about. And naturally, I wish you and Fionn much happiness."

"How long will you be staying in France?" I enquired, as I turned round for one last look at her.

"Just long enough to read my story in France-soir or La Monde," she said with a smile. "Bon Chance, Byrney."

I breathed a huge sigh of relief, once I'd left the cool, shaded jungle of the mangroves behind me. Just beyond the clearing of White House Bay I could see our little bar waiting for me. The news I had for Fionn was a bit of a double-edged sword. On the one hand, Iko and Ilena would be gone by tomorrow and on the other hand I'd agreed to post Ilena's controversial films. Fionn was almost as pleased as I was that they were both safe. It was difficult to imagine what a close shave we'd all had with the American who had been unmasked as a Nazi war criminal.

The main security command centre at St. John's international airport was hidden in plain view, by a series of ordinary, mirrored windows, immediately behind the prominent information desk. Passengers and staff were unable to see inside, but anyone inside the long command room had a clear view of all those who passed in front of them. The room itself had half a dozen soundproofed cubicles whose intended purpose was for interviewing passengers deemed to be acting suspiciously, or who had been caught smuggling. But, in practice, they were mostly used as glorified, lost property shops. At the hub of the room, behind a large semi circular desk, were two, dry wipe boards, containing flight details of the daily schedule of arrivals and departures. Sat next to the white plastic coated boards was a row of multi drawer filing cabinets, which contained personnel lists, vetting reports and medical records of all three hundred and fifty employees who kept the planes and passengers moving happily and efficiently: from baggage handlers to catering staff, from the girls at the check-in desks to the sub contractors who cleaned the windows. Everyone who worked there was given a security number and was indexed inside the relevant drawer. So, full passenger lists were, of course, held on record as a matter of routine. Antigua had set itself goals and standards for boosting its economy through tourism and the international airport, they believed, was the gateway to its success.

P.C Throup had phoned through to the security desk in advance, to request access to a certain passenger list, so when the two men presented themselves to the clerk at the information desk, they were soon met by the daytime supervisor, George Hardman. Throup introduced Ben Hansen and they were quickly ushered inside. Hardman already had the exact passenger list, waiting on top of his in-tray: Flight KIA 59, 4th February 1980. It didn't take long for Ben to suss out who Arfield's accompanying colleague was as there were only six names on the Kahbuna Island Air flight from Puerto Rico. On the way over to the airport, Ben had worked up a sweat trying to memorise the names of the people whom he'd shared a table with at that first meeting with Arfield, in Santa Barbara: Allan Klein, Jim McGarry, somebody Glendenning, Robert Stickley, or Stockley and the Austrian guy nearest him had been Felix Schwarzkopf. None of the above appeared on the flight list. However, the last name, the one directly below Arfield's, belonged to a man whom Ben had already met, albeit briefly - Robert Fagg. Fagg had handed Ben the report on Ilena Romero, just prior to his own flight from Phoenix to Puerto Rico, the day before on the 3rd of February.

"This is our man," confirmed Ben confidently.

Throup thanked Hardman for his punctual assistance and stepped back into the noisy reception hall to catch up with Ben.

"Are we going to arrest this Fagg person?" Enquired Throup.

"Not just yet, Clarence. We'd best play this by the book. How long will it take to get a search warrant organised?"

Throup thought for a moment. "Well, if the judge is at the DPP's office in St. Johns, we can go there right now. But we'll need to get my bosses authorisation. I'll put a call through to the station. He should be back at his desk by now."

Chapter Ten
It Ain't Over, 'Til It's Over

The airstrip at Coolidge International airport, in St. Johns, Antigua, had been first laid down by the U.S. air force when they entered the Second World War in 1941. Several bomber squadrons were stationed there, until the air base was handed over to the British for commercial use, around eight years later. However, the American military retained a small complex of buildings, inside the perimeter fence at the north-eastern shoreline. During the sixties and early seventies, these buildings had been used by NASA, as a tracking station for the Apollo Space Program.

Bob Fagg was aware of its existence from the time during his stint of working at Kennedy Space centre, in Florida. As part of its security team, Fagg had had a wide range of responsibilities. He was never one to miss a trick when it came to opportunities, especially those that involved get-rich-quick schemes. During the run up to the Apollo 11 mission, Fagg was put in charge of the LOX farm. When he learnt that the Saturn V launch rocket, which was being used to launch the lunar space capsule, required almost two million kilograms of liquid oxygen, he knew there had to be a way of skimming a little off for himself.

He made contact with the manager at LINOX, Jacksonville, whose company supplied the rocket fuel for all NASA rockets and together they struck upon a loophole in the supply chain, which enabled them to sell back to NASA the liquid oxygen they'd already paid for. Their clever scheme ran undetected for over two years, until the Apollo 13 disaster. Fifty-six hours into that fateful flight to the moon, one Saturn V's main oxygen tanks exploded in space. The security authorities at Cape Kennedy were asked to investigate whether sabotage had been responsible. During their extensive search of the LOX farm and its paper trail, they fell upon Fagg's fraudulent activities. He was arrested and interviewed by government intelligence officers who were impressed by Fagg's aptitude and capacity for lateral thinking. Instead of sending him to jail, they made him a permanent member of their criminal investigations branch.

When the Apollo Space program was terminated, at the end of 1972, the tracking station in Antigua reverted back to it's original, post war role of underwater, sound surveillance, monitoring Soviet submarine movements in the Caribbean Sea and the Gulf of Mexico. The current station commander was forty-eight year old, Frank Schaeffer. Schaeffer had volunteered to take up this newly created post after having had a belly full of COT, the U.S. Covert Operations Team, whose operatives were sometimes referred to as 'Dustcoats'. Their game plan involved performing a dastardly array of dirty deeds, such as: burglaries, witness intimidation, wiretapping, nuisance phone calls, aggressive surveillance and a lot more nastier stuff too, which occurred under two main classifications: 1, 'Double Top Secret' and 2, the most infamous classification of all, which covered just about any unlawful, or sinister act of perverted justice, 'In The Interests Of National Security'.

Life was much less complicated at the sleepy station on the breezy, northern shore of Antigua. It was almost too quiet. That was until Bob Fagg showed up recently. At first Schaeffer was only too happy to welcome a former colleague. Having a familiar face from the states call in for a friendly natter had made Schaeffer feel homesick for the City of Dreams and for Santa Monica beach, where they served the best burgers in the Golden State.

He'd known Fagg, back in his COT days, as a slick operator and for being an expert at role-play. Their chitchat and reminiscences had been fairly routine stuff to begin with. Fagg later asked about the number of men under his command and what facilities they enjoyed, operational as well as recreational. Then, towards the end of that first visit, Schaeffer's memory was suddenly jogged into the recollection of Fagg's annoying persistence with borrowing expensive bits of kit and never handing them back.

So, when Fagg stepped into his office for the third day in a row, Schaeffer made out he was tidying his desk, in the hope of making a quick getaway for the afternoon. But when he recognised that unwelcome look on Fagg's face, his perfected hangdog, cap-in-hand expression, he knew exactly where it was leading.

"Oh god. What is it this time? Another phone tap?" Schaeffer left no time for Fagg to answer before adding, "and by the way, I've already set up the audio tape again for you, from this morning's conversation."

"It's good to see you too, Frank," replied Fagg, holding up the palms of his hands submissively. "I'll go and grab a chair next door." Fagg turned away then remembered the tin of polymer clay, rubbing against his leg inside his trouser pocket. "Oh, just one last thing, Frank. Can you run me up a key from these impressions?" Fagg handed the small, flat tin to Schaeffer, who opened it out of curiosity.

"What am I supposed to do with this?"

"Come on Frank. Just get one of your lab boys to make up a mould. I'll pick it up same time tomorrow."

Schaeffer shook his head in disbelief. "Anything else, Bob?"

"A black coffee, if you can spare one? I'll be next door."

Fagg knew just how far to push his luck. He settled into his seat, placed the headphones over his ears, switched on the big, cumbersome, reel to reel tape machine and adjusted the volume, until the recorded voices came through loud and clear. 'Perfect'.

About a mile and a half away, Ben and PC Throup stepped out of the front of the main terminal building and walked to the end of the taxi rank, to where Throup had parked the police Land Rover. He picked up the receiver of the in-car Motorola radiophone and called up the station. After thirty seconds, Hawkeye's cheerful baritones rang out of the dusty speaker, which to Ben's ears sounded like someone was frying a pan full of sliced bacon in the background. But Throup had obviously grown accustomed to the crackly reception.

"Where are you Throup?"

"We're just leaving the airport, Sarge."

"Excellent. I've got some very good news. Marcia has agreed to go on a date with me. And if I can locate her pussy who knows where it might lead?" Ben began laughing uncontrollably, leading Throup to cover the mouthpiece with his hand, to prevent his own giggles from being transmitted across to Charlestown.

"Hello Throup, are you still receiving me?" Hawkeye's voice being oblivious to the mayhem was still coated in a childish innocence. Throup recovered his composure and updated his boss with their current findings.

"You mean to tell me Hansen is accompanying you?" Hawkeye's voice had quickly reverted to type.

"Yes Sarge, we're on our way to pick up the search warrant for Padgett House."

"Well call me again when you collect it and don't do anything until I get there. I'll phone through to the judge and request it right away."

"Okay Sarge. Over and out."

Throup started up the engine and pulled away from the busy drop off point. "Sounds like Hawkeye will be joining us after all," reflected Ben. Still it would work in his favour. He was confident he'd be able to win back Hawkeye's trust, once he'd handed over the old flintlock pistol; provided, of course, that it was still hidden where he'd found it yesterday.

We had a party of four new guests, fresh from Florida, arriving at Bar Amigo's. They were typical, travel weary holiday makers, struggling with their over loaded suit cases. Someone should write a comment in our brochure, I thought, advising guests to bring a minimal amount of clothing. If they were anything like me, two pairs of shorts and three t-shirts would be more than enough for a week of sea, sand and sight seeing.

We checked them in, escorted them to their rooms and waited for the inevitable complaints about the rudimentary, rustic surroundings. What the rooms lacked in modern conveniences they made up for in charm. Well, that was how we explained it. "By the end of the week they'll have forgotten all about the things they missed to begin with," commented Fionn.

With the bar temporarily to ourselves, Fionn asked me to explain how things had gone earlier at Fort Anderson. After summing up the situation and offering her my view that we'd probably seen the last of Ilena and Iko and the American, Fionn was still none to happy.

"For Pete's sake, Byrney. Why did you agree to post those bloody films?"

"For the simple reason that, once they're in the post, it'll all be over."

Fionn gasped in disbelief. "Well, when are you going to post them?"

I looked at Fionn and knew she wasn't about to like my answer. "Ilena said to leave it for a day or two."

"Well, you're not keeping them here. Who knows who else is going to turn up next looking for them?" she said irritably and turned away toward the veranda.

She had a valid point, of course. I removed the envelope from my pocket and stared once more at the address. "Oh bollocks," I said to myself. "It's now or never." I followed Fionn outside and told her I'd ride up into St. Johns right away and drop them off at the General Post Office.

"Finally. The pennies dropped," gasped Fionn. "Promise me when you get back, you'll forget all about other peoples troubles for a while. Let's concentrate on running our own business."

"And having some fun too," I added with a cheeky grin on my face..

Sergeant Fred 'Hawkeye' Hawkins was stood outside the door of the old colonial villa, itching to get inside. He was having a good day. So far he'd charmed his way into Marcia

Hirst's affections, having shared a pot of Lapsang Souchong black tea and enthralled 'the little woman' with his daring do and his vast knowledge of the current weekly run of TV detectives. "Once I've written my own memoirs, they'll be queuing up in Hollywood to make a serial of them," he'd assured her. But all Marcia really wanted, at that moment, was to have her missing cat back where it belonged - sat in her lap.

Hawkeye was rattling Orr's bunch of keys as the dry, dust covered Land Rover squeaked to a halt. Throup handed his boss the search warrant and after checking the details, he was ready to proceed, that was, until he saw Hansen alighting from the passenger door of the police vehicle. Hawkeye's eyes narrowed suspiciously as he pursed his lips. "I'm not sure we require your kind of help, Hansen." Hawkeye announced.

Throup stepped forward and informed him that Hansen had already found Orr's flintlock, hidden in a drawer. On hearing this confession Hawkeye knew that Hansen had probably acted unlawfully, and therefore was jeopardising his investigation. He stared at Hansen and asked angrily. "When exactly did you make this discovery?"

"Yesterday afternoon, whilst Throup was checking the museum. I took the liberty of taking a quick look for myself."

"Well you're not taking liberties with me. Did anyone see you enter?" Hawkeye wasn't ready to congratulate Hansen's actions just yet. If there'd been any procedural negligence, then it'd be his own neck hanging at the end of the line.

"No one saw me arrive and no one saw me leave either. I was alone the whole time," replied Ben impatiently. "Can we get on with it, now?"

Hawkeye paused for half a minute to dwell on the facts, knowing this would leave Hansen feeling uncomfortable. "Well, in that case, let us proceed." Hawkeye unlocked the door and the three men entered in single file, with Hansen at the rear.

The house was as lifeless as an abandoned tomb. The three men paused, statuesque-like, inside the stately entrance hall to listen for any sounds. After a few seconds, Hansen took the lead towards the kitchen. "This way, gentlemen."

Once the flintlock pistol was bagged and labelled they continued their search upstairs. At last, they found signs of recent occupation, inside Arfield's bedroom. There was a strong odour of stale cigar smoke and his belongings had been scattered untidily, as if he'd left in a hurry. Hawkeye jumped to the incorrect conclusion that there must have been a burglary then turned his accusations toward Hansen. "Is this mess your doing?"

"Of course not. It was the same yesterday, before I arrived."

"I've found his passport," confirmed Throup, enthusiastically. "And a jar of pills."

"That would suggest he hasn't left Antigua, yet," replied Hawkeye. "Let me see them?"

A thought flashed through Ben's mind that Arfield's passport hadn't been there the day before. But more strangely perhaps, when he came to think about it, where was Arfield's leather diplomatic pouch? It was nowhere to be found.

Hansen stepped back into the upper corridor and searched the remaining rooms for any evidence of Fagg, but disappointingly, apart from a crumpled bed cover, found no other physical evidence to prove he'd also been staying there. Hawkeye's voice bellowed across the empty corridor, "This other man, Robert Fagg? You told my PC that you'd met him before? We're going to need a description of him."

Hansen returned to Arfield's bedroom, empty handed. "There's nothing at all in any of the other rooms."

"Are you sure Arfield has an accomplice? Could be they just travelled together and then went their separate ways?"

"Absolutely not. I'm one hundred per cent sure there must be two of them," replied Ben. "There's no way Arfield could have moved Orr's body by himself."

"Well, let Throup have his details: height, weight, age, hair colour etcetera; you know the kind of thing. If these two men are still here on the island, then we must apprehend them as soon as possible. I'll raise another APB and if they or anyone matching their description tries to leave by the airport, or our marine ports, then, they'll be arrested on sight."

Fagg had replayed the taped conversation in full, three times and was now studying his notes. It was apparent to him that he to wrap up his mission in Antigua within the next twenty-four hours. The changing situation was becoming more complicated than he would have liked, but not impossibly so. True he'd need some help, but most of all he'd also need a fast boat. He looked through the connecting glass window between the data room and Schaeffer's office and began to figure out a resilient plan. He picked up the phone and dialled COT headquarters at Fort Jeremy USA using the military network. Once he'd agreed to act in the best way forward, he slowly put down the receiver, switched off the overhead light and stepped back into the room next door.

Schaeffer had wisely stayed behind to make sure Fagg had no more last minute requests. Although he found Fagg's presence somewhat tiresome, there was no getting away from the fact that Fagg held a higher position in the chain of command. "Everything to your liking?" he enquired, tentatively.

"No. There's been a change of plan. I need to borrow the Hydrofoil later this evening," said Fagg stoically.

"Not possible, Bob. She's due into dry dock in Puerto Rico tomorrow, for an engine overhaul. Sorry, but that's how it is."

"No problem," agreed Fagg. "I only need her for two hours, three at the most. Then we can sail direct to the maintenance dock immediately afterwards."

Schaeffer rubbed his chin and mulled over his priorities. Fagg could see he still wasn't convinced. "Look, I'll be heading in the same direction," he lied.

"I'll have to run it by the skipper, Gene Lowry. He's a stickler for regulations and, I'll definitely need a signed operations order from COT before I can let you have her," replied Schaeffer.

"Already on its way." Said Fagg, confidently. "Oh, and that key, I've asked for?"

"Yeah, don't tell me. You need it yesterday? Lucky for you I've already sent your mould over to Strawberry. It'll be ready in one hour.

"Bravo, Frank."

Fagg felt a definite buzz of expectation, like all the pieces of the puzzle were finally clicking into place, tomorrow he'd be Scott-Free and on his way back to sunny Arizona. He took the vacant chair, at the opposite side of Schaeffer's desk and sat down for a moment. "Okay, listen up. Here's the plan for this evening. The timing is going to be crucial for both of us."

After sliding Ilena's padded envelope across the counter at the general post office I was surprised to find there was a package addressed to me, waiting to be collected. It was a box of seven-inch singles sent over to us from England, by my brother Anthony. I had a quick delve inside and noted it was the usual handful of ex-jukebox records, with their centres snapped away. I was looking forward to adding them to our jukebox as soon as I returned. Knowing I'd some new music to listen to really put me in the party mood and it was a welcome addition to the relief of finally getting Ilena's films out of Antigua. In the end, it had been an easy decision for me to send them on their way, first class to Washington.

I'd a little spare time left to myself, after leaving the post office. Fionn wouldn't be missing me just yet, so I went to one of my favourite places in Antigua, the fresh produce market. The stalls were laid out under makeshift shelters, on either side of Market Street, for as far as the eye could see. The hustle and bustle hung in the air like static electricity and even if you didn't need to buy anything it was a great place to take your eyes for a walk. It felt like the life-hub of the island. It attracted eagle eyed locals as well as the more cautious tourists, gawping at some of the more unusual items on offer: black pineapples, mangoes, sugar cane and live sea snails, all weighed, on time-worn, bashed and battered copper scales. There was such a glorious abundance of fruit and vegetables and spices to choose from and the local farmers and vendors were just as proud and colourful as their produce. Each stall had its own scent, which I found inspiring. I spotted some blood orange coloured, Scotch bonnet peppers and instantly I had the idea of having a Jerk chicken bar-be-que night at Amigo's. It would be a great way to get back into the swing of entertaining our residential guests and drop-in's. I was in my element, sampling and breathing in the intoxicating atmosphere. It was at times like this that I really wished I had Fionn beside me. We'd been so 'full on' at making a go of our business that we'd almost forgotten to take some time out. It would be nice to have a break from our bar for a while.

With a full shopping basket, strapped to the back of our little Honda, I sped back to Cross Green with great expectations. Even when Fionn drew my attention to the fact Jerk chicken had to be marinaded overnight I couldn't be persuaded to wait any longer.

"We can skip the overnight bit by cooking it slowly." I said, with the authority of someone who was clearly making it up as they went along. "I'll pour some wood chips over the barbie to keep the heat down. It'll only take an hour to cook at the most."

"I suppose it would be a daft question to ask if you've got all the proper ingredients?" she said sarcastically.

I showed her the chillies. "And I've got limes, allspice, ginger and some coconut milk. I thought we'd have it with rice and peas."

"Wow you have been busy. Okay then, why not, it's a lovely idea, Byrney."

My theory was: spicy hot food encourages you to drink more too. "You'd better stock up the bar." I suggested. "I'll go and chalk up the blackboard and put it out at the front of our veranda. Let's get the party started."

With Orr's old flintlock safely stored away in the evidence locker, Throup removed the thirty-five mm film from the official police camera. He offered to hand it in at the path lab for developing and then later he would add the prints to Orr's case file. Between the three of them: Hawkeye, Throup and Ben Hansen, they had more or less pieced together the events surrounding Orr's death. Ben's take on the affair was the closest to what had actually occurred two days before. The only missing elements were the two suspects.

Hawkeye sent out descriptions of both men to the central police station at St. John's and asked them to pass the details along to the port authorities and the airport security team.

Whilst Ben was sat at Throup's desk, he picked up the phone and dialled up his old office at the DEA (Western) headquarters in Los Angeles. He had the direct number for his former colleague and friend, Mike Dooley. He'd very generously supplied Ben with departmental background information from their data base, on the odd occasion in the past and Ben was hoping to get a bit more of a handle on Bob Fagg: his home address, who he worked for and if he had a criminal record. When the person at the other end of the line answered, Ben immediately recognised the voice of his old boss, Bill Chadwick who explained, to Ben's disappointment, that Dooley was currently on secondment in Costa Rica.

"So, how's the private eye business shaping up?"

Ben couldn't help but feel slightly downhearted over the best way to answer. The 'Romero' case had been taken away from him, Orr's murder case in Antigua had come to nothing and soon he'd be heading back to California to an empty diary. On top of that, Ben had come to realise he wasn't happy at playing the lone wolf.

He kept his reply short and sweet, "I'm doing okay."

Chadwick detected a note of despondency in Ben's voice. "Gee, as bad as that, eh? Listen, you won't have heard, but Chief Calhoun has been forced to take an early retirement. They finally got rid of him." The mention of Calhoun's name brought a shiver to Ben. Jack Calhoun had been the reason Ben had quickly resigned from the drugs administration team, after Chuck's untimely death. He'd been convinced, rightly or wrongly, that Calhoun was behind it. He was more crooked than any villain Ben knew.

"Yes, it's all change over here at the moment," continued Chadwick. "We're creating a new culture within the whole department, proactive rather than reactive. And we're building a new team too, hand picked of course. Mike's already signed up and wait for this, I'd like you to be a part of it too. It'll mean promotion too of course. I'll be running things my way, that is to say we'll all have an input as to what procedural changes are needed. What do you say?"

It sounded too good to be true. Returning to the DEA was a massive step backwards, of course. But Ben had come to realise leaving the DEA hadn't led to the better life which he'd hoped for.

"Can I think about it for a day or two?" He answered. "I'm in Antigua right now."

"Antigua? This is no time to be taking a holiday. Yes, sure. You can call me on this number. I'll be counting on you, so get yourself back here pronto." Chadwick ended his conversation with a burst of warm laughter.

When Ben put down the phone and surveyed the quiet police office he knew his time on Antigua had all but fizzled out. All that was left for him to do was to say his goodbyes.

I was being heavily distracted as I fired up the barbeque, just a few feet away from the external side door to our tiny kitchen. I had one eye on the sky, which was already much darker than it ought to be at this early stage of the evening. Normally, the sun set around six p.m. and then there'd be at least thirty minutes before the first star began to twinkle. As the thick, grey, clouds formed into one, impenetrable mass I was thinking that, after all the preparations we'd arranged for tonight, it'd be a shame if we were rained off at the last minute. I raked the contents of our dissected oil drum and was pleased to find that the buried embers of woodchips were nicely glowing away. Fionn appeared, carrying a tray of spice-rubbed chicken thighs.

"Don't you think it's a good idea to rig up a plastic sheet, in case you get drenched?" She suggested.

"Nah, nothings going to spoil our fun for this evening," I replied, optimistically. "How's it looking inside the bar? Nice and busy?"

"Yes, most of our guests have stayed behind. I think they're all feeling a bit jet lagged."

I smiled at Fionn. She was looking the part, like a real Caribbean queen in her loose fitting floral dress. I was always proud of her dress sense. "Listen Fi, I've been thinking. Isn't it about time we had a little holiday?"

Fionn began to laugh.

"What's so funny?"

"No, I just thought you were going to propose something else."

"It's been non-stop for the two of us since we started out on this big adventure. I just thought it'd be nice to get away together for a week."

Fionn stepped closer and helped to place the food over the hot grill. "Where do you have in mind? But more to the point who's going to run this place while we're away?"

"I've not really thought it through yet. It's just an idea. Give ourselves a break and maybe visit another Caribbean island, or catch a plane to California."

"Ooh, I like the sound of that. I've always fancied going to Malibu, or Acapulco. Is that in California?"

"No," I laughed. "It's in Mexico, but we could go there too, instead. Why don't you cadge a lift off Leyda tomorrow and have a look inside the travel agents in St. Johns?"

I could hear our jukebox pipe up inside, playing something from Anthony's latest batch of records. It was a new song by Queen, called 'Crazy Little Thing Called Love'. I grabbed hold of Fionn and did an impromptu 'step and jig' soft shoe shuffle.

"You'd better keep your eye on the food," she said gayly breaking away from our embrace. "I'd better go and see what our guests are doing."

The jerk chicken and rice was going down better than I expected, despite Fionn making fun of me for lacing the chicken with far too much chilli. I hadn't realised I was supposed to remove all the seeds from them. But the after effect amongst our guests was reaping rewards inside our till. Every occupied table had a growing collection of empties, at least three for each guest, so far.

We had a surprise 'pit-stop' visit from Leyda, who'd just returned from her second visit of the day to check up on Pug's progress. "I was amazed to find him, sat up in bed," she happily informed us. "And he was able to give me a partial description of the man who'd attacked him. He was one of the Americans staying at Padgett House."

I was only half listening as the volume blasting out from the jukebox was making it difficult to concentrate on what Leyda was telling me. Padgett House, it would seem, had a habit of attracting some very dodgy characters.

"The hospital has said that if Pug continues to make the same progress overnight, then he should be allowed home in the morning. But it's a shame he lives by himself."

"Yes, I know. He's a bit of a loner."

"Well, I'm going to suggest he stays with me for a couple of days, just to make sure he has some nourishing meals."

It was a great relief to know that Pug was going to be okay.

As the evening wore on there wasn't a spare seat to be had, either inside or out. The rum and beer was working its magic on everyone present and the music crept noticeably louder and louder. About an hour before closing time, we had our second surprise visitor of the evening - Ben Hansen

I was looking through the kitchen and saw Fionn behind the bar wave him over. I wasn't sure about stepping back into the raucous mayhem of the bar area. My wobbliness told me I ought to stay put and sit it out by smoking oil drum..

"Ben's come to say goodbye," hollered Fionn in my direction.

I tipped the remaining contents of my bottle of Red Stripe over the dying embers inside the homemade grill and when I was satisfied the heat had been drowned out I looked up to find Ben standing in front of me. He looked oddly out of place, smartly attired and freshly shaved.

"I'll be off tomorrow," he said, holding out his hand. "Back to Silver Lake in L.A."

"I'm sorry to hear that," I said doing my best not to slur my words. "I guess things haven't worked out for you in Antigua, this time round." I commented, smiling to myself.

"How do you mean, Byrney?"

"You know. Not finding those films."

"Yeah, well. Win some, lose some."

"That's true. In any case I think those films will probably reach America before you do." My words fell freely with drunken bravado. Unable to reel them back in, I was stopped from saying more by an oncoming bout of hiccups.

Ben's tone immediately changed down a gear or two and both his heads (I wasn't aware I was seeing double), had the same serious expression.

"Why, what do you know about them?" He asked in a casual controlled manner, coaxing an answer from me.

"I dropped them in the post, ages ago."

Ben suddenly became angry. "You did what? You stupid young fucker. Why for heavens sake? Surely you realised the damage they could do?"

I stood up as straight as my legs would allow and said, "I did it, to make the world a safer place. People have a right to know what's going on in the world."

Ben put his face right up to mine. "You dumb fool. Do really think those films are going to make any difference? Sure they're gunna cause a stink for the government for a day or two and no doubt a few heads will roll. But they'll just be replaced by men even more determined to preserve the American way."

I was stumped for an answer. I'd expected Ben to be a bit cross with me, but now I was feeling like I'd been taking all those risks for nothing. Ben pulled back from me. His self-controlled voice returned.

"It wouldn't surprise me if that package is picked up by the FBI before it reaches its final destination. Then of course they'll be running all kinds of forensic tests on it. You didn't handle it yourself, did you Byrney?"

'Oh bollocks,' I thought, suddenly having a sobering moment. I'd not taken any such precautions. Shit, I should have worn gloves. But then again, how would the FBI know that some of the fingerprints belonged to me? I passed Ben's comments off to the fact he was just trying to scare me.

I shrugged, as I gave Ben my reply. "It wouldn't matter if I'd touched the envelope or not. The FBI doesn't have a record of my fingerprints."

"That's not entirely true, Byrney. Remember your role in the drugs bust two years ago in Puerto Rico? Your hands were all over those sacks of marijuana when you hauled them out from the back of the van. D'you know what I'm saying?"

'Oh god yes.' I instantly felt burdened with guilt, like those heavy sacks were actually being pushed down onto my shoulders once more.

"Well, I'll leave you to your thoughts, Byrney. Say farewell to Fionn for me."

I stood outside, alone, for ten minutes, worrying about what Ben had said to me. More than ever I wanted those revealing films to reach their destination at the Herald and Chronicle in Washington. I wasn't entirely one hundred per cent taken in by Ben's fingerprint theory. I think he was just getting his own back on me. The more I thought about it, the more I was convinced it was just a wind up.

It was just after midnight when the last of our residential guests waddled back to their rooms and I was able to switch off the lights and drop the latch on the front door.

Fionn and myself were both feeling shattered and worn out too. I didn't even recall falling asleep, but it only felt like a matter of minutes before I was awoken by Fionn's startled voice.

"Byrney, our room's filling up with smoke," she said, as if consumed by panic. My eyes were slow to focus, but the haziness wasn't imaginary, it was all too real. I saw the source of the grey fog seeping through the walls and through the gap in the door-sill.

"Bloody hell. I think we're on fire. I'll go and sound the alarm." As I rushed to put on my shorts and t-shirt Fionn asked if I'd remembered to check the barbeque was properly extinguished. "Yer, of course I did."

When I opened the door I was met by an overhead blanket of flames spreading quickly across the rush matting, which lay beneath the roof. I shouted for everyone to wake up, knocking on all the bedroom doors and warning our guests to get outside as fast as possible. I made my way to the kitchen, crouching to avoid the descending blades of heat and smoke. The ceiling was well and truly ablaze. I found Fionn by the telephone trying to dial 999.

"It's no good, Byrney. The bloody phones not working again." I looked at her in desperation. We had two fire extinguishers in the kitchen, but the fire had gone beyond anything the extinguishers could throw at it. We heard coughs and screams coming from the rooms at the back, as some of our dawdling guests began to choke and panic with fear.

"The best thing we can do now is to make sure everyone gets out onto the beach. I'll go and grab the register from behind the bar, then at least we can check everyone's accounted for."

"Okay," replied Fionn. "I'll go to Cross Green and try to get some help." There was no time to argue.

"Be careful," I shouted as she went out through the front door and round the opposite side of the building to try and reach our moped. But it was no use. She returned to the beach, almost immediately.

"The fire is just too fierce and I think I've singed my eyebrows too," she commented ruefully. "Has everyone made it?"

"Yer, they're all safely out."

Our guests stood silently in little family groups with some of their valuables and belongings dumped at their feet. I looked behind and saw all their faces, illuminated in the bright orange glow. They looked dazed and worried. Their fearful, anxious gaze was firmly fixed on their disintegrating holiday accommodation. Fionn and I paused to get our breath back too. We were both covered in a black film of soot. There was absolutely nothing more we could do, but hold onto one another. A gathering storm of a thousand unanswered questions awaited us. We backed further away from the intense furnace as the flames grew higher and higher, mercilessly destroying everything we had worked for. I felt Fionn begin to tremble and shake as she began to sob uncontrollably. I saw her face was consumed with grief. "On Byrney," she blurted painfully.

I let her head fall into the nape of my neck as I held her in my arms. Her sadness was total and pulled heavily on my heart strings. I tried to console her but struggled to find an answer other than to say, "hey Fionn, we still have each other." I lifted her head, carefully wiped her tears and whispered, "God, I love you. We'll get through this one way or another. I promise."

Chapter Eleven
Ships That Pass In The Night

It was precisely one a.m. when Fagg breezed into the assembly room outside Schaeffer's office, looking like he was prepared for a siege. To say he was a scant unpopular at that precise moment was like being voted into third place in a three- way beauty contest between himself, Fidel Castro and Mao Zedong. He dropped all his bags by the steel entrance door and stood to face the welcoming committee. There were two hungry, lean looking men, standing either side of Schaeffer like they were his personal bodyguard. They were wearing crisp, U.S navy uniforms. Fagg had seen neither of them before. Schaeffer made a point of tapping at his watch before speaking to Fagg. He was three hours later than the agreed time.

"Is there any point in asking where you've been? What happened to that crucial timing you were at pains to refer to earlier in my office?"

Fagg gave a wry smile and replied, "There isn't time to get into that now." The three men opposite him shuffled their feet, restlessly as he looked over at Schaeffer's desk and noticed the navy blue, camouflage set of navy fatigues. Fagg's eyes lit up at the sight of a Colt semi-automatic pistol, resting beside them. "Those are mine, yeah?" he asked, pointing at the neatly folded uniform. Schaeffer nodded.

As Fagg began to pull on the two items of military gear over the top of the lightweight clothes he was wearing, he asked about the current location of the El Alca.

The younger of the two men next to Schaeffer, Lieutenant Tom Ritchie, was holding a sheet of paper with the most up-to-date information available. He realised Fagg's last question had been directed at him. Tom Ritchie cleared his throat and replied that several small vessels had arrived at anchor in Falmouth harbour so far that evening. The last one was just over one hour ago; it had been stationary, close to White House Bay, for approximately thirty minutes.

"That sounds like the one," Fagg interjected as he picked up the pistol and checked the firing action. "Ammunition?" he said curtly.

Schaeffer stepped behind his desk and took out a box of fifty .45 calibre bullets. But before handing them over to Fagg, he gave him a copy of the inventory sheet and ensured Fagg signed it first. "These must all be returned after tonight's operation and that's non negotiable. I must insist."

"Okay," beamed Fagg cockily. "What are we waiting for? Let's go."

Captain Gene Lowry had been the most impatient and the least impressed with having a G-man aboard his command. He quickly turned on his heels, leading the way and headed straight for the door. He threw it wide open to the point of making it's steel hinges groan at being over stretched. He wasn't sure of what to make of Fagg. He was both curious and cautious towards the stranger. But at the same time he knew he had an important job ahead of him, although he wasn't happy about the obvious conflict of his orders: help to locate and stop the El Alca, but above all else, to make the rendezvous at the military dock in Puerto Rico in exactly eight hours time. And thanks to 'last minute' Fagg, the schedule was getting tighter by the hour.

Schaeffer helped Fagg pick up his baggage. His attention was drawn to the dark green, leather diplomatic pouch. It was a further indicator that's Fagg's stature had risen meteorically since they'd last worked together as Dustcoats. He was about to enquire what Fagg was carrying inside, but then thought better of it. He knew Fagg would only spin him a barefaced lie. He followed them all out to the parked jeep and waited until the rest of Fagg's kit was loaded into the back. As the jeep sped away in the direction of the 'Restricted Coastal Area' where the US Hydrofoil was moored. Schaeffer was mightily relieved to see the back of them, especially his former colleague. Things would be back to normal tomorrow and he was already looking forward to some peace and quiet and a pleasant afternoon, fishing on the shore.

Between the hours of eleven and midnight, Ilena and Iko had both been silently standing at the small, square window, on the ground floor of Fort Anderson:
They were staring out to sea, waiting for the arrival of their rescue boat, the El Alca. As if perhaps the act of staring itself would somehow bring their ship closer to them. Both their kitbags had been packed and stored inside the Dory speedboat, in readiness for a hasty escape. Their prisoner was sat tied to the iron framed bed, which Iko had earlier dragged down from the upper floor. The only chair in the room was being used by each of them in turn to keep an eye on their convict.

In the long, stagnant hours since his capture, Arfield had gradually recovered his senses and although he was still gagged about his mouth, he felt very alert. It was only a matter of time before Fagg would come to his rescue. Arfield had worked out that all Fagg had to do was pay a visit to Amigo's bar to learn of his whereabouts. The young English couple who ran the bar had both witnessed him leaving with the young kid who'd been wearing the makeshift uniform of the Marine Observation Team. And likely as not, the couple would probably also know exactly where he was based.

Iko checked his watch again and turned to Ilena.

"Another thirty minutes at the most and the El Alca should be here. You'll feel much safer once we're all aboard," he said carefully.

"I think we should move Friedla into your boat, as soon as we have sighting of this fishing boat of yours." She replied.

They both glanced over their shoulders to check their prisoner was still behaving himself. When they were satisfied and had looked away, Arfield continued to wriggle his arms, wrists and hands in an attempt to loosen the knotted restraints that bound him. He wasn't making any significant progress and could feel his skin burning and starting to blister. The more his struggles became hopeless, the more his anger was channelled toward the incompetence of his would be rescuer. What the hell was keeping Fagg? Arfield cursed his luck for having been lumbered with him in the first place. Since the day he'd closed his office door in California, at the start of their trip, Fagg's clumsiness had been the root cause that had hampered Arfield's mission in acquiring the films. The best he could hope for now was to be back in his bedroom at Padgett House, by dawn. In the meantime he realised he was heading for a long night. He tried to calm his nerves with some deep breathing exercises. All this stress was playing merry hell with his blood pressure.

    The partially obscured light of a waning moon was fading ominously. Its hazy reflection barely illuminated the nearest waves as they broke against the jetty at the rear of the fort. The only other sound to penetrate the darkness was the easterly trade winds, bumping down the terraced slopes of Arawak Hill. These narrow gusts continued their descent, combing through the spikey canopy of nearby palm trees before gushing out to sea, mimicking the faint cries of lost souls.
    Ten minutes ahead of schedule, both Ilena and Iko heard the rhythmic chatter of a marine engine. "That sounds like the El Alca approaching now," commented Iko with a broad smile across his lips. He moved away from the window and over towards the back of the room. "Come on Ilena, help me get Friedla to his feet. You walk behind him and if he starts to resist, just give him a few encouraging jabs to his backbone."
    Ilena picked up Arfield's pistol and watched him closely as Iko unleashed their prisoner. The loose end of the rope was used as a leash to drag him forward by his tied hands. Iko had no intention of letting Friedla come within striking distance. Once inside the Dory, Iko transferred the loose end of the rope, making a reef knot to one of the securing brackets, which ran along the top edge of the aft bulkhead.
    The El Alca was now lying stationary, about forty yards away. Her deck lights had been switched on, creating a pool of milky light around it's hull, which was gently rising up and down on the tips and troughs of shallow waves.
    Iko fired up the outboard on the ignition key and checked that Ilena was seated against their kit bags before shifting into

forward gear. He gently eased along, up to the stern of the fishing boat and tied off, at midships, against the El Alca's diving ladder. The lone, dark figure of Luis Fredericks was already in position at the top rung, waiting to help haul the pieces of kit on board.

Had Arfield been twenty years younger, he would have risked jumping overboard. But he was in no condition to risk attempting an escape beneath the inky waves and their submerged currents with both hands tied. It was futile to resist, and much less painful too. 'Where the hell was Fagg? A greenhorn fresh out of the academy could have done a better job so far at locating him'. Arfield cursed his luck once more and made a promise to himself: that when he was finally rescued he would kick Fagg's ass from here to Alaska.

Ilena was the last to be helped aboard. She watched Iko lead Friedla down to the forward cabin, the very same one that Iko had slept in, on his initial, overnight voyage from Grenada to Antigua, just four eventful days ago. How his world had changed in such a short space of time; he'd captured an important fugitive and in the process he'd probably captured the heart of a beautiful young woman from the dreamy metropolis of France. He rightly supposed he had made a good impression with his superiors too. Perhaps he'd even done enough to earn the right to live out his life under his own terms. If this former Nazi criminal turned out to be the person the Soviets thought he was, then who knew what valuable information could be learnt from him. And if he was responsible for certain atrocities committed during World War Two, as Ilena suspected, then the publicity surrounding him would be enormous. The only reward Iko intended to claim for himself was the freedom to live his life peacefully from that day forward.

When Iko was satisfied that his prisoner was well and truly secured, he climbed back out onto the boat deck. He had one last thing to do before they could head out to sea. Iko stripped down to his briefs and returned the Dory back to the jetty in front of Fort Anderson. And finally, he gathered his strength to swim back out to the El Alca. It took all his nerve and effort to make the short distance. Luckily the El Alca had drifted slightly closer to the shore. When he climbed the ladder for the last time, it was Ilena who was waiting to meet him with a dry towel.

"Okay Captain," she said. "Take us to Grenada." She wrapped the towel over Iko's shoulders and they were both held together by the excitement of the moment.

The El Alca's inboard engine thumped into life, happily chattering away to itself as Luis swung the ship's wheel and headed for home. The pilot's wheelhouse was enclosed on three sides by half glazed panels. There was a comfortable high chair for the captain and a short wooden bench seat for his clients. The floor hatch beneath his feet allowed access to the motor; it was never locked. It was kept that way as a lucky omen to keep the gremlins at bay. Deep-sea fishing couldn't possibly function successfully without observing a few superstitious rituals.

Luis had been given the El Alca four years ago, when his father retired. It was handed down to him to keep the family tradition alive. And although the El Alca was getting a little long in the tooth, she was still a reliable old girl. Provided you summoned the protection of 'Aganju' with a few voodoo chants, whenever the engine misfired, or the ship rolled alarmingly.

In recent times, it had become harder to locate the prized, big fish and to supplement the El Alca's income Luis had taken up charter work for the Queen Conch travel agency. These random trips normally involved taking tourists out to uninhabited, tiny islands so that they could indulge themselves with bathing and barbequing and copious amounts of beer. It was easy money as far as Luis was concerned. And of course he ran other 'no questions asked' errands for Des Riley too, like picking up and delivering a selection of odd-looking characters. As long as he was paid on time, Luis kept his mouth firmly closed.

As he steered clear of the headland, he checked his chart and set a compass bearing of two hundred and seventy degrees. His two companions were sat quietly behind him. Then, a chink of light caught Ilena's attention. She stood up and looked behind her as the old fort fell away from view. Luis studied the distant shoreline too. It had a definite, orange glow.

Ilena tapped Iko on the shoulder. "Is that a fire or something?" She looked puzzled and continued to stare at the shoreline, to the east of the fort. Iko took out his field glasses and focussed on the intense arclight. It appeared to be coming from Cross Green. He could see flames and smoke shooting up from the roof of a building, but its ground floor was obscured, by the mangrove in the foreground.

"Yes, it's definitely a building that's on fire. Maybe one of the Chandlery Shops," he suggested.

Ilena made a grab for his binoculars. "Can I see for myself?"

She aimed at the glow in the sky and worked her way down. "Oh merde," she said. "I think it's Amigo's Bar. I hope everyone's okay." She could tell from the height of the flames that the fire must be out of control. She handed the binoculars back to Iko as a cold chill drifted in and around the wheelhouse. Directly in front of the bow pulpit, the sea fell away to nothing. It was an even stranger view than the one they'd just witnessed behind them. Out of nowhere, the El Alca was heading straight into a flash fog. Ilena and Iko were mesmerised by the incoming, ghostly veil of dense cloud.

"I'm going to have to reduce our speed for a while," commented Luis. "Don't worry. These fogs normally go away as quickly as they appear." He asked Iko to take the wheel and went forward to sit at the bow pulpit, to listen for any other vessels in the immediate vicinity. The sea was becalmed and the breeze had disappeared, along with the topographical outline of Antigua.

Ilena settled down again on the bench seat and watched Iko, who had both hands holding the handles of the wheel. His eyes were fully focussed on the compass, making sure the needle remained on their set course.

The sight of the fiery sky over Cross Green had upset her. Was it her fault? But she'd no reason to suspect it was at all connected to her. The only malevolent agent who'd wished her any harm had been the man they'd held captive since early afternoon, long before the fire would've started. She was concerned for her films and hoped that Byrney had them stored somewhere safe.

The El Alca's rhythmic heartbeat thumped away unhindered and without the slightest fluctuation. It was a comforting sound. For as long as it remained, their destination was slowly moving closer.

The USS Aquarius was a Pegasus-class hydrofoil and one of the latest interceptor vessels to enter service in the United States Navy. She had a top speed of forty-five knots in foilborne mode, which gave her an edge: the capacity to outrun most other vessels that passed through the Caribbean Sea. And any that were foolish enough to evade her could be 'brought to heel' with one of her eight, Harpoon, surface to surface missiles. They had a firing range of over one hundred kilometres, together with a sophisticated radar system that was so advanced, a craft not much bigger than a bathtub could be located seventy-five nautical miles away.

Captain Lowry was in his element, in command of the bridge. The American government ensured that their service men and women had the best kit in the world. It was pointless engaging the enemy with anything less. The only disadvantage was that this could sometimes lead to a less experienced sailor making an error of judgement, through being overconfident.

Fagg was stood back from the business end of the bridge as the six alert Naval officers stood by their stations. Besides Lowry and Ritchie, each of the four other officers had their own area of expertise: piloting, navigation, tracking and communications.

Inside ten minutes of launching, the Aquarius was set into foilborne mode. The ship stood up out of the water, powered along by its Boeing, gas-turbine engine. She was literally jetting across the waves. The sudden unexpected increase in thrust had caused Fagg to lose his balance, sending him back a pace or two, until he collided with his own baggage. Lowry and Ritchie looked at one another and smiled at his misfortune.

It was only a matter of minutes before the tracking engineer announced he had a fix on a potential target, approximately twenty-five miles nautical miles ahead of them. He passed on the bearing to the pilot, who made a fractional adjustment to their course setting. The Navigator advised Lowry that the target was moving unusually slowly, about thirty miles north of Guadeloupe.

"Keep your eyes on her and let me know if anything changes," advised Lowry. He looked at his watch and turned to Fagg. "We should be alongside in thirty minutes."

Fagg nodded his head in agreement. The ride was not exactly a smooth one. The one thing he'd not taken any precautions against was feeling seasick. At least it would only be a relatively short-lived experience. Fagg knew he couldn't just sit there and do nothing. He needed a distraction and forced himself into a conversation with the man closest to him, Lieutenant Ritchie.

"How will you recognise the El Alca?" He asked.

"We've boarded her twice before," he replied stoically. "The last time was only a few months ago, in November. We routinely board vessels travelling from Venezuela to Puerto Rico, that's the main narcotics route. The El Alca is registered in Grenada to a Captain Luis Fredericks. He's just a fisherman, chasing yellow fin, tuna and the like."

"What about Fredericks? Did he give you any trouble?"

"No, not as yet. Might be different this time though. If he's carrying what you say he is."

"What about guns? Is he likely to be armed?"

"You can never be sure. That's why we're always tooled up, ready for the unexpected before boarding any suspicious vessel."

The El Alca had been making a snail's pace through the fog for at least thirty, agonising minutes. Luis returned to the wheelhouse, looking slightly more anxious than before.

"I thought I heard something in the distance," he said anxiously. The web-like mist had stuck to his dark curly hair and his clothing was coated in a shiny film of water droplets. "Did either of you hear anything?" They all stood perfectly still, listening over and beyond the El Alca's heartbeat.

"There," shouted Luis. "I think it's behind us."

There was a distinctive, whoosh-like sound still some distance away. Luis cut the engine, to get a clearer impression of which direction the sound was coming from.

Ilena heard it too. "It sounds like an aircraft, but it must be flying very low." They all moved right up to the stern handrail, peering into the gloom. "It's a pity we can't see anything," she sighed.

The noise was getting alarmingly louder and undoubtedly sounded more and more like a single engine jet. "Could be a helicopter," offered Iko.

Luis disagreed. "No it can't be. There are no nearby airports open at this time of night." Then, suddenly, Luis recognised the sound of the water jet. "Fout toné. I know exactly what it is. It's the U.S Navy hydrofoil. I think it's going to pass us by."

The sonic noise suddenly subsided. "Perhaps you're right," replied Ilena with a sigh of relief. But it was short lived. The three of them were forces to take a step backwards as the dark steel bow pierced the grey wall of gloom with an ominous foreboding. Then the silence was broken by a new sound. The roar of a powerful marine motor grew closer and closer, followed by a few sharp words of command hailing to them through a P.A system, like the voice of a god, unseen and ethereal.

"Stay exactly where you are. Prepare for the U.S Navy boarding party. We are taking control of your vessel."

It wasn't God after all, just people who enjoyed playing at being him. However, the words spoken by the American military automatically set everyone on edge. Iko unclipped his pistol from his gun belt and checked it was fully loaded. Luis peered at them both as Ilena followed Iko's lead and checked over her borrowed firearm. Iko helped Ilena to locate the safety catch and demonstrated the on/off position.

"Listen to me carefully," announced Luis. "Don't do anything stupid. It's probably just a routine check. Please, you must put your weapons away and try to act normally." Luis waited for Ilena and Iko to respond. They had no reasonable alternative course of action other than to follow his advice. Luis was the one in charge. It was his vessel and he'd been through this type of experience before.

"They usually just ask to see our passports and permits. So we're cool. Right guys?"

Iko wasn't entirely convinced. His right hand was still firmly clenched around the grip of his pistol. He wasn't the sort of soldier to surrender before the fight had begun. But he guessed he would surely be outgunned in this conflict. His emotions were getting the better of his instincts. They were telling him to protect Ilena at all costs. He let his pistol fall back inside its leather holster, but left the securing strap unclipped. Ilena had already tucked hers half inside the front of her jeans and had buttoned up her denim jacket to conceal it. Iko suggested he'd better go and check on Friedla and make sure there was no way he could call out for help."

The hydrofoil was now crushingly close and dwarfed over them, like a giant sea monster. There were two armed combatants standing on the wings of its deck. The monster moved in alongside ready to strike, like it was about to devour their fragile fishing boat, whole.

A rope ladder was thrown down, unfurling as it fell towards them. The voice on the loud speaker commanded them to secure the end of the ladder and stand aside. Luis hurried down the port side of his ship, setting three cork fenders in position to prevent the hydrofoil from smashing against the wooden hull. A powerful beam of light illuminated the base of the ladder as the two American servicemen began to climb down. Their armaments could be seen from the deck below. They were fully loaded with grenades, gas canisters and side arms, well prepared for any eventuality.

Iko just managed to return in time to see the leading figure set foot on the aft deck. Iko took up his stance slightly to the rear of Captain Luis, hoping to shield his pistol from view as they waited for the second figure to reach the deck. Luis instantly recognised Lieutenant Ritchie and this put him slightly more at ease; there was at least a chance that the inspection would pan-out in the usual way. "It's okay guys," he whispered. "I know the one at the front, just let me do all the talking."

Ritchie stepped forward towards the Captain and made his opening enquiry. "It's a little late to be out fishing. Who are your two guests?"

Before Luis could answer, the second armed combatant stepped in between them raising his pistol and pointing it at Iko. "Hands in the air, now."

Iko quickly glanced at Luis for an indication of what he should do, but he just quickly frowned and shook his head, sensing that Iko was about to do something foolish. Iko reluctantly and slowly raised both his arms.

"Well, Soldier Blue," said the second one. "What have we got here?" He lifted Iko's pistol from its holster and examined it quickly, pulling a face like he'd a mouthful of soggy tobaccy. "What's a kid like you doing in possession of a Soviet made Malarov pistol?" Without waiting for an answer, the inquisitor tossed it overboard and raised his voice in anger. "Passport, now," he demanded, pointing his weapon at Iko's forehead.

Ilena and Luis both flinched at the aggressive action. It wasn't panning out as expected. What next?

Iko very carefully removed his passport from his shirt pocket. The second one handed it back to the Lieutenant who examined its contents. "You're Eldridge Delgado?" enquired Ritchie.

Iko nodded in agreement.

The second one now turned his attention on Ilena. She stood her ground defiantly. She wasn't about to show any fear. She looked straight at him as he began to smile full of confidence. He waved his pistol loosely and gleefully said, "Hands up, Miss Romero."

Ilena's cool took a heavy blow at discovering this nasty piece of work knew her by name and she was none the wiser as to his identity. He began frisking her, slowly, as if he was enjoying himself. His right hand located her pistol. He wasn't the least bit surprised to discover it was Arfield's Smith and Wesson model thirty-nine. Fagg pocketed the weapon and tutted audibly at the photojournalist.

"I don't suppose you have those incriminating films with you either?" he asked, with his pistol still waving casually in her general direction.

"You're too late. I've already handed them over." Ilena spoke the truth, knowing that a lie would possibly get her into more trouble. This man opposite her, whoever he was, was not only well informed, but he also had the might of the U.S navy to back him up too.

"I guessed as much. Okay little lady, hand me your passport."

It was passed back to the Lieutenant who gave the French passport the same attention that he had shown with Delgado's. Ritchie noted it contained several interesting immigration stamps. "You're quite a busy traveller, Miss Romero," he commented.

Fagg stepped away from the girl and turned his attention to the man in charge of the El Alca. "So, my Grenadian rebel, where are you hiding him?" The question caught everyone by surprise. Luis decided to play dumb until he could think of a better way out. He shrugged his shoulders and spoke submissively. "I've no idea what you're talking about. We're just on our way back to Grenada and got caught up in this fog. As you can see, there's just the three of us onboard."

Fagg opened the cylinder of his pistol to show it was fully loaded with six rounds then snapped it shut and stepped to one side, pointing it straight at Ilena. "Tell me where your prisoner is now, or the bitch dies."

The deathly silence was broken, almost immediately, by Iko, who replied that the man he was looking for was in the forward cabin.

"Thanks sonny," said Fagg with a grin. "I'm glad someone's being sensible at last." He weaved his way forward around the wheelhouse and ordered Ritchie to shoot the first person that tried to follow him.

The forward cabin was cramped and stuffy and smelt of engine fumes. He found Arfield gagged and bound to a chair. As soon as Fagg entered the room, Arfield began to wriggle and mumble when he recognised the person who'd come to his rescue at last. Fagg pulled down the gag from Arfield's mouth, which produced an undesirable if not totally unexpected tirade of venomous expletives.

"And about goddam time, you imbecile. I've been trussed up like the darn thanksgiving turkey for the last twelve hours, you fuckwit." Fagg stood back with his arms folded to allow Arfield to finish his rant. "And I hope for your sake you've remembered to bring along my medication? Well don't just stand there you idiot, untie me."

Fagg stepped forward and lifted the gag back across Arfield's mouth causing his eyes to practically pop out of their sockets. His forehead too turned into the blackest shade of red and shone like an over ripe kidney bean.

"Change of plan, Arfield. You've been declassified as surplus to requirements. You were right about us requiring a scapegoat down here. You're it." Fagg displayed a psychotic grin for a moment or two to let this new information 'slow burn' its way through to Arfield's brain, which was still set in overload. Fagg pulled back the hammer on his pistol and took aim. Arfield shook from side to side, attempting to dodge what was obviously coming next.

"I've been ordered to liquidate you," Fagg announced calmly. He carefully adjusted his aim then fired two deafening shots into the bulkhead immediately behind his target. "That should sound convincing enough," he sniggered into Arfield's face. "Hey smile, you're heading out on vacation Arfield, all the way to Cuba. I'm sure you and El Loco will get along like a house on fire."

Fagg turned and quickly climbed back on deck. He marched over to Ritchie and informed him that everything appeared to be in order. "Please, let these tourists have their passports back." As Fagg walked past Luis, he patted him on the shoulder and wished him a pleasant voyage.

Within minutes, the two naval combatants were climbing aboard the hydrofoil and the ladder was being hauled up. The roar of the engines indicated the monster was about to depart. It nimbly reversed clear of the El Alca's stern then turned away for the final time into the mysterious grey shroud.

Iko, Ilena and Luis were still in a daze, trying to figure out what had just occurred. It was incomprehensible, even for the Yanks, that they should kill one of their own. Then again if Arfield was Friedla, perhaps he'd worn out his welcome. There was obviously a limit as to how many times you could wash away the blood from your hands before the stains became permanent.

"Well, it's just the three of us, after all," said Luis with a hint of irony as he started up the motor.

"I'd better go and clean up the cabin," said Iko ruefully, not wishing the distasteful task upon anyone else. Then, as an after thought, he turned to Luis and asked what he should do with the body?

"Just wrap it in a bedsheet for now," replied Luis.

Ilena watched Iko graciously head off to the forward cabin. She had no desire whatsoever to see another bloodied and mutilated corpse. But, she was more disappointed that Friedla had been spared the ordeal of answering for his crimes. It was an agonising, hurtful shame for the remaining few, who had survived the consequences of coming up against an evil executioner like Friedla, that they would now be denied the opportunity to see him get his just deserts in a court of law. Ilena was still tussling with these thoughts when Iko threw open the forward hatch again and shouted back to the wheelhouse.

"He's alive. Friedla's alive and well. The gun shots have missed him completely."

When Fagg returned to the bridge, he handed over his armour and artillery. Lieutenant Ritchie ticked each item off the list and Fagg was given a copy of the signed inventory as proof that all his equipment had been accounted for this time and returned to stores. When Captain Gene Lowry saw that the paperwork was done and dusted he asked Fagg if his quarry had been terminated?

"What do you think?" Replied Fagg. "He won't be causing us any more irritation again."

"Excellent, well done Fagg." sneered Lowry. "If there's one thing I can't abide, it's someone doing harm to the United States of America, especially an incompetent asshole who thinks he's above the law."

Fagg allowed those words to drift over his head as Captain Lowry stepped back from his command post. It was time for him to loosen his starched collar and turn in for the night.

"Lieutenant Ritchie, you're in charge. Set our course for Puerto Rico and make sure the navigator has plenty of black coffee at hand. By my reckoning we should arrive at the military dock, bang on time. Wake me a good half an hour before we arrive."

Chapter Twelve

Aftermath

It had been the worst night of my life. From around one p.m. when we'd first noticed the smoke filling up our bedroom, Fionn and I had had no sleep whatsoever. The Charleston fire brigade had finally come to our rescue when the inferno had already reached its height. The first we saw of the rescue team was when a small, red, pickup truck drove onto our beach and came to a halt in the midst of our huddle. And, along with our weary clients, we all saw the fire chief's worried look when he clapped eyes on the raging size of the flames. His immediate plan was to use the fire hydrant down by the chandlery shops, but this hit a severe setback due to their lack of equipment: despite rolling out every single length of hose they had, they were still fifty yards short. Luckily, they also carried an engine driven pump with them, which the fire chief eventually set up at the edge of the shore. If they weren't able to use fresh water, then seawater would be just as effective. But, sadly, the old engine proved difficult to start, due to its infrequent use and the fact that they had to manually wrap a strap around the drive pulley at each attempt. There was much huffing and puffing, but not a single drop of water was seen. The pointy end of the fire hose remained as dry as the scorched sand.

The primary concern now switched to the finding of alternative accommodation for our stranded guests. With the fire left to burn itself out, the fire chief insisted on everyone being moved off the beach.

Fire Chief Ken Duerden sent his right-hand man down to the 'Victory Holiday Resort' at English Harbour. They had a night watchman there who manned the reception desk outside normal office hours. It was also common knowledge that they'd recently built a new extension, at the southern end of the complex, based on Jericho Padgett's original redevelopment plans. These shiny, modular buildings hadn't yet been unveiled, but they had all been fully kitted out in readiness for the grand opening. When the nature of our emergency was conveyed to the off duty manager, he agreed at once to open its doors.

Not long after Fionn and I had first opened our bar, almost two years ago, we'd spent a fact-finding day out, at the resort village in English Harbour to 'check up on the opposition', as it were. We soon discovered they had some very strange, old-fashioned ideas about family fun, which they'd obviously borrowed from one or two of the more tacky, home-grown, seaside resorts, back home in England. Their events notice board had given us the giggles. Their guests were being invited to compete as drag artists. First prize was a bottle of Blue Nun, which made us wonder what sort of drag acts they were encouraging. It was all very kitsch. Next to the outdoor pool, they had a kiosk size souvenir shop, which sold one-armed plastic dolls resembling Horatio Nelson, complete with eye patch. The shop was also brimming with a selection of beach inflatables: king size bananas, life rings, Loch Ness monsters and lilos. They even stocked 'Kiss Me Quick' hats, like the ones sold on Blackpool prom, only their version read 'Kiss Me Hardy'.

We came to the conclusion, very early on, that our humble establishment would be the exact opposite. We wanted our guests to relax in a more authentic, Caribbean style. What was the point in travelling half way around the world to be entertained by sad imitations of Bernie Clifton and Jimmy Clitheroe?

Around 4.00 p.m in the morning, Chief Duerden's blushes were spared when it began to rain heavily. Luckily our guests had been shipped out to English harbour one hour before the downpour landed. At least they were in a much more comfortable place at the Victory, despite Fionn's and my own misgivings that their Caribbean experience was about to be dunked in candy floss.

There was nothing more the fire crew could do in attendance at Cross Green. The rain was now doing their work for them, slowly dousing and soothing the charred, skeletal framework of our embattled bar. Chief Duerden very kindly offered to put us up in the 'night duty' rooms back at the fire station.

He explained that he would carry out a thorough investigation at first light. "You might as well get some sleep for a couple of hours. We can return to Cross Green together later on. However, I'll have to carry out a safety assessment first before we can let you back on site."

To accept Ken's offer was the most sensible thing to do, although it proved impossible for either of us to switch off. We discussed how the fire would impact on our finances. We'd have to compensate our current clients, which meant returning their accommodation fees, or at least paying for their remaining stay at the Victory.

Fionn reminded me that the Island Tourist's Association, which we were members of, would pay up to half towards re-siting holiday makers in the event of a crisis, such as a hurricane or a flooding. Fionn was sure that being forced out by a fire would also count as an emergency. This would mean we'd only have to cover half of the re-accommodation costs out of our own pockets. Luckily, one of the things Fionn had remembered to do, before we evacuated our burning bar, was to empty our till. Takings-wise it had been a record evening for us and together with our meagre savings, we were fairly confident we could at least survive for the immediate future.

We were both adamant about rebuilding Amigo's from its ashes. According to Leyda, when we'd last spoken about our legacy, the reward money for finding the Potosi cross, and the larger amount we could now expect to receive would finance a rebuild as well as our initial loan for purchase of what had been Bijoe's Bar. We'd made lots of improvements over the past twenty months, reinvesting our profits with better quality fittings and equipment. It was going to be a hard slog to start from the ground upwards, but we were both fully committed to keeping our dream alive.

Ben Hansen was also on the move at early doors that morning. He checked out of the Ocean Edge Hotel and Spa and took a taxi direct to St. John's international airport. He'd foregone his ritual swim at dawn, in order to catch an early flight to Puerto Rico. And as a small compensation for missing his morning work out he wound down the car window and filled his lungs with the cool fresh breeze. He watched ordinary, everyday people going through their daily motions: shopkeepers opening their shops and decorating the pavements with their wares, school-kids chatting at bus-stops and housewives queuing up for fresh bread. The journey ahead, he hoped, would be kept to schedule, and if that were the case, he'd be back in L.A by early evening.

There were two early flights to Luis Muñoz Marín International Airport in Puerto Rico available to him. He'd already experienced a hairy-scary flight with Kahbuna Airways on his way out to Antigua, so he was determined not to use the same airline again even it was with a different pilot. Instead, he paid a little extra for a ticket with T.A.C.A. It was the exact same type of aircraft as before, a six seater Cessna 206, but the red, white and blue livery reminded him of home.

As he waited for take-off, an American businessman in the seat next to him was attempting to crack a few jokes. Ben took it in good humour despite learning that T.A.C.A wasn't an acronym for The Antiguan Charter Aircraft company. Oh no, according to this loud-mouthed joker, it stood for 'Take-A-Chance-Airways'.

Happily, the lightweight, twin-engined Cessna's take off was the smoothest Ben had ever experienced. It circled the island at a steady altitude, well below the level of the imposing, grey clouds. The pilot had an easy touch with the controls inside the cockpit; turning and climbing with the most gentle of movements, the plane banked at forty-five degrees to port and skirted around the southern edge of the island before heading westward again.

Ben looked down at the jagged coastline that changed, seamlessly, from green to gold, from the native mangroves to sand covered beaches. Despite the sea reflecting the greyness of today's sky, the landscape still roused the senses to its idyllic, unspoilt beauty. He recognised the old fort and the lone white house and the line of chandlery shacks leading to the busy marina in the distance, at Cross Green. But, between the white house and the first shack, he saw what looked like a scorched footprint, at the edge of the beach. He turned into his window to look again, counting the properties along the dusty track. The black footprint, he anxiously noted, was the charred remains in the exact place where Amigo's bar should be. He'd stood there yesterday evening and now it was gone and although he'd parted on adverse terms with Byrney, he wouldn't have wished this outcome on them. Was this Arfield's doing, or perhaps Fagg's? 'The dirty, rotten bastards,' he thought.

The small plane continued on its journey, at a constant speed of one hundred and fifty knots, passing over the last views of Antigua. The honeybee hum of its engines was a familiar sound to those below on the ground. You could almost set your watch by them. Outside the sleepy police station in Charlestown, opposite St. Michael's church, Hawkeye paused on the worn, bare wooden steps. He looked skyward at the tiny, two barred cross, buzzing along under the clouds, then dropped his gaze upon his wristwatch - almost seven o'clock.

He unlocked the station door and turned the flip-over sign to read 'open'. As usual, he was the first to arrive, armed with a brown paper bag containing his favourite, warm croissants. He put them down on top of his desk and twisted the venetian blinds, allowing the daylight to filter across the office. On went the kettle and the overhead fan. It might feel a little cool to start with, but by midday it would be baking hot. It always paid to start the air circulating long before the heat became too sticky to dislodge. He poured himself a cup of char and waited for young Throup to arrive. He looked across at the Fax machine. The light was on, but there were no new messages, nothing with regards to the two men wanted for Orr's murder.

He picked up the phone and called his opposite number at St. Johns central police station, but Inspector Larry Brown had no news to report either. No one matching Arfield's, or Fagg's description had been seen at any of the main exit ports. At the end of the call, Hawkeye rubbed his chin then raised a croissant to his mouth, consuming half of it at first bite. When his munching subsided and a merry whistling tune ascended outside in the street, Hawkeye knew it must be Throup, of course. Seconds later, the smartly dressed constable marched in through the entrance door and up to his desk. As he sat down his whistling was replaced with a smile and a look of eager enthusiasm. "Morning Sarge. Anything new in?"

Hawkeye picked up his mug of tea and washed down the remnants of his breakfast. He thought young Throup possessed the kind of attributes that, one day, with some honing and coaching on his part, would produce a well-accomplished police sergeant, just like himself.

"After you've had your cup of tea Throup I'd like you to go down to Padgett House and gather up all the American's belongings and bring them back here; here's the keys. When you leave, lock the door again and place a seal across it. I believe that old plantation house to be cursed. It's had such a chequered history; it's high time someone drove a bulldozer at it."

Hawkeye stood in front of the window and stared into space, gathering his thoughts towards that forthcoming day when he could finally hang up his helmet.

"What's happened to our two fugitives, Sarge?" enquired Throup.

Hawkeye shook his head and continued to stare out into the quiet street. "It's as if they've vanished into thin air." Then he turned on his heels and looked straight at his eager assistant. "There is one, important thing you can help me with," commented Hawkeye sincerely.

"Of course, I'd be glad to," replied Throup with great expectation. "How can I help?"

"What do you think I should wear tonight for my date with Marcia."

We were both still wide-awake when one of the firemen knocked on our door. "Rise and shine," called the voice.

"Glad to hear someone's merry," said Fionn drily.

"I suppose we'd better face the music," I replied half-heartedly. In my mind I'd been going over and over how the blaze could've started. We wouldn't know for definite until the fire chief had carried out his examination of the burnt remains. Perhaps we'd never know. But I was having grave worries that perhaps it was linked to Ilena and her films after all. Even though I knew Hansen and the American guy were nowhere near at the time, I had to mention it to Fionn, the way I was feeling, and that somehow the fire was my fault.

"I'm starting to wish I'd listened to you about going to the police with Ilena's films," I confessed.

Fionn stopped what she was doing and looked directly into my eyes. "I've been thinking about that too, and for what it's worth, I don't think it would've made any difference if you had or not. Come here you fool." Fionn held out her arms and we hugged each other tightly. It meant a lot to me to know she was firmly with me. "I think you did the right thing posting them to America. Watching our livelihood being burnt to the ground has made me realise how awful it must have been for all those poor people who were burnt to death in San Albarra City. If the world doesn't get to hear about what happened there, then their deaths would have come to nothing."

When we arrived back at Cross Green we were met by a small gathering: inquisitive onlookers and one or two nosey-parkers. Most of those we knew were from the chandlery shops. We spoke to Sly as we watched Chief Duerden and two of his colleagues begin to search the ruins. They each carried a short handled axe and didn't waste any time in bringing down pieces of the framework that were hanging dangerously. The flames and smoke had all but died away. Mostly, the hot embers just hissed at the odd spot of rain.

"Really sorry, Byrney," said Sly, solemnly. "If there's anything I can do, you only have to say the word."

"Thanks for coming over. I'll let you know," I replied gratefully and shook his hand.

The firemen continued with their assessment, in full protective uniforms and steel helmets. They dragged, kicked and stamped on the foundations testing their sturdiness. It was a dirty, individual task, which had no clear deadline. Their assessment would conclude only when they deemed it safe for us to enter. Sly and most of the onlookers had returned to their own doings as we continued to watch from the edge of the beach.

All our furniture had been consumed. Only their tubular steel frames were recognisable, but even these were twisted beyond use. There didn't look to be anything that we could salvage.

When the fire chief eventually allowed us back on site I noticed our old jukebox, still standing in the corner, but partially hidden by fallen debris. The horizontal glass display screen was cracked and when I wiped away the soot to look inside, I found an even sadder sight. All our records had melted and congealed. They were stuck to each other like the contents of a forgotten packet of Pontefract cakes.

Ken called me over to the rear of the building. He pointed to the telephone wire. "Do you see that?" he asked, indicating to where it had broken away from the steel junction box.

"Yer, you mean it's snapped."

"No. Look carefully. Notice the edges of the inner strands of cable? How straight they are? That's been deliberately cut."

"So that's why we weren't able to call for help."

"Exactly." Chief Duerden moved further around the outer wall to where the side door leading to the kitchen had been. The only thing that remained of it was the charred doorsill. There was nothing left of the door. Its steel fittings, handle and hinges were buried under a mound of black dust.

"Do you keep any petrol out here?" he enquired.

"Only what's in the tank of our moped, why?"

"In that case, I've no hesitation in saying that this fire was started deliberately. Right here. Just bend down and put your nose to that sill."

I did as he asked. There was a faint whiff of petrol.

"You can smell that too, can't you? I'm going to write up in my report that this is unmistakably a case of arson. It'll be passed onto the police, of course. So they'll probably want to take a statement from you both, ask you if you saw anyone loitering about, etcetera."

The thought occurred to me that this was the same spot where I'd had the barbeque set up. Apart from Fionn, the only other person to have visited me here was Ben. I was a pretty good judge of character and in my experience Ben was not the sort of person to set fire to a building full of people. He might have been a bit miffed with me when he left, but he was no psychopath.

By lunchtime, Fionn and I were the only two people left plodding through the wreckage of our home. We found some wooden crates of Red Stripe beer in one of the outbuildings furthest from the rear of the bar. Miraculously, it had been left unscathed by the blaze. The internal rooms however were non-existent. Our bedroom furniture and their contents had been reduced to wafers of ash. The only clothes we possessed were the ones we were wearing and these were now practically ruined, stained with charcoal and stinking of smoke.

We wandered around in a daze, each new, beleaguered discovery dragging us deeper into a pit of despair. Then we heard a familiar voice calling to us. It was Leyda Friday. She greeted us with a grave expression on her face.

"Oh you poor darlings," her eyes were welling up with tears. "I'm so sorry, I'm so sorry. I didn't expect it would be such an awful mess. I wish I could have come sooner, but as you know I'm looking after Pug and I had to practically lock my doors to stop him from coming over to help you."

"How is he?" Asked Fionn.

"He's getting stronger by the day. I'd say he'll be ready for going back home in a day or two. His face is still swollen, but he is talking a little more."

"That's good," I replied. I looked at Leyda and I could tell she was holding something back. Maybe it was coming face to face with all this destruction that had pushed her into an uneasy silence. Then, she suddenly turned to face us both and grabbed a hand from us both, which she began to squeeze, to summon up the strength needed for what she was about to tell us. She had our full attention. Whatever it was, it couldn't possibly be any worse than the fire.

"I'm afraid I'm the bearer of more bad news." I saw a tear roll down her cheek.

"What is it, Leyda?" asked Fionn anxiously.

She took a deep breath and drew her lips together to prevent them from quivering. "There's been a theft at Manners Bank in St. Johns. The Potosi cross has been stolen."

I could feel myself go light-headed. I grabbed Fionn as she turned towards me, straight into my arms. As I hugged her I felt her shoulders shaking as she sobbed with tears.

"Are you sure? I mean, how?" I replied, facing back towards Leyda. "It was locked inside the vault, in a safety deposit for Christ's sake." I let go of Fionn and put my hand to my mouth. "I'm sorry Leyda. I didn't mean to shout at you. I just don't understand. Does anyone at the bank know what happened?"

Leyda shook her head in pity and comforted Fionn with a hug too. "I'm so sorry, darling."

When our emotions had settled down somewhat, Leyda explained what Gilbert Chivers, the chairman at Manners Bank had told her. They keep a register of course, of everyone who holds a safety deposit box at the bank." Leyda paused and shook her head again. "I'm sorry, let me start again from the beginning. Earlier this morning, some technicians from the University arrived at the bank to carry out some more tests on the cross. The bank had contacted Raoul and asked if he'd mind opening up the box with the manager. When both keys were fitted into their locks and the safety deposit box opened, they found it was empty. The manager checked the register of course. It appears that only one customer visited the vault this week. The customers name was, John Arfield.

"Who the hell's John Arfield?" I asked.

"Wasn't he the American guy who left with Iko, yesterday?" asked Fionn. "I'm sure he introduced himself as John when he first came to our bar."

"But that's impossible." I stopped short of speaking any further, realising immediately that I should keep my thoughts to myself.

"I've spoken about it to Pug of course," continued Leyda. "And he thinks he may have lost his key when he was beaten up outside Padgett House."

'Oh bloody hell.' I thought, 'this get's worse.' "But how did this Arfield guy get hold of the banks key? I thought you needed both keys to open a safety deposit box?"

"I haven't a clue," replied Leyda. "The bank isn't saying either. Look, why don't you two drop what you're doing and accompany me back to my place? Have you got anywhere to stay tonight?"

I looked at Fionn and I could tell we were both thinking the same thing - we hadn't thought that far ahead.

"That's very kind of you, Leyda," replied Fionn, drying her tears.

"Yer, I guess we're really up the creek without a paddle, now," I commented.

"Yes, we all are. I think Raoul was planning to get married and buy a house, soon. Even Pug was hoping to retire on the reward money."

We were both too tired to take it all in. We followed Leyda across the sands of White House Bay, not knowing what our future held or if our sanity would survive, or more to the point, if our love would survive.

My body felt almost normal again after a reviving shower and a change of clothes. It was now almost thirty-six hours since I'd last had any sleep. Leyda had put out some of Joe Fernandez's (Raoul's deceased father's) old clothes for me to choose from. Leyda wasn't the type of person to throw anything useful away. By her own admission, she'd been a bit of a fashion diva back in the swinging Sixties. Even on Antigua back then there were parties where a young girl might bump into a British rock star, or a famous actor.

Fionn followed me out onto Leyda's west facing veranda. Pug applauded us as we made our entrance. He was full of apologies.

"It's not your fault," I said. "Besides, there are always plenty more riches in the ocean just waiting to be found." That sounded really naff, I thought. I wasn't convincing anyone, least of all myself.

Out on the horizon we could see a brighter weather front, which promised to return an azure blue tint to tomorrows dawn and although the sky was still overcast directly overhead, the temperature was warm enough to sit out comfortably in just a t-shirt and a pair of jeans. Fionn had borrowed one of Leyda's treasured cast offs and there was genuine approval as to how well it suited her, hugging her hour glass figure.

"I wish I could still squeeze into that dress, darling. I'd forgotten just how much I adore it," lamented Leyda. "You look beautiful, Fionn."

Just after four-thirty p.m. the tall, tidy, figure of Sergeant Hawkins was spotted walking across the sands, briefcase in hand and making a beeline for Leyda's veranda.

'Oh bloody hell,' I thought. 'This is all we need right now to make our day complete.'

Leyda had obviously noticed me slump a little lower. "I'll make sure he sticks to the point with his questioning, then we can all get back to the art of relaxation."

"A little bird told me I'd find you here," announced Hawkeye, removing his dress cap and wiping the sweat from his brow with a white handkerchief. He eyed us all up for size, as if he was measuring us for one of his cells. "I know you've had a rough time, so as soon as I have your signed statements I'll leave you all in peace."

'Well, at least that was a promising start'.

Leyda brought him an old milking stool to sit on. It was quite a tricky balancing act for him, attempting to write up his notes and maintain both cheeks on a space small enough for one. Watching him fidget from one cheek to the other helped to lighten our moods.

"Firstly, I have to inform you that the fire chief has submitted his report and has recorded your fire as an act of arson. So, what I need from you Byrney, and you as well young lady, is to tell me in your own words if you saw anyone suspicious outside your bar around midnight? Which one of you locked up?

"I did." I replied. "It was dead quiet outside when we eventually switched everything off. We'd had a barbeque evening."

"Yes, I'm well aware of that."

I wasn't sure if Hawkeye understood me, or whether he thought I was conveying a coded message that I'd set fire to the bar myself.

"Was anyone else at all outside with you that evening?"

"No, just Fionn bringing out the marinated chicken."

"No one else?" retorted Hawkeye in one of his suspicious tones.

"Well, the only other visitor we had was Ben Hansen."

"Hansen, you say. That's interesting. What was he doing there, was he invited?"

"No, he sort of turned up out of the blue to say farewell," replied Fionn, in her own words.

"Is that so. And what time did he leave?"

Fionn looked at me to answer. She'd not seen Ben leave.

"Around eleven p.m., long before the fire started. I know we'd had a disagreement about a girl he was looking for, but Ben wouldn't have burnt down our bar over it."

Hawkeye scratched away on his note pad.

"Mmmm. What about you Fionn? Did you hear anything around the time the fire started?"

"Not at all. The first we knew about it was when I could smell smoke, drifting into our bedroom."

"What about your telephone? When did you first notice it wasn't working?"

"When I tried to call the fire brigade."

"And before that, did you see anyone else using it?"

"No one last night, but it has been playing up for the last couple of days. We even had a visit from a telephone engineer three days ago to say the line had come down. But it was working again later that day."

"Can you remember which telephone company it was? He didn't leave a card or an invoice?"

"No, I only saw him briefly when he popped his head around the corner of the bar to say he was off and that the line had been reconnected."

Leyda interrupted the questioning. "Fred, don't you think Fionn and Byrney have had enough for one day? They haven't had any sleep since the night before last."

Hawkeye checked his watch, purposefully. "I only have a couple more questions."

"What more is there to say about the fire? They've given you chapter and verse," Leyda argued.

Sergeant Hawkins turned over a new leaf in his note pad and scribbled a new title and drew a line under it. "Actually it's not about the fire; it concerns yesterday's theft at Manners Bank. My opposite number at St. Johns Central has asked me to check with you all regarding the safety deposit box. I understand that all three of you each had a key? That's you Byrney, Mister Walker here and young Raoul Fernandez. Is that correct?"

It was Pug's turn to shuffle uncomfortably in his chair. He raised his hand almost immediately. "I've lost mine," said Pug, stuttering with embarrassment.

"Mmm is that so." Hawkeye looked at Pug for a second, then continued. "My colleague would like to know, what was inside your box? If you can give me a list, I'll pass it on to St. Johns."

I looked at Leyda, hopefully. Should we own up? As far as I was aware it was still a state secret.

"Well now, that should be easy enough," replied Leyda. "There was only one item in it, an old, religious relic."

Hawkeye stopped writing and looked across at everyone in turn. He didn't appear to believe us. "Is that correct?"

We all nodded in agreement. The less we said then the less we'd have to explain.

Hawkeye continued writing up his notes. "Can you describe it? Big, small, what it was made of?"

"It was just an average size cross like you might find in any church. It was a sort of a brassy colour."

"Mmm, nothing else?"

"No," repeated Leyda. "As we've said, that's all there was."

Hawkeye looked anxiously at his watch again and stood up to leave. "Well, thank you. That'll be all for the moment. I'd just like to add how sorry I was when I first heard about the fire at your bar. Everyone I've spoken to has said what a wonderful establishment it was. Rest assured we at Charlestown police station will do our utmost to catch the person or persons responsible."

Leyda touched Hawkeye's arm for a second and asked if there was anything else he could tell her about the theft from the bank. "You see it's an old family heirloom of sorts."

Hawkeye stiffened his back and clasped his briefcase under his arm. "I'm not at liberty to say. The investigation is still on-going."

"Oh come along Fred. You're amongst friends now. Surely you must know the names of the bank's customers who visited the vault yesterday. I know for a fact they keep a register." Leyda winked at me. What was she playing at? We already knew the guy's name was John Arfield, but I guessed there was no harm in playing dumb. Maybe we'd get to know a little bit more. Maybe it would help us to relocate the Potosi cross again. I watched Hawkeye rub his chin as he deliberated over whether to give us any further details.

"Okay," he said. "But you didn't hear this from me. Our chief suspect is an American called John Arfield who visited the bank vault yesterday, just before the bank closed at five p.m."

"Do we know who this Arfield is? Is he dangerous?"

"Mmm, perhaps. He's some sort of Federal agent who's been staying at Padgett House. If it was down to me, I'd have that building demolished. There must be a voodoo curse on it."

I saw Pug roll his eyes at the mention of the word voodoo. Hawkeye had stepped down off the veranda and stood with his shoes submerged in the soft sand. "Try not to worry," he continued. "We have a warrant out for his arrest, together with his accomplice. So far they have evaded our efforts to capture them, but we are almost certain they're still on the island, possibly hiding somewhere near."

I went bright red in the face at Hawkeye's parting comments. I knew exactly where Arfield was, but I couldn't say anything, not even to Leyda or Pug. I looked at Fionn and she was keeping her head low, also. But who was Arfield's accomplice? I had an awful feeling Hawkeye believed it was Ben Hansen.

"Thank you, Fred," said Leyda as a parting farewell. "We'll keep our eye's wide open."

Hawkeye carried on trudging through the sand with large, flat, footsteps. We watched him climb into his Land Rover at the opposite end of White House Bay.

"Well now, what do you make of all that?" Asked Leyda. She was quite a sleuth on the quiet. "A Federal agent, no less. Just the type of person to get away with cold blooded murder."

'How right she was,' I thought. Who knew just how many he'd had a hand in killing, either as John Arfield, or Johann Friedla?

But there was no way he could have stolen our priceless relic. I was a witness to that. At the time of its theft, he was inside Fort Anderson, securely tied to a chair and being closely guarded by Iko and Ilena Romero.

Chapter Thirteen

Synchronicity

To understand the way in which synchronicity can interact with random and unconnected events, one must first be aware of the historical origins of populous migrations, be they individual, or en masse.

Take, for example, two particular individuals and their pathway to a connection with current events, such as those affecting the inhabitants of Cross Green: It can be shown that the circumstances leading to the fire at Amigo's Bar and the murder of Norman Orr were set in motion decades earlier.

In the final days of April 1945 the unthinkable began to dawn on the leaders of the Third Reich, that they were actually going to lose the war in Europe.

From the 25th to the 29th, inside the headquarters of the Gestapo on Prinz-Albrecht Strasse, pandemonium reigned supreme. Its ruthless leaders had already fled, but not before issuing orders that all documentary evidence of their evil must be totally destroyed, including material with the signatures and counter signatures not only of those who held positions in the high echelons of office, but also those of police chiefs, government administrators and foreign officials.

There was a mountain of paperwork: secret files covering the Nazi's experimental work in science and medicine, as well as transportation and extermination orders, death warrants and executions relating to civilians, spies and allied servicemen. Those left to deal with this inedible task, the adjutants, administrators and secretaries were scurrying about like frightened rats in the drowning pool, emptying shelf after shelf, destroying the truth that they were all as guilty as each other, perpetrators and collaborators, in crimes against humanity.

In the final, raging hours of the Battle of Berlin, against a background of advancing artillery fire, each new bombshell brought about an even greater urgency. As the soaring sounds of doom grew louder and ever closer, rocking the foundations and obliterating buildings, just streets away from the Tiergaten, the bureaucratic monster which the Nazis had created was literally choking on it's own words.

With the Russian storm armies beating at the door, Johann Friedla and Felix Schwarzkopf had locked themselves inside one of the empty offices to determine a plan of escape, or at least conjure up a story with which they might hoodwink their advancing captors.

Up until this moment in time they had pursued their military careers with a zealous appetite, neither shying away nor shrinking from any task, no matter how gruesome or cold bloodied their duties had been. They'd washed away the malodorous aura of death many times. And by presenting a clean slate and a clean pair of hands they were hoping their own, youthful faces would lend them an air of innocence. It was now or never if they were to cheat the hangman's noose. Had it been the American army who'd entered the 'arena of despots' first, then perhaps Friedla's and Schwarzkopf's chances of a life after surrender could have been more easily swayed.

Their life journey together began in 1938, at the university of Vienna. It had been a seismic year for the Nazi party. In Austria too, their populist propaganda was gaining momentum leading up to the German annexation of their closest neighbour. It's effects were felt immediately at the university, when all Jewish professors were removed and dismissed without notice. Even Jewish students were barred from classrooms and lectures and at least ninety were murdered. It's impossible to say for sure whether Friedla and Schwarzkopf were directly involved in these skirmishes, but soon afterwards they became willing members of the Nazi party, carried along by racial policies of a so called Aryan supremacy, that a powerful nation could pick and choose to end the lives of an entire race of people if they spoiled and soiled the Nazi vision of the new world order.

In their own way they were both gifted and ambitious. Friedla was the most vocal and intuitive, whilst Schwarzkopf's skills were his pragmatism and foresight. Within a few short months they found themselves rubbing shoulders with the generals and commanders whom they'd set out to impress.

By June 1940 most of the independent sovereign states of mainland Europe had surrendered to the German army. What little resistance they encountered capitulated in a matter of days. The speed of this 'all out victory' had surprised everyone. And now, with theses conquered lands and the populace at their mercy, the Nazi's could put their prophecies into action - a final solution.

With the bulk of its armies heading out to new fronts, it was left to the newly formed death squads to mop up those displaced by the destruction of their towns and villages. In the course of the following eighteen months these Einsatzgruppens were responsible for over half a million deaths. Friedla and Schwarzkopf were leaders of the highly successful group G, which employed thugs and parasites from the very same communities that were being hunted. As a result they were quickly able to identify those selected to die. It was blood thirsty and tiresome work for these machine-gun wielding mobs, moving from one territory to another, travelling deeper into eastern Europe, beyond the Carpathian Mountains and on to the vast plains of Ukraine.

By the end of 1941, when the Nazi's began using concentration camps, the need to kill undesirables by hand and the digging of mass graves became almost superfluous.

Both Friedla and Schwarzkopf were rewarded and decorated for their unwavering determination and as members of the SS they became part of the vast organisation responsible for administering the occupied territories of western Europe.

In November 1942, when the demarcation line, which separated Nazi governed northern France from the free zone in the south was withdrawn, they were posted to the regional capital of Lyon. Here, they ensured that Nazi rule was indisputably upheld. Together, they helped to devise ways of infiltrating the underground movements, winkling out its members, often at the expense of innocent bystanders.

In all, they had done more than their fair share of maintaining the oppressive success of the occupying forces.

And now, as their hour of reckoning was but a hare's breath away, they had only one option available to them - survival at all costs. So when Schwarzkopf announced that they had no choice other than to surrender, they quickly adopted a plan to match their current predicament, one that would lead to the most lenient outcome.

Rifle fire could clearly be heard in the rooms below them on the ground floor, with screams and shouts thrown into the alarming mix.

"Of all the allied armies surrounding us, it had be the Soviets peasants who came knocking first," announced Schwarzkopf as he ducked down behind the desk beneath a shower of shattered plaster, which continued to tumble down from the ornate ceiling. He looked at his friend with grave concern for their safety. "They must never learn the truth of what we did to them..."

"Quick, take off your jacket," replied Friedla, sounding the cooler of the two. "A rank of power will prove to be our undoing. Whatever happens in the next few days we must both stick to the same story: we're only foot soldiers following orders, destroying files of papers. Look, we're both still only twenty- four years old, no one would expect a couple of youths to have committed any crimes. Perhaps one day humanity will congratulate us." Friedla opened one of the desk drawers and quickly stuffed their decorated jackets inside. He tipped a few, loose documents into the paper bin and tossed his identity card inside, then set it ablaze. Schwarzkopf threw his into the flames too.

When the door to their office burst open they faced a Soviet soldier who looked even younger than themselves. His face was frightened, startled and surprised, at having got this far along the chase of kill, or be killed. When the two young Germans raised their arms instantly, the Soviet stood perfectly still, staring at their clean white shirts, which contrasted starkly to the smoke filled dusty room. He aimed his rifle at shoulder height whilst he recovered his breath, waiting for the others to catch up and relieve him of his prisoners. He preferred that someone of higher rank determined whether these two, clean living, German soldiers should live or die.

From the back of the open truck, the stench of Sachsenhausen varnished their nostrils, well before they reached its iron gates. The latest truckload of captives was added to the crowd of hatless and shoeless prisoners inside the wire-fenced compound. Each was waiting their turn to be questioned; the longer they waited the more hungry and cold they became. What little food there was available had already been handed to the walking dead and any confiscated greatcoats were used to cover their dirty rags.

Friedla was still angry at being taken by the Red Army. He realised his prospects, should he survive interrogation, would promise nothing more than a life of misery, confined to a Gulag in some forgotten, frozen wasteland. His only reprieve was to somehow make an escape. Having made a quick assessment, it appeared the only route out was the same as the one they'd entered by. Somehow, he had to get back on board that empty truck and take the place of the driver. His only opportunity came when he was being escorted to and from the interview hut. As Friedla and Schwarzkopf had been captured together they were interviewed at the same time.

Whilst they waited in line, Friedla suggested to his friend that in order to distract their inquisitors, they should admit to being high-ranking members of SiPo, the Nazi security police. It would be easy enough to convince the Soviets that they were the genuine article, having had knowledge and experience of rounding up Jews and resistance leaders in southern France. This would surely lead to a transfer to face a more serious investigation team. When they were led back outside again they made a run for the transport truck, ejecting the driver and steering the vehicle straight through the gates in a hail of rifle fire. The Soviets had been too lackadaisical, believing their

German captives had given up the fight. And, more naïvely, they hadn't placed any value on what useful knowledge their German prisoners might possess.

Friedla and Schwarzkopf headed into the sunset and within one hour, on the north-western side of Berlin, they ran into an American road block, where they surrendered to the guard. The American soldiers were bemused by their enthusiasm and were genuinely surprised they had done so, willingly, even commandeering a Soviet truck to assist them.

In the days that followed, the more they talked, the higher up the inquisitee ladder they climbed, until eventually they were brought before Captain Edwin Erstgaard, at McNair Barracks in West Berlin. He was a shrewd judge of character and an innovative maverick in the Army Intelligence Corps. With the German surrender now a formality, he'd been hurriedly flown into Germany with the specific directive to seek out 'performer' Nazis. Men and women who fulfilled roles on his shopping list: rocket scientists at the top, down to administrators who had access to secret files. Friedla and Schwarzkopf fell somewhere in between and although there was nothing that linked them to a specific role which he'd been asked to find, Erstgaard recognised that they were persons of special interest.

They were sent to the nearby Wilhelmina Hotel and housed in separate rooms on the sixth floor, which had been the former servants quarters; as such there was no lift access. This meant the American military police only had to guard the end of the corridor at the top of the dusty, narrow staircase. But Erstgaard knew darn well that Friedla and Schwarzkopf had no intention of escaping.

Two days later they were interviewed, by two unnamed men from the C.I.A, who made extensive notes. Nothing in their military careers was left out, from their university days through to the death squads, details of their torture techniques on the French resistance, suppression, psychological warfare, the works.

On the eighth of May 1945, at the conclusion of their interviews and following the German unconditional surrender,

Friedla and Schwarzkopf were sent back to McNair Barracks and imprisoned at the American military base, without trial. They remained incarcerated until their release in 1951.

Just prior to their release, they were seen again by Captain Edwin Erstgaard. The three men hardly recognised each other. Both Friedla and Schwarzkopf had lost a considerable amount of weight, whereas Erstgaard had grown a bay window around his waist. The American officer had an offer of employment for the two Germans to either, 'come and work for the intelligence services in America, or be sent to Russia as part of an exchange deal'. The American foreign office had drawn up plans for an operation across Latin America to counter the influence of communism, which had already taken up a foothold in several neighbouring countries. It was a no-brainer for Friedla and Schwarzkopf to begin working for a new master, especially one as powerful as the United States of America.

Johann Friedla was trained for active fieldwork as an agent in the CIA and at his own request he was given the new identity of John Arfield. Felix Schwarzkopf slipped into an administration role, organising and processing data on potential targets and helping to create an effective strategy for overseas operations. Their first target was just a few months away: the ousting of the democratically voted in president of San Albarra, in 1952. This was just the beginning of covert operations, sanctioned by Washington, to ensure that any Latin American country within striking distance of a task force represented a bias towards North American businesses and North American ideals.

During their time with the company, the CIA was backed by a succession of Republican presidents into the late Nineteen-Sixties and through until 1976. The intelligence community had financial backing and the armed resources to protect the borders of America from any Soviet threat, be it real or imagined or even presented to the government to appear threatening. In their neighbouring countries alone, there was an abundance of natural resources just waiting to be tapped into. And a purported Soviet threat was a proven tactic to win over the

United States Congress, which allowed America to take home a bigger slice of the pie.

Then came the Carter administration. American foreign policy had never looked so weak and ill organised. The final nail in the democratic government's coffin came in November 1979 when fifty two American workers were held hostage at the US embassy in Tehran. And so far, all diplomatic attempts to free them had failed.

Arfield hated being idle as much as he hated having to curtail his plans to influence events further into South America. At the start of the election year of 1980, he realised he had a chance to make America a world leader and a world-beater once more. He had formed a professional friendship with the Republican candidate. If he could guarantee him the top seat at the White House, in return he'd be handed the mandate to crush the growth of communism, which was practically perched on their own doorstep. Arfield understood it to be a gentlemen's agreement; I get you elected and you give me a free hand. In doing so, Arfield had by-passed the elitist military powerhouse at the Pentagon.

Immediately after the presidential campaign meeting to discuss the Ilena Romero crisis, in Santa Barbara on 1st February 1980, Schwarzkopf returned to his home in Oak View to find a black Lincoln limousine waiting for him. He was handed a written subpoena to attend a meeting at Fort Jeremy in Arizona. Before he knew what was happening, he was hauled into the back of the car and driven out to the desert; it was not so much a subpoena in a judicial sense, but more like a rendition. There was not an explanation, nor a word spoken, by any of the occupants during the five-hour journey. He arrived in the hours of darkness and was placed in a single occupancy cell.

At six a.m the following morning, he was handed a breakfast tray and was told he had thirty minutes to make himself ready for an interview. After eggs and bacon, coffee and a juice, Schwarzkopf freshened up his face by the sink and patted down his suit jacket. He'd had ample time to turn over recent events in his mind, but as yet he was still none the wiser as to what questions he faced. Whatever it was, someone had gone to a lot of trouble to grab him from outside his home.

At the precise, given time he was escorted down a long and winding, dimly lit corridor to the rhythm of marching feet until he eventually came up against a solid looking fire exit. His escort reached across him and slammed down on the bar, unlocking the door and giving Schwarzkopf an encouraging nudge from behind. If was as if he'd just been delivered through the gut of the building and out through it's arsehole into a brightly lit, porcelain white room. Before him, in the centre of the room, he saw an empty, folding, wooden chair. In front of the chair, about ten feet away, stood a long console table and behind this sat a panel of seven, high ranking, military figures. Their uniform jackets were ten per cent material and ninety per cent medal ribbons. The differing colours denoted the service to which they represented: white for the Navy, blue for the Air Force and green for the Army. The power which these men wielded was so strong Schwarzkopf could almost smell the cordite on their breath.

"Thank you for choosing to join us, today," commenced the olive green one at the centre of the seven. "We're sorry to drag you away from your family on a Saturday. Please extend our apologies to Isabelle and the two boys, what are their names?" The army General glanced down at his notes. "Ah yes, Ryan and Carl." The General took off his reading glasses, looked up again at the interviewee and came straight to the point. "We're picking up some disconcerting news relating to the presidential election and we'd like to hear your take on things?" The General looked directly at Schwarzkopf as he spoke until the final words of his sentence, when he turned his head right then left to indicate those beside him would also like to hear what was about to be said.

Felix raised his eyebrows as if to say, 'is that all?' "What exactly would you like to know?"

"Specifically, what Arfield intends to do about this rogue reporter, Miss Ilena Romero? We're aware she's in possession of some photos, appertaining to the arson attack on the Spanish embassy in San Albarra. We believe them to be of a toxic nature." The General nodded to affirm it was the view of his fellow panellists.

"John's hired a PI called Ben Hansen to locate the girl."

The General made a note of the name whilst Schwarzkopf carried on speaking. "We believe that she's in hiding on the Caribbean island of Antigua. That's as for as we've got."

The General looked a little disappointed at what he'd just heard. "Well, that sounds like you're being somewhat economical with the truth. We're fully conversant with Arfield's personnel file and it's not in his nature to take a back seat. In fact, it wouldn't surprise us if he flew out to Antigua himself. What have you got to say about that?"

Schwarzkopf had the feeling these Chiefs of Staff no longer regarded Arfield as being part of their team. Up until now he'd always been loyal to his friend and colleague, but the seriousness of his current situation was beginning to make him question whether he shouldn't be putting himself first. The truth was he'd no idea John intended to fly down to Antigua and he said as much to the men in front of him.

"We're glad to hear that, because we're of the opinion that Arfield intends to kill the reporter and we just can't afford that kind of scandal at this delicate stage." The General loosened his tie and began to relax his tone. "Look Felix, we like how you're handling the presidential campaign. Your IOD thing, what's that again?" The admiral seated to his right supplied the answer, "idea of the day."

"Yeah, right," continued the General. "We think you can put our man in the hot seat. We like what you're doing with the campaign strategy, such as the catchphrases you've put out, like, "Is America better off now than it was four years ago?" And we especially like the way you're handling the TV and media with the buzzwords, "Let's make America great again." The General paused again to look at the men seated either side of him who all nodded in agreement, then he turned to face Schwarzkopf once more. "And on a personal note you've integrated really well into the American way of life. Married to

Isabelle for twenty-eight years and both your boys are enrolled at universities. So, as of now, we'd like you to take over as campaign director. It was a straightforward choice that we have all agreed on. The time has come for Arfield to be put out to grass."

The General's last sentence was like an alarm bell to Schwarzkopf. Put out to grass, or did he mean put him six feet under the grass?

"Just leave the rest to us, Felix. We have one of our Dustcoats lined up to join up with Arfield should he step out of the country. We'll contact you if and when that happens and give you our operative's details. We just need to keep a tight lid on compulsive individuals like Arfield until our man's elected. Then, after the inauguration, we can give the good people of America the kind of protection they need and deserve. That's all for now Felix. We'll be in touch."

The side-door was opened by a sharp-suited agent. Schwarzkopf recognised him as one of the men who'd picked him up yesterday. Felix rose to his feet and headed towards the exit, but before he reached the door the General had one last thing to say to him.

"This arrangement is strictly between you and the men in this room. If Arfield contacts you, just play him along. And remember, we'll be listening too."

When Schwarzkopf left the room the General turned to his colleagues and sought their appraisal of the meeting. The overall consensus was that they now had the situation totally under control. "Right then gentlemen," announced the General with an air of expectation, "It's time to bring Bob Fagg into the room."

'There are no such things as coincidences.' It was one of the maxims that Ben Hansen always believed in, especially in his line of work. Usually, bad man did bad things and hopefully, in the end, they got their just desserts. This was proved to be the case, when he learnt of John Arfield's demise.

Chapter Fourteen

The Fagg End

Bob Fagg had a natural flair for picking the pockets of any given situation. Had he been in the film 'The Great Escape' he would undoubtedly have slipped neatly into the part of 'The Scrounger' - the James Garner role. Not that Fagg could have passed for a Hollywood heartthrob. His pock marked facial skin and this, together with being slightly goofy in the dental department, wouldn't have left much of an impression at a screen test with any of the top studios. But, given the chance, he could easily have made a living with his acting skills. Looks apart, he had the uncanny knack of coming and going largely unseen and easily dismissed. He had a habit too, of entering a room quietly and on the occasion of meeting up with Arfield at his office in Sunnydale, he was able to stand right behind his boss, completely undetected, thus allowing him to make a mental note of the combination lock of Arfield's diplomatic pouch.

Before setting foot in Arfield's office, Fagg had received a head start from General Lubbock at Fort Jeremy. He'd been given details of the best-case scenario regarding the photographs and the likely outcome for pensioning off Arfield's services. In addition to this, a day earlier, he'd had ample time to read the full dossier on Miss Romero, prior to handing over her file to Hansen at Phoenix Sky Harbour airport.

Fagg possessed a larger than average mental capacity and already he was departmentalising the different aspects of his mission. So far there were only three people who would be involved directly: himself, Arfield and Ben Hansen and of the three, Fagg was the only one withholding knowledge of all the facts.

Once in Antigua, Fagg wasted no time in locating the necessary back up resources at the Undersea Sound Surveillance Station and a productive, fifteen-minute chat with Frank Schaeffer laid down the foundations for any support and favours he might need.

Then, just twelve hours after arriving at Padgett House, in the early light of dawn, Fagg was able to seal Arfield's fate with the opportunity of framing him for the murder of the nut-job from the museum, Norman Orr. Fagg had first heard raised voices coming from the direction of the kitchen. He quickly unlocked Arfield's diplomatic bag and took out Arfield's pistol. When he saw Orr pointing the flintlock at Arfield, he made no mistake, shooting Orr in the back of the head from a little more than six feet. It made Fagg's plan much easier to manage with only one body to dispose of, rather than two, which would have been the case had Orr killed Arfield first.

Leaving Arfield to clean up the mess, Fagg took Orr's body and dumped it just far enough away from Arfield, but close enough to implicate him. He was more than satisfied with how things were progressing. When he rolled Orr's body into the ditch, he heard the distinctive rattle of a set of keys. There was ample time for a small diversion, he thought as he removed the keys and headed over to the dockyard museum. Fagg always enjoyed the breaking and entering side of his activities; only this time there was no need to break down any doors. He slid Orr's key into the lock and moved quickly inside the gallery, scanning the contents of the museum for any items of high value. The museum pieces, he deemed, weren't worth the trouble. Moving swiftly on, he soon located Orr's quarters on the top floor and ransacked every drawer, nook and cranny; there was nothing to be had. Realising he only had a short window of opportunity to work with, until Orr's body was discovered, he quit his search, locked the museum door and returned the keys once again to Orr.

Fagg's turn of fortune came later that morning, when the American private detective, Ben Hansen, arrived at Padgett House, to update Arfield with his verbal report. He stood on the balcony directly above Arfield and Hansen, to eavesdrop on their conversation. He heard Hanson mention that Miss Romero had been staying at Amigo's bar and that from evidence he'd found in Byrne's and Miss Terry's personal effects Hansen had learned that they were in possession of a very valuable prize indeed, one that had paid for the purchase of their bar, according to the documents Hansen had seen. Not only that, theirs was only a third share. The other two thirds belonged to a Raoul Fernandez and a James Walker. And whatever this mystery object was, it was currently being stored at Manners Bank in St. Johns. Having learnt of its existence and location, Fagg's focus of attention was now firmly fixed on getting his hands on it.

Returning to the Undersea Sound Surveillance station, Fagg requested a tap be installed on the phone at Amigo's bar. This would be invaluable for picking up further clues and putting together a time-plan for fine-tuning his activities. When Fagg replayed the first tape recordings, he hadn't reckoned on discovering enemy intelligence, that there was also a Soviet agent staying close by and that Orr had been his handler.

Whilst in St. Johns, Fagg's latest scheme had required him to obtain a safety deposit box of his own at Manners Bank. In so doing, he created an additional false implication by using Arfield's passport instead. Fagg had nabbed it from Arfield's bedroom, after noticing that the back and white photo on the first page showed Arfield as a much younger man with dark hair. Fagg calculated that if the bank clerk didn't look too closely at it, he'd probably get away with it.

Once inside the vault, Fagg planned to create a diversion to allow him to take a quick impression of the bank's safety deposit box key. However, this goal was achieved before he'd even left the front desk. Whilst he was filling out the application forms, the young bank clerk had unintentionally left his key on his side of the counter whilst he went to retrieve the register. In the thirty seconds that the clerk was absent from his desk, Fagg took out his tin of polymer clay and expertly pressed the key down on both faces to produce two, perfect impressions. All Fagg required now was a copy of Byrne's key. Then, on his next visit to the bank vault and on the pretence of opening up his own safety deposit box, he could take a peek inside Byrne's and discover what the valuable item amounted to.

Fagg's first attempt to obtain a key to Byrne's deposit box was made at the Barracuda dive shop where young Fernandez worked, but this proved to be a dead end as the lad was currently in Barbuda. But a further chance came the following morning, when he stayed behind at Padgett House whilst Arfield went to stake out Amigo's. From out of his bedroom window, Fagg observed a local man at work in the garden. Parked close to him was a homemade dogcart, which carried his tools and equipment. On the side of the cart was the printed name - James Walker.

'How many James Walker's could there be around this deserted part of the island?' He thought to himself.

Fagg struck up a difficult conversation with the quiet man, who was obviously more intent on carrying out his work, rather than talk to strangers. Once Fagg discovered that Byrne was a friend of the gardener's, Fagg supposed that this must indeed be one of the three shareholders to the fortune, which lay inside Manners Bank.

When Pugg turned away, Fagg struck him about the head and body several times with the flat end of his spade and when he lay, unconscious and bleeding Fagg worked his way through the big man's pockets, until he found what he was looking for.

On Fagg's next visit to Schaeffer's office, later that afternoon, he discovered more incredulous facts from the latest tape recording on Byrne's telephone. The conversation between Iko and his English speaking contact in Grenada had revealed Arfield's true identity and that they planned to kidnap him. Fagg at first thought it too incredulous to be true, that the man he'd known for the last twenty-five years, as John Arfield was actually a former Nazi, named Johann Friedla. And then he sniggered at the obvious connection between the two names; the surnames were anagrams of each other. Arfield's destiny had now changed and he knew he had to bring his own plans forward. He figured all that was required were a few minor adjustments, but to cover his own back he needed to inform

'The General' at Fort Jeremy. Assuming that Arfield would be taken alive, they decided together that if a rescue operation wasn't feasible then Arfield must be silenced and no leaf must be left unturned to ensure the films were also destroyed.

Immediately after organising a rescue mission with Schaeffer and after obtaining a duplicate copy of the bank's safety deposit box key, Fagg headed straight over there, arriving just before closing time. When Fagg was left alone to open the box in Arfield's name, he instead located the box belonging to Byrne and Co. He inserted both keys, the one belonging to the unfortunate James Walker and the bank duplicate that he'd had made. Both keys turned smoothly, without the slightest resistance, as if they were floating on air. When Fagg withdrew the box and looked inside he was completely blown away. Never in his wildest dreams had he encountered nor imagined a relic of such rich reward. He placed it quickly inside the green leather bag and headed back to Padgett House, to clear out the rest of his belongings.

Around nine p.m., he was strategically hidden to observe the coming and goings outside Amigo's bar. He had one eye on the time and one eye on Hansen, who was stood talking to Byrne at the side of the building. Fagg was cutting it fine for time if he was to make his next appointment - his final visit to the Undersea Sound Surveillance station and the boat journey to rescue Arfield. But he knew he must take care of the films first. If they were still inside the bar then, as ordered, he would leave nothing to chance.

Just after midnight, he crept around the back of the bar, located the outside telephone wire and cut it with his pocket-knife. Then he emptied a can of petrol over the side door, dowsing it thoroughly before setting it alight. If the films were hidden somewhere inside, it was only a matter of time before they went up in flames. Fagg had calculated the films could only be in one of three places and he'd taken precautions to cover them all. If Byrne had them they'd soon be turned to ash, if Miss Romero had them, then he'd catch up with her later and if they'd already been sent in the post, he'd already advised the General to intercept all mail from Antigua destined for the

Washington and district sorting office. Finally, any letter, specifically addressed to The Herald and Chronicle, should be opened up by one of his local agents.

Fagg had run out of excuses when he eventually faced Shaeffer and the crew of the Aquarius. He decided to play it straight from 'here on in', especially in their strict company. The last remaining detail of his mission was to find and rescue Arfield.

When the Aquarius caught up with the tiny fishing boat and tied alongside, Fagg began to sense a moment of victory. Apart from feeling slightly green behind the gills, he had total command of the situation and was fully prepared for dealing with the twitchy reception he was likely to encounter from Iko Kaloode and Ilena Romero. The Aquarius towered over the narrow deck of the El Alca. His only nervous moment came when he followed Lieutenant Ritchie down the flimsy rope ladder. Fagg was eager to get this show over and done with. He had a lingering picture of the jewelled cross shining brightly in his mind's eye. Ever since he'd clapped eyes on the dazzling treasure, it had completely taken over Fagg's endgame.

When he saw Iko and Ilena standing in front of him he wasted no time in making their acquaintance, although he was conscious of not referring to Eldridge Delgado as a Soviet agent, or by his real name. The least Lieutenant Ritchie knew of their true identities, the quicker they could all return to their own destinations. But he couldn't help feeling a thrill of conquest at having finally met up with Ilena Romero. He, of course, asked her if she had her films about her person and when she gave her reply he half believed she was telling the truth, but he had to frisk her carefully to be doubly sure. He smiled to himself, with the knowledge that the films would soon be intercepted and prevented from making the wrong headlines, if they hadn't already been burnt to a crisp in the inferno of Amigo's bar.

Luis, Iko and Ilena's resistance was no match for the threatening behaviour of a trained assassin. Once inside the forward cabin, Fagg had no intention of rescuing Arfield. He was prepared to execute him on the spot. That was until Arfield began mouthing off. Fagg had taken all the verbal shit he could take from this arrogant, Nazi criminal. He took great delight in despatching Arfield onward, to continue his journey into the welcoming arms of the communists, the very people Arfield despised the most. Once in Cuban hands, it wouldn't be long before the Russians learnt of his capture. No statute of limitations would prevent the Soviets from exacting their revenge.

Back onboard the Aquarius Fagg felt the fatigue of the day's events catching up with him. When Captain Lowry turned in for the night, Fagg headed down to his own cabin too, but before turning out the light he couldn't resist looking inside the diplomatic pouch, for another glimpse of the numerous gemstones, which covered the golden cross.

When dawn broke, Fagg looked out of his porthole to find the Aquarius stationary in the water. He saw the flat surface of sea turn cloudy and sand colour as the Aquarius turned up the force on its bow thrusters. In his half awakened state, he was suddenly struck by the awful feeling that the ship was marooned on a sand bank. He dashed out to the open deck where his anxieties were put to rest; the Aquarius was making a reversing manoeuvre into it's berth at the US naval dry dock. It had arrived bang on schedule.

Fagg declined breakfast in the ship's galley and instead gathered his bags and belongings and walked ashore. There was no point in allowing the ship's hospitality to hinder his return home. Once clear of the military port, he climbed into a waiting taxi and headed straight for Luis Muñoz Marín International Airport. There was a flight to Los Angeles departing at ten-thirty a.m., which gave him ample time to clear customs and relax, in one of the bars inside the departure lounge.

Inside the busy, stuffy airport Fagg proceeded through the various check points, hassle free. The green leather diplomatic bag that he clung to seemed to bring him the same courtesy as a VIP ticket. It never left his side, nor did anyone enquire as to its contents. The Puerto Ricans certainly knew which side their bread was buttered on and especially so in the presence of what they believed to be an American ambassador. So far, Fagg's illicit bit of smuggling was going very smoothly.

He stared out of the first floor lounge bar window at the taxiing aircraft. He had a table to himself, just as he preferred. He'd just finished his eggs and bacon and was about to down the last dregs of his Schlitz beer when he turned to face a growing commotion at the entrance to the departure lounge. A group of six nuns in their black habits were being ushered through the busy crowd of jet setters. A path was carved out for them through a chaotic obstruction of random luggage, duty free carrier bags and lounging backpackers like the parting of the Red Sea, allowing the saintly creatures to shuffle past. 'Heaven forbid if one of them should trip up,' thought Fagg. Unconsciously, he'd been captivated by their serenity and perhaps it was this conveyed feeling of guilt that had blindsided him from seeing an approaching American citizen. It wasn't until the tall, lean figure was just a few feet away that he recognised his face. 'Bloody hell, it's Ben Hansen,' screamed a voice inside Fagg's head.

Hansen held out his hand. "I thought it was you, Bob Fagg, am I right?" From the first moment he'd spotted Fagg, sitting eating his breakfast, he had decided to play a coy hand. "What are you doing here in Puerto Rico? The last time I saw you was back in Phoenix."

Fagg stood up to shake Hansen's hand then invited him to sit at one of the three, empty, blue Dralon seats, which Fagg had commandeered for his luggage. The green leather bag immediately caught Hansen's attention, but it was tightly locked and sealed, of course. "Another messenger drop is it?" commented Ben, acknowledging Fagg's diplomatic pouch.

"I've learnt not to ask questions," replied Fagg, abruptly. "It was handed to me in Antigua; that's all I know about it."

Hansen wasn't going to give up that easily. "You're a lucky man, Bob. I'm sure you're aware that I've just left Antigua too, but I'll bet you didn't know there was a warrant out for your arrest." Ben allowed himself a smile. He'd already alerted one of the airport security guards and as he rose to his feet, he waved his arm in the air and two armed guards came rushing forward. They firmly seized Fagg's arms, twisting them, painfully, behind his back.

"Señor Fagg, you're under arrest."

Fagg tried to struggle free and faced up to the guard, angrily. "On what charge?"

It was Hansen who supplied the answer. "Aiding and abetting the murder of Norman Orr."

Whilst he was led away to the main security office, Hansen and the second guard gathered Fagg's belongings. Hansen made sure he carried the diplomatic pouch, which was surprisingly heavy. It obviously contained more than just paperwork.

"You're making the biggest mistake of your career, Hansen," growled Fagg as he was frog-marched ahead.

Inside the office, the waiting security chief emptied Fagg's pockets. His passport was inspected and scrutinised. The photo matched, the date of birth: 13th September 1932; it looked genuine too. Next to the line for occupation it simply stated, 'Government Service'. Fagg had calmed down considerably. He was confident that it would only take one phone call before he'd be free to continue his journey.

The security chief picked up Fagg's wallet. But, before he opened it, Hansen's impatience got the better of him and he called for the security chief to open up the diplomatic bag.

"I'm sorry; we're not allowed to do that Mister Hansen. It's against international law and Mr Fagg here is an American citizen. You must understand, we have to play by their rules."

It was Fagg's turn to smile. "That's right, open up my wallet and have a good look."

The silver shield of Fagg's CIA badge had the desired effect; the security chief's eyes lit up with blind surprise and a tint of fear. Fagg's manner now grew as cocky as the US bald eagle, which stared back at the Puerto Rican official. He could see that the security chief suddenly felt out of his depth.

"I suggest you call my boss, right away. His number is inside the right hand flap. And it's General Calvin Lubbock, of Fort Jeremy, just so that you know who you're speaking to."

When the security chief left the room, Fagg turned to Hansen, confident of his imminent release. "Nice try Hansen. Has no one ever told you, it's not what you know, it's who you know?"

Ben could feel his blood boiling. Right now, there was not a more distasteful sight than the smug son-of-a-bitch in front of him. "I thought John Arfield was your boss?"

"Ha! Arfield, that two-faced bigot! He's a dead man. You've been had Hansen. You've been working for the losing team all along. If you want to join the winning side, maybe I could put in a good word for you."

Just then, the door to the security office opened as the airport security chief returned. He handed Fagg his wallet and passport and ordered his deputy to uncuff him. "Please accept our apologies Señor Fagg. We're sorry to have delayed you. You're now free to leave."

Fagg grabbed his belongings and bundled his way out of the door. Hansen looked on in disbelief. Fagg had been proved right about one thing, about being favoured by powerful friends. But, Ben wouldn't be joining what Fagg referred to as the winning team anytime soon. There was no place for murder and corruption in Ben's work ethic. If that's what you have to do to keep one step ahead of your adversaries, then looking for a alternative way was long overdue. Maybe Ben was a dreamer, but his way would have been for America and her enemies to gather around a negotiating table with the aim of reaching a compromise that suited everyone. But getting these powerful forces to come together with one truthful aim in mind, in today's world, was still the stuff of dreams. John Lennon had written a most incredibly moving song with that one theme in mind and yet, five years on, the world was still no closer to a global solution. Perhaps it never would be.

As Hansen stepped towards the office door the security chief blocked his path. "I'm sorry Señor Hansen, but we have to insist on you catching a later flight back to California. Señor Fagg must be allowed to leave first."

Chapter Fifteen

Every Cloud

On our first night sleeping in Leyda's spare room we were both dead to the world, not waking until noon the next day. The other rooms, spaced within the ground floor, were all devoid of chatter. No doubt Leyda was at her place of work, at the university library in St. Johns. And Pug, either he was skulking about in the garden or maybe he'd gone back to his own digs. As I lay there, my thoughts were drawn to last night's visit from Police Sergeant 'Hawkeye' Hawkins. There was some casual remark he'd made which had me puzzled and for the life of me I couldn't recall what it was. However, right now my appetite was telling me to get out of bed and look for some food.

On finding we had the house to ourselves we decided to take breakfast out on Leyda's terrace. We both sat facing the empty, narrow bay. The sea glistened in the bright sunlight, which shone down directly above our heads. Its intense warmth cheered our moods as we crunched on our toast and slurped black coffee.

"That's it." I said out loud.

"What is?" replied Fionn as she brushed away a few crumbs from her bare knees.

"The thing that's been bugging me since we woke, Arfield's accomplice. Do you think Hawkeye's referring to Ben?" I said, looking at Fionn for an answer.

"Who else could it be?" she replied with a puzzled look. I must admit I was struggling to think of anyone else. One thing's for sure, if it wasn't Arfield who set fire to our bar, then it must have been his accomplice. Perhaps it had been Ben after all.

Fionn had other more pressing issues on her mind. The night before, Leyda had kindly offered to let us stay with her for as long as we wanted. But Fionn didn't feel comfortable taking advantage of her generosity. "I simply think we shouldn't be a burden to her when we've no means to repay her."

"I know, I feel the same, but it's like Leyda says, something always comes along. I reckon we could both find temporary work," I suggested, trying to maintain a positive outlook on our dilemma.

"Yes, but where are we going to live in the meantime?"

I hutched up my chair next to her, put my arm around Fionn's shoulder and rested our heads together. It was going to be a long, hard slog before we were back on our feet again, financially speaking.

"Let's just enjoy this peace and quiet for a minute," I said softly.

Before long, we noticed Leyda herself, striding purposefully across the dry, white sand. She carried a woven wicker basket on her arm and knowing how talented Leyda was, she could have probably balanced it on her head without spilling any of the contents. She waved and smiled happily. She was pleased that we'd helped ourselves to food and were treating her home like our own.

"I have some good news for you two," she said teasingly. "I've spoken to Gilbert Chivers, the chairman of Manners Bank and he's assured me you won't have to pay for the damage to Amigo's bar."

"So what exactly is he saying? I tell yer, we should all be suing him for allowing our cross to get nicked."

Leyda pulled up a chair next to mine and gave me a look of dismay. "Calm down, Byrney. You have to see things from their side too. We all know that in its present condition the property at Amigo's is worthless, but, since you and Fionn bought it, in the last two years the price of land has risen dramatically, especially vacant land with a sea front view."

"Okay. But that still leaves the money we owe the bank for the initial purchase of Amigo's. We can't possibly afford to pay it back, we're practically skint."

"Oh this is awful," commented Fionn.

"Not quite," replied Leyda. "The value of the plot of land which Amigo's sits on is worth slightly more than you owe. Gilbert has agreed to take back the land in exchange for writing off your loan."

"Well I guess that's okay," replied Fionn, carrying the banner for our cause. "But we still won't be able to support ourselves."

"Well you're both fine here for the moment. I'm sure new opportunities will present themselves soon enough."

"Thanks for explaining it all to us Leyda. I've been worrying myself silly about it."

Leyda placed her hand on Fionn's arm and said calmly. "The worst is over now, darling. You can look to the future again and plan what you'd both like to do next. But really, there's no rush. You both need to give yourselves a little time to recover from the shock and the stress of your recent misfortunes."

Leyda disappeared inside mumbling about how all this talk makes one thirsty. I heard the spirit bottles rattle together as she opened up her booze cabinet. "I think she's gone to get some drinks," I said cheerily to the sad looking girl next to me.

"Byrney, I know it's really lovely of Leyda wanting to look after us, but we can't stay here indefinitely. I just feel so miserable. I've been thinking of asking Leyda to lend me the money to fly back home. I can't see any other way out. We'd such a lovely life here. Even all the hard work seemed worthwhile."

"Well we were brought up on it," I said, muscling in on her thoughts. "Working at the Friary in Crowston after school, Madge and Joanie taught us not to be afraid of getting stuck in. Mind you, they did run us all around ragged." This fond memory brought a smile to Fionn's face. "That's more like it. Let's see what happens over the next couple of days and take it from there. I don't know about you, but I feel like we've been dragged through a mangle in the last seven days."

The day started well for Ben Hansen. He'd had a long journey the previous day, with numerous delays. Eventually, having driven the final leg of his journey straight from the airport, he reached the sanctuary of his home in the Huntington Park area of Los Angeles, just before midnight. All that travelling, cooped up inside an aeroplane or sat in an airport departure lounge, had given him ample time to consider his future and whether to go back to his old job at the DEA. When he'd last spoken to his former boss, Bill Chadwick, he'd made it perfectly clear that Ben would be welcome to return. And more than that he'd actually made Ben's old job sound exciting. Modernisation was going to be central to a lot of changes. Rather than sit at home waiting for the phone to ring, Ben knew he had at least to give the DEA a try, once again.

And so, the very next morning, he took a cab down to the Parker Centre at 150 North Los Angeles Street, which was also the home of the Los Angeles Police Department. The DEA had offices on the third floor and when Ben walked in, he received an unexpected round of applause from his former colleagues and a firm, welcoming handshake from Bill.

"There's a spare office, next to mine, with your name over the door," he said invitingly. "Well, the name plate can be added later. Why don't you try it out for size, Ben?"

The office suited Ben down to the ground. He had a good view of the shop floor; Bill's Office was to his left and his old buddy Mike Dooley's was the next one down to his right. The view away from the rear of the building was long and uninterrupted. It was a clear, sunny day and he could see the floodlight towers sticking out above the Dodgers Stadium. The bright sunshine flooding into his office also sent his thoughts racing back across to the Caribbean. He glanced down at his watch and calculated that if it was nine-thirty a.m. here, then it was twelve-thirty midday in Antigua. He picked up his phone, listened for the ring tone then dialled up an outside line.

Over at Charlestown, the phone rang inside the police station. PC Throup lifted the receiver and was genuinely surprised to hear Ben Hansen's loud voice at the other end of the line, calling from California.

"Is Fred with you?" inquired Ben.

Throup looked across at the empty seat behind his boss's desk. "Sorry Ben, but he's not here right now. He mentioned something about acting on impulse, said he had a sudden urge to buy a bunch of roses and take them round to Marcia's house. He's been behaving very strangely these past few days. I don't know what's come over him."

Ben smiled to himself. He knew exactly what Hawkeye's motivations were about. "Have you ever been in love, Clarence?"

"I don't think so."

"Well you'll know all about it when it happens, believe me." Ben lifted the phone from his desk and carried it over to the rear window. "Listen up Clarence, I've some new information for you, regarding your two suspects for the Orr Murder."

"Okay, give me the details and I'll pass them on to Sarge. Oh and by the way it's not just a murder. There's also a case of arson to answer to as well."

"Arson?" replied Ben with surprise.

"Yes, Amigo's bar was burnt to the ground two nights ago."

This latest piece of news caught Ben by surprise until he recalled seeing the dark stain, on the ground near the marina at Cross Green, when he'd flown over it on his way to Puerto Rico, yesterday morning. So it was Byrney and Fionn's place after all. "Oh that's a shame. Are they both okay?"

"There were no casualties. Luckily, everybody was able to evacuate the building before the fire destroyed everything."

"That's a blessing. Well, next time you see either of them, please pass on my commiserations and tell them that if they need any help or anything to give me a call."

"Of course Ben. So what's this new information you have for us?"

Ben reported what had occurred at the airport when he'd confronted Fagg and how he'd suddenly become immune from prosecution. Ben went on to explain further that Fagg had hinted that Arfield was now dead. "He didn't elaborate as to what he meant by that, but I've no reason to disbelieve him."

"I've written everything down," replied Throup. "So, it doesn't look as though there's anything more we can do," he added, almost as an afterthought.

"I'm afraid so. I'll send you my signed statement in a day or two, so that you can add it to the file. But as far as I can see, it looks like you'll have to close Orr's murder as case unsolved."

The conversation ended with Ben wishing PC Throup the best of luck. He knew that Clarence would do alright for himself as a detective. And on top of that, Ben had made a true friend. The feeling was mutual.

On the same morning, at ten-thirty a.m. Mountain Standard time, Bob Fagg opened his eyes and found himself staring at a half full bottle of Schlitz beer. It was the remnant of a long journey back to his upmarket home in the Arcadia district of Phoenix. His home telephone had been ringing upon his arrival, even before he'd inserted his front door key into the lock. General Lubbock's secretary had been calling his number for the past two hours. When Fagg picked up, the call was transferred to General Lubbock, who was keen to learn the outcome of his mission. Fagg spoke very briefly. He was practically dead on his feet, having hardly slept a wink for the past forty-eight hours. He'd not slept at all on the USS Aquarius. It had been too noisy and too bumpy. Then he was far too preoccupied, keeping an eye on his diplomatic bag at all times, to have nodded off on his flight. So when the General asked Fagg if he had dispatched John Arfield, Fagg was able to answer in the affirmative, without hesitation or word of a lie. However, he let the General believe Arfield had been dispatched to his death rather than dispatched to Cuba. Fagg, of course, remembered the General's gratitude and his parting words - 'there'll be a cheque in the post'.

As the daylight filtered into his bedroom, Fagg slid across the edge of his bed and rubbed his head. He enjoyed listening to the silence of his quiet neighbourhood on the northern fringes of Phoenix. Nestled between forty-fourth and sixty-eighth streets, he could come and go as he pleased without having to explain himself to his neighbours. And as he lived completely alone, he'd the freedom to leave at the drop of a hat and not return for weeks, sometimes months at a time.

His bedroom was on the ground floor, to compensate for the fact that daytime temperatures often reached forty degrees Celsius. Life would be unbearable without air conditioning and there was a unit in each of the main rooms. One end of the room he slept in also served as his office. He was a gadget freak. He'd the very latest IBM computer, which was also wired up to his home security system. He checked the multi-screen monitor for peace of mind and when he was satisfied all was well, he climbed the stairs to his lounge. The first floor rooms at the top of the house were stuffy, having been sealed shut for six days, so he walked over to the balcony doors, opened them fully and stepped out into the warm, morning sunshine. He never grew tired of the familiar view northwards: the dark outline of Camelback Mountain and the surrounding air so clear and still and laced with the aroma of citrus trees.

Inside the modern, furnished living room, everything had its tried and tested resting place. The glass and chrome made a pleasing contrast with the elegant, black leather upholstery and the wooden teak frames of his sofa and chairs. The shelves and cabinet surfaces were devoid of any womanly touch. They were bare of any ornaments and there were no famed photographs of family and friends; he didn't have any. The only portrait to occupy a dedicated space on the wall was an oversized, framed photographic print of the Apollo Eleven launch, taken at the moment of ignition. It was a powerful image, one that Fagg had studied many times, over the last ten years. It conjured up a feeling of unstoppable momentum.

Having filled his nostrils with the fragrance of oranges and lemons, he returned to the sofa and slumped down on the middle cushion. The green, leather, diplomatic bag lay at his feet. He rotated the combination lock to the set code - 21769. As the pin sprang open, Fagg looked inside the bag. With both hands, he withdrew the stolen cross as if it was a newly born child.

He eyed up the jewels, in turn, to decide which one he should choose first. Settling on the large green emerald at the intersection of the crucifix, he withdrew his pocketknife and carefully levered the gold clasps until they released their grip. Once the jewel had been extracted Fagg held it between his forefinger and thumb and turned it under the light. As the glittering rays struck his constricted pupils, he felt his hair tingle on the back of his neck. He was so thrilled that he spoke to himself out loud.

"Well now my little beauty, how much might you be worth?"

He had no qualms over the destruction of a sacred object. He intended to pluck out each jewel one at a time, with intervals of perhaps weeks or even months in between. And when they had all been fenced in exchange for cash, then, as a final act of desecration, he intended to melt down the gold and silver frame as well.

Fagg's actions summed up everything that was bad in the world: a total lack of respect and a polluted appetite for greed.

The El Alca had not performed well on its return journey to Grenada. First it was the fog then the motor's sea water intakes had been fouled by a belt of Sargassum, a vast field of brown seaweed, which can sometimes stretch for miles. Iko volunteered to slip overboard and clear the intake valves, which were positioned on the fishing boats hull, just below the surface, on either side of the stern. It had been a tense situation. Things were bad enough having a former Nazi tied up in the forward cabin, without having to prolong their ordeal. But when Iko descended beneath the waves Luis and Ilena kept a vigilant watch for him, in case there were any nearby sharks. When daylight broke, the sea appeared to be covered in a brown rug for as far as the eye could see. They had little choice other than to remain on their set course. There was no telling which direction would lead to clearer seas.

By the time they reached the commercial basin in the port of St. Georges they had been at sea almost thirty-eight hours. Inside the large port, it was a scene of chaos as massive reconstruction work was in progress. With all the comings and goings involved with the expansion program, it allowed the El Alca to slip in unnoticed.

Iko wasted no time in making his way to the Queen Conch travel agency, whilst Ilena nipped ashore to buy food and fresh water. When Iko reached his destination he first peeked through the large, front window, to check there were no clients sitting in front of Riley's desk. For a minute, he watched Des, who was standing behind his desk. He appeared to be moving from side to side, in an animated way, as if he was rehearsing for the stage. When the doorbell chimed, Des sat down quickly then smiled at the person entering. "Come in Iko," he said cheerily. "Do you have you know who?"

After Iko had confirmed that Friedla was still aboard the El Alca, Des picked up the red 'top secret' phone and spoke in a series of numerical codes until he was transferred to Alphonso Chinquata. After identifying himself, Des's conversation with the spymaster was remarkably brief as preparations for handling Friedla were already in place. One of the army's military speedboats, a Soviet built PG-127, would be launched immediately to pick up the 'package'. It was clear that Alphonso was greatly impressed with Iko's performance and the fact that he'd carried out the snatch successfully.

Iko waited for the call to end before announcing that he'd something very important to say. "I want to quit."

He looked at Des who'd dropped his pen and had begun to whistle. In the past few days of living independently, Iko had matured in his attitude and ambition. And meeting Ilena and sharing in her company had given him a palpable 'raison d'être'. He was now more determined than ever to force the issue. "They have what they asked me to do. And now," Iko paused to make sure he was fully understood, "I want to move on, with my new companion."

Des started to smile. "Oh aye. What have you been doing, me old flower," he said sarcastically. Iko began to blush with embarrassment as Des put two and two together. "You've met a girl?"

""Yes, we have plans, together." Iko began to grow more self-assured. "This time my feelings are real. She is a brave woman and we have talked about returning to Africa." Iko checked Des's reaction before continuing. At least Des now looked to be taking his request seriously. "Can you speak to Comrade Chinquata tomorrow, after Friedla has been handed over."

"Sure, I can try. But what are you going to do in Africa that you can't do here in Grenada?"

Iko stuck his chest out with pride as he spoke. "Ilena, who's my girl, has spoken about the civil war in Ethiopia which has been raging for the last five years. It was going to be her next project before she was forced to go into hiding. She says there are many people there who have been displaced and that they will likely starve to death if the West doesn't come to their aid. She wants to go to ensure their desperate cries for help are sent around the globe. It is a worthy cause and I feel I must help her in any way I can. Africa was my home too, once upon a time."

Des found Iko's request very moving. "Okay Iko. Leave it with me and I'll do my best. You'd better head back to the El Alca and tell Luis to stay put."

Before he left, Iko handed over the documents relating to the false identity of Eldrige Delgado and in exchange Des handed back Iko's Cuban passport.

When Iko walked out of the Queen Conch travel shop, he'd no intention of waiting to hear Havana's answer to the request he'd just made through Des Riley. 'Tomorrow,' he thought, 'when the Cubans arrive for Friedla, Ilena and I will be leaving for a different ship, one that is destined for the port of Marseilles.

At the Alamo, later that evening, we had a visit from Raoul. He had come to offer his commiserations, having seen for himself the mountain of ash that used to be our bar. He carried a humble expression, which sort of summed up the helplessness of our catastrophe. Having said hello to us both, he slumped down next to us, in one of Leyda's wicker chairs.

"Cheryl was angry with me when I told her we were going to have to put the date back for our wedding," he announced, with the weight of his solace resting on his shoulders. "She's already had a fitting for her wedding dress too."

"Crumbs," replied Fionn. "Are you still going ahead with it?"

"It'll be more than my life's worth to back out now. I'd never hear the last of it from Cheryl's mum. It's just not going to be the big, fancy wedding that we both wanted."

Leyda was on her way through from her drinks store. "Is that Raoul's voice I can hear? I'd better fetch an extra glass."

When Leyda appeared with the rum and cokes, she instantly set about cheering us all up. She'd had an sudden idea, and went back inside to find whatever it was she was looking for. Five minutes later she reappeared, carrying an old Decca portable record player and a dust covered box of seven-inch singles. "Let music be the food of life," she said joyously. "Come on Byrney, put one on. There are some timeless classics in that box of delights." She grabbed the three-pin plug and stuck it in the nearest socket. I held back, just in case it blew a fuse. Almost immediately, the turntable began building up to speed. "What are you waiting for? Fionn once told me you do a very amusing sand dance."

I had always been a believer that music can really take you out of yourself. We'd always had a record player and records at home, for as long as I could remember. Mum was a fan of Elvis. She used to dance with my brother Anthony and me, holding our hands and spinning us round to songs like Hound Dog and Jailhouse Rock. Dad, on the other hand, preferred classics, which we had to listen to quietly, in a more reflective mood, but they still stirred our young imaginations.

It was difficult to sit still and do nothing upon hearing the harmony in a song. It's like your bones and muscles were taking control. I couldn't stop myself from getting into the rhythm. As they say in Antigua - 'dance, do the reggae'.

Most of Leyda's records I'd never even heard of. They were mainly from the sixties. One record in particular made me lean into the record player to find out what is was called.

"Do you like this one, Byrney?" she asked.

"I love it. Put it on again. What's it called?"

"I'm in the mood for Ska by Lord Tanamo. His real name is Joe Gordon. He used to be in a band called the Skatalites."

I looked at Leyda blankly. I'd never heard of them. "I'm not very good at naming sixties bands," I replied.

Leyda looked at me with a bemused smile. "Aha, but this song is much older than that. It's from the 1930's."

As the song started up again, Leyda grabbed hold of Fionn and myself and together with Raoul, we danced in a circular chain, on the sand in front of her veranda as the night drew closer and the stars began to shine.

I had this daft idea. Maybe it was the effects of the drink or maybe it was because I couldn't stop smiling, but my idea was to play this song at the next world summit. And before anyone could speak they should be made to listen to 'I'm in the mood for Ska' by Lord Tanamo. The song would be played over and over again until all the leading delegates got up on their feet and danced. Only then could they sit back down and discuss a solution. I reckoned it would come to them much faster that way.

The next morning started up like a repeat of the one the day before. I could feel a pattern forming, although I could tell that Fionn was nursing a sore head. "How does Leyda manage to get herself off to work after the night we all had?" She bemoaned.

"I think she must have been weened on rum," I replied.

"Oh please, don't mention rum again." Her attempts at laughter were painfully half hearted."

"I'll go and make us a cup of tea."

As we ventured out onto the veranda, the sea and sky remained timeless. 'Stuck in their Caribbean groove', I thought. We sipped our hot drinks and watched the morning ebb and flow.

"I think we should take one last trip down to Amigo's," I suggested. "See if there's anything we've missed."

The scene of destruction was still just a bad as anything I'd ever witnessed. The burnt and twisted structure was unrecognisable as to its former state. It was still powerfully shocking. It reminded me that we'd all been lucky to escape from the inferno. Had we been asleep and overcome by fumes, then not everyone would have survived. We stepped through the charred scraps of wood. The only things still standing in their original position were the two porcelain toilets. They had been sited back to back with a dividing wall between them, although there was little evidence of that now. The firemen had disconnected the water supply and the bowls were full of ash. I found a half burnt piece of plywood and rested it over the two toilet basins to form a bench. We sat down together and stared down at the beach.

"I'm glad we can leave all this mess for someone else to clean up," lamented Fionn. "I wouldn't know where to start."

"Well, it's the bank's problem now, that is once we've signed the agreement to hand over the land."

"Mmmm, yes, I suppose," replied Fionn like she was caught up in a daydream. I followed her line of sight and noticed she was watching the lone, slim figure of a man, walking in our direction across the sand. He appeared to be skipping, rather than walking with his arms hanging by his sides, exaggerating the springiness of his gait. With his body angled forward he would not have looked out of place in a painting by L S Lowry. As he came closer I could see more of his facial features. He had a warm, friendly face with weathered tones and a greying 'Van Dyke' beard, which framed his natural smile. With his fixed smile and his unique swagger gave me the impression he was in possession of a gaggle of jokes which he kept stored beneath his rolled up sleeves. I was looking forward to hearing his greeting and although he was a total stranger to the two of us, I'd made up my mind that if he didn't speak then I would introduce ourselves to about him. However his look of harmless self-composure almost took a tumble as he tripped over the edge of our sandwich board advertising the entertainment for what had turned out to be our final, fateful evening at Amigo's. He stopped to read the chalked lettering. I'd forgotten the board was still out there. He looked directly at us then picked his own path through the debris.

"It must have been some barbeque?" He commented with in a friendly, southern accent. "My name's Jim, Jim Osman." We made a move to greet him. We must have looked a strange sight, sitting together across two old toilets. "It's okay, stay where you are. You both look very comfortable. You must be Byrney and Fionn. Sly, down at the Barracuda dive shop told me I'd probably find you both here."

Fionn and I looked at one another as Jim momentarily glanced out to sea. Then he quickly returned to fix his gaze upon us once more. "Look, I'll come straight to the point. Our yacht is due to sail out of here at the end of the week. But there's just one problem. Well, two actually. Our cook and deckhand have just deserted us. Up sticks and eloped together. So I was wondering how you're both fixed? Sly also mentioned you both have good sailing experience."

As Jim spoke I had to smile to myself. He had the bushiest eyebrows I'd ever seen. They seemed to have a life of their own, like they were dancing to the sound of his own words.

"What type of vessel is it?" I asked, but before he could answer Fionn chipped in with a question of her own.

"Do we get a uniform?"

Jim's eyebrows slowly formed a perfect Norman arch as he looked at her and smiled sympathetically as she tried not to appear self conscious about the borrowed clothes she was wearing.

"Yes, we have some nice clobber. Some of it will probably fit you properly too." He joked. "And as for the vessel, she was built fifteen years ago by the Psarros shipyard near Athens. She's a seventy-two foot motor sailer, with a crew of four. At the moment there's just myself and my wife, Liz and maybe your good selves, if I can persuade you both to join us. We have a fully booked season of charters, in and around the Aegean Sea."

I looked at Fionn and she looked back at me, wide-eyed. It sounded too good to be true. A free ticket out of here and we'd be paid wages too.

"What are the wages, if you don't mind me asking?"

Jim smiled again. "I'm glad you asked. I was hoping you would. We'll start you off on one hundred and fifty pounds a month, each. Then see how you go from there." He looked at us for a reaction, but I could tell he was having difficulty reading our thoughts. We'd recently been taking that amount of cash per night at Amigo's, but that was all in the past now. We both accepted that we'd have to start over again from scratch and it was a case of sooner the better.

I noticed Jim was starting to look a little restless and awkward; he began to talk some more. "Look you don't have to decide right this minute. Have a think about it for a day or two." Jim tapped the side of his head as a new thought came to him. "No, I've a better idea. Why don't the two of you come along tomorrow evening and join Liz and myself for a meal on board? You can meet Liz and have a look around our yacht. See if it meets your requirements." The three of us all smiled. It sounded like a great idea.

"By the way, have you ever been to Greece?" He asked. We both shook our heads.

"No, but I've heard it's a nice place." Replied Fionn in typical Fionn style. Everywhere abroad was a nice place to her.

"Nice?" said Jim, teasingly. "Greece is the land of gods and goddesses, where we lavish our guests with ambrosia and nectar." He looked at our puzzled faces then continued with his tribute. "Do you know your Iliad and the Odyssey?"

We shook our heads again, like beguiled infants.

"Argh, wonderful. This adventure is going to be an education for you both, too. There are hundreds of islands that make up the Cyclades. Some are uninhabited, lonely places, with deserted olive groves and yet they are the most beautiful in the world. Since the dawn of the ancient civilisations of the Minoans and the Mycenaeans, the Greeks have been renowned for their inimitable hospitality. Will six thirty be okay? We're moored at the marina down the road. You can't miss us. Just look for the Maya 'B'."

We watched Jim skip back down the beach, towards Cross Green as we excitedly discussed our next move. The decision had already been made. Fionn was so pleased, she could hardly contain herself and had to go and find shelter behind a lonely coconut palm.

When she returned she was carrying a bottle of red wine. "I found this out the back. Heaven knows how it got there. It was sticking out of the sand. I took the bottle from her and it felt reasonably cool.

"Pity we haven't got a corkscrew," she sighed.

I looked down at my feet for a pencil size stick of wood. "We don't need one. Woody once taught me an old Navy trick about how to remove a cork from a bottle with just a pencil and a shoelace. Never fails. Works every time according to him."

I removed the lace from one of my trainers and tied a thick double knot in the end of it. Then, taking hold of the pencil shape stick, I pushed the cork into the bottle. Fionn looked at me 'gone out'. "Oh, well done Byrney, I could have done that."

"Hang on a minute. Here comes the clever bit. Pulling the cork out," I boasted. "The trick is to leave the cork floating near the neck of the bottle." I lifted the bottle to my lips and took a tiny nip of the wine. It tasted surprisingly good. Then, I pushed the knotted end of the lace down inside the bottle until the knot dropped just beneath the cork. I showed Fionn. "Now watch." I wrapped the opposite end of the lace around my right hand and started to pull gently. The cork moved back into the neck of the bottle. Then, as I continued to pull harder on the lace the knot dragged the cork clean out. "Hey presto."

"Well done," she said and as a reward planted a kiss on my cheek.

"I don't just pop my cork for anyone, you should know that." I joked.

Fionn blushed. "Byrney," she said, in a friendly, scolding tone.

We passed the bottle between us as a few spots of rain began to fall. I looked up and saw a rogue grey cloud. The rain was warm and gentle. It must have wanted to join our little party too.

On the next pass of the bottle our gaze met and something knowing and intimate passed between, in perfect silence. It was one of those calming and sublime passages of time that seemed to linger forever, leaving an indelible imprint in my memory. The wine was warming our thoughts and although we didn't have a single cent or any possessions to our name, those material means were magically dispelled. We'd travelled halfway around the world together and right here, right at this moment, it was now just the two of us again.

"Fancy going for a swim?" I asked with an encouraging smile.

Fionn turned her open palms to the air. "But it's raining."

"I know, we'll be much wetter in the sea." I laughed.

I took hold of Fionn's hand and realised I never wanted to let it go.

As we walked towards the sea I glanced around and had this sudden, perception shaping my senses: that, if I was to return to this very spot in maybe ten, twenty or even thirty years time, it would still be here, the thing I'd unknowingly left behind.

I would find - a part of my soul.

Milton Keynes UK
Ingram Content Group UK Ltd.
UKHW022018131124
451149UK00013B/1189